NYTE TERRORS

NYTE PATROL, BOOK 2

ALEX P. BERG

I SAT ON MY SUITCASE, BACK TO THE WALL, GRUNTING AS I drove my weight into the bunched clothes underneath. The halves touched and my heart soared. I leaned over to grab the zipper, but in doing so, my weight shifted, giving the luggage the opportunity it was waiting for. As I slipped backward, the suitcase popped open, dumping me ass on the ground and feet in the air with a pile of crumpled shirts in my lap.

I heard a snort. "You want some help with that, Lexie?"

Heather stood in the doorway to my room, a loose UT sweatshirt hanging from her frame. She held a bowl of Frosted Mini-Wheats in one hand, a spoon protruding over the edge.

I blew a strand of hair out of my face. "I mean, sure. *If you're up.*"

Heather had long everything. Long lustrous blonde hair, long eyelashes that were perfect for batting, and long legs made even longer by the tiny pink athletic shorts she wore. "Don't say it like that. It's barely nine."

"You going to help or not?"

Heather set her bowl on the desk and strode over with gazelle-like grace. She gave me a hand and pulled me up. "You almost had it. How about you sit again and this time I tackle the zipper?"

I gave her a cheeky smile. "Why should I do the sitting? You saying I have a big ass?"

"I mean, I'll take some if you're willing to share. I see the way boys look at it. Hell, sometimes *I* can't stop looking at it."

I gave her a playful shove. "Shut up."

I sat. Heather gave me an assist with her elbow and tugged the zipper shut with a few sharp pulls.

"There. Hopefully it holds." She stood and returned to her bowl. She grabbed it as she looked around the room, now populated only by suitcases and boxes. "Looks like you got just about everything."

"That's what happens when you wake up at seven. You get things done before lunch."

Heather hopped onto the desk and waved her spoon at me. "You realize I never said you had to take off first thing in the morning."

The university closed the dorms at the end of the spring semester, but since our softball season extended a few weeks past that, I'd needed temporary housing. "I know, but this is your place. I don't want to feel like a third wheel."

"You mean a second wheel? I'm the only one who lives here. You're welcome to stay as long as you want. Seriously."

Heather was an awesome friend. Heck, maybe *the best* friend. She'd put up with a lot of my crap over the past season, what with me injuring my shoulder, suffering a crisis of confidence, erupting at practice, and nearly getting kicked off the team before learning a few lessons about responsibility and humility. She's seen me at my worst, and I knew she meant every word she said. She'd let me stay at her apartment all summer if I needed to, and her parents wouldn't bat an eye at the prospect, either. They were even more charitable than Heather, but the fact of the matter was I didn't want anyone's charity. My family's financial situation wasn't the best. The fact that I was still living at the dorms in my junior season was a constant source of embarrassment, one that I couldn't talk to Heather about. Staying at her place cultivated a sense of jealously within me, and I wanted none of it.

"I appreciate the offer, Heather. Really, I do, but it's time. The season's over. We got bounced. I should do the same."

Heather snorted as she spooned Mini-Wheats into her mouth. "I'm still salty about that. We were an out away from Super Regionals. *One.* That's going to haunt me all summer."

I shrugged. "There's no shame in losing to Florida State, especially on a walk-off. We beat expectations. A lot of people didn't even think we'd beat Cal."

Heather smiled. "Yeah, well we showed them, didn't we?"

"Damn straight." I held out a fist. Heather bumped it. "I think we made a hell of a comeback, especially considering the start to the season we had."

"We killed it, girl. And all we needed—or should I say all *you* needed—was a little confidence." Heather shook her head as she spooned down another bite. "You know it pains me to say this, but I think you getting tangled up with those Nyte Patrol folks made you a better softball player. You were so listless and depressed before you met them."

It was true, at least to a degree. My shoulder injury and the self-doubt it had instilled in me vanished upon teaming up with Larry, Dawn, and Tank and taking down Ivan Romanov. I'd finished out the season strong with the best two month batting average of my life, but at the same time, getting beaten by Florida State felt *final*. More than the end of a season, our loss to them felt like the end of one chapter of my life and the beginning of another. It concerned me because I still had my senior season awaiting me. I should've been the most excited I'd ever been about softball, yet somehow I felt the opposite, like I'd be okay with it ending. I'd never felt that way before. Ever.

I hadn't told Heather about it yet. Perhaps it was better not to. I don't think she shared the sentiment. "Yeah. I'm glad I met the Nyte Patrol, too."

Heather paused with her spoon in the bowl. She raised an eyebrow, her voice cautious. "So... you sure you're going to be okay living with them?"

Ah. Now I understood why she'd brought them up. Normally, Heather was happy to pretend my supernaturally-inclined friends were a crazy fantasy. "Heather, trust me. I'll be fine. They're good people even if they're quirky."

"That's not what I meant. I don't think any of them are going to take advantage of you. It's more that... Well, shouldn't you be more focused on something else? Like, your school work?"

"You're one to talk. You're not doing summer session, either."

Heather smiled. "In my defense, I have a tan that's in serious need of evening out."

A buzz in my back pocket accompanied the rhythmic ringing of my phone. I pulled it out and checked the number. "One sec, Heather. I've got to take this." I answered the call and headed into the hall for more privacy. "Hey, Mom. What's up?"

"*Hola, mi amor*. How are you feeling?"

"I'm fine." My parents had travelled to see me at Regionals. Based on their reactions, they were more bent out of shape by our loss to Florida State than I was. "You and Dad make it home last night?"

"It was a long drive, but your *papa* pushed through. We'll be spending most of the day on the couch, I think. How about you? You're moving out today, right?"

"Just finished packing the last of my things. Heather helped —a little."

In the background, I heard Heather's voice, muffled by Mini-Wheats. "I heard that."

"Is she helping you move, too?"

"I don't know. We haven't gotten that far yet."

"*Que maravilla.* I love that girl. You make sure to thank Heather for everything, understand?"

I wandered into the kitchen, trailing my fingers across the stone countertop. "You think I haven't?"

"I'm just saying. Speaking of Heather, has she met the people you're moving in with? Does she approve of them? Because if *she* doesn't..."

"Mom, I told you. They're nice folks. Everyone at the new house is going to be interning alongside me."

"I know, but it seems like you haven't known them very long, certainly not as long as you've known Heather. I mean, if you only met them at that career fair—"

"*Mom*. Please."

"*Oye! Mira,* I'm just happy for you. Your first internship. It's exciting, isn't it?"

"Yes, very exciting. Look, I've got to get going. Lots of stuff to move."

"Of course. If you need any help, give us a call. I know your *papa* is tired, but we can make the drive up I-35 if we need to."

"No, mom, I've got it under control."

"Okay. Take care. *Te quiero.*"

"Love you too, Mom. Bye."

I hung up and turned to find Heather entering the kitchen. She put her bowl in the sink and turned on the faucet to rinse it out. She gave me an off-kilter look.

"What?" I said.

Heather hesitated. "Look, I'm not normally the snooping type—"

"Liar."

"—but did I overhear you tell your mom you were *interning?*"

My heart rose toward my throat. "With the Nyte Patrol, yeah. It's a job."

"I thought you said you were more or less leading them now."

"Technically, I'm still a junior partner, but yeah. It's sort of like an internship."

Heather turned the water off and cocked her head at me, lifting her eyebrows at the same time. "Lexie, you *did* tell your parents what you're doing this summer, didn't you?"

I sighed and threw up my hands. "Ok, fine! I *may* have lied a little and told them I'd accepted an internship with Westlake Design and Engineering."

Heather knew how to strike a reproachful pose. She planted a hand on her hip and made her eyebrows stretch higher. "Lexie Rodriguez, there are things I fully support lying to your parents about, namely whether or not you're sexually active, how much you drink, and if you've ever smoked pot, but your summer job is definitely not one of them."

"In general, I agree, but what was I supposed to tell them? That I'd decided to move in with a wizard, a blade master, a werebear, and a severed zombie head to help them solve mysteries and fight against the forces of evil? I mean, do you remember how batshit crazy you thought I was when I told you about the Nyte Patrol?"

"I've met most of them, and I *still* think you're halfway off your rocker."

"Which is exactly my point. You're my best friend, the only girl on the team I've told, and even now you only sort of believe me. Be honest, somewhere inside that head of yours you still think I'm moving into that house to join a cult or become a crack whore or that I'll disappear and you'll never see me again."

Heather moved around the edge of the countertop. "I never said any of that."

"But you've thought it, right? And why wouldn't you? Everything about the Nyte Patrol is crazy. It's unbelievable in every way. So imagine how my parents would take it if I tried to explain it to them. They're hardcore Catholics, and they're not even particularly hip. They don't watch *The Walking Dead* or *Game of Thrones* or anything. If I tell them I'm moving in with a wizard and a zombie they're either going to try to have me institutionalized or exorcised. Maybe both."

Heather reached out and took me by the shoulders. "Lexie, I wasn't trying to guilt trip you. You're capable of making your own choices, and for the record, *I believe you*. I've always believed you, and I'll keep believing you until the day you tell me you can out-pitch me."

I swallowed Heather in a hug. "Thanks. I appreciate it."

Heather let the hug linger for a moment before pulling back. "So. You need help moving stuff to your truck?"

I smiled. "What was that about not snooping?"

Heather laughed. "I'll grab my flip-flops."

2

I PULLED MY '94 CHEVY SUBURBAN INTO THE DRIVEWAY AT the house on West 21st and killed the engine. Even now, after having frequented the place for two and a half months, I was still embarrassed by its shabbiness. There were four different colors of paint on the front of the house alone, the lawn consisted of the occasional tuft of grass amid a field of dandelions and clover, and plywood boards covered the front door and adjacent window. At least someone had pressure washed the spray-painted political graffiti and phalluses from the boards, but it was still a far cry from the brightly painted, gated community Heather lived in. Good thing my parents weren't tech savvy enough to look the place up on Google Maps—though they *would* drop by sooner or later. San Antonio was only an hour or three drive away, depending on traffic. Maybe I could get Tank to help me spruce the place up. Oddly enough, he was the most domestic of the bunch.

I hopped out of my truck, moved around back, and popped open the hatch. While I generally hated driving around downtown Austin in my Suburban, it did have the benefit of being able to fit a metric buttload of cargo. Thanks to it, I'd hauled everything I had at Heather's in a single trip. It was also one of the reasons Larry's spell had initially picked me to join the Nyte Patrol. Strange to think that if I drove a Corolla I'd probably be blissfully unaware of the existence of magic, vampires, and werewolves and still be as miffed about losing to Florida State as Heather and my parents were.

As I rummaged in the back of the 'burban, trying to figure out where to make the first dent, I heard a metallic rap. I looked up to find Tank standing next to the truck. He smiled and gave me a nod. "Morning, short stuff."

"Right back at you, big guy. Hear the truck coming?"

"Hard not to."

At six foot six, Tank loomed over me. I'd never seen him step on a scale, but I guessed he weighed in the range of two-sixty to two-eighty, assuming his tightly-knit were-flesh weighed the same as the normal human kind. He always wore muscle shirts that showed off his bulging biceps and massive chest. Today's version was a white compression shirt, and thanks to his dark complexion, *everything* was visible underneath, including a ridiculous set of washboard abs. They were mesmerizing. Like Lego Batman, I think he had an extra ab or two smushed in among the rest.

Tank smirked at my wandering gaze. "You doing okay?"

"You're distracting sometimes. What the hell is that anyway? Gauze?"

Tank laughed. "Something-prene. I forget. I bought it online. I think it's meant for someone four sizes smaller than me. Put it on just for you." He winked at me.

When we'd first met, Tank had barely talked to me, much less cracked a smile or laughed, but we'd come a long way. Like an onion, he had a lot of layers and took a long time to peel. I think he got a kick out of teasing me about his body because he knew there was no spark between us. That said, I didn't mind looking. I'd even been lucky enough to see him naked once, though his head had been in grizzly bear form at the time. If ever I needed cold water thrown on me, I pictured that and it did the trick.

"Instead of flexing for shits and giggles, you want to help me move stuff in?"

"Why do you think I came down, Lex? Move aside and let me grab a few boxes."

I tugged out my largest suitcase and pulled up the handle while Tank reached in and collected the heaviest boxes he could find, stacking them one atop the other and lifting them as easily as if they contained packing peanuts. He headed around the side of the house toward the back door. I followed him, my roller bag's wheels clacking over the cracked pavement.

"So I'm going to propose something and you tell me what you think, okay, Tank?"

He glanced back over the pile of boxes in his arms. "This sounds ominous."

"It's not, I promise. I just think we should remodel a little. Get someone to come out. Fix the glass and front door. Repaint. Heck, we could do it ourselves."

"Well, we'd have to clear it with Larry..."

We approached the back door, which wasn't boarded up, though the intercom at the side was still burnt to a crisp, made nonoperational by Larry's inability to use electronics. "Be honest. You can't like living in a dump like this. I know Larry claims his obfuscation spells work best when the house is in disarray, that people will look away and scuttle off faster as a result, but I think that's bull. He could just as easily set up spells to keep people away if this house looked the same as every other. He's simply too lazy to change them."

Tank nudged the back door open with his foot. "You didn't let me finish."

I pulled my suitcase up the steps. "Oh. Sorry."

"What I was going to say is, we'd have to clear it with Larry, but I love it. This place is about thirty years past its prime. You've got my vote."

I smiled. "Oh. Awesome. Well, that's one down."

I followed Tank into the house, which true to the man's word was at least a quarter century out of date. Shag carpet, once a vibrant grass color but now a muddy artichoke, covered the floor. Thick paisley drapes hung over the windows that weren't boarded up. I pulled the chain on a desk lamp atop the console in the entry while Tank paused at the foot of the stairs, not at all bothered by the hundred pounds of gear in his arms.

"Bill!" he shouted into the adjacent room. "Lexie needs your vote of confidence. She have it?"

In the living room, past the end of Larry's massive desk on his own dedicated end table, Bill startled and blinked—although the startle was more of a mild roll. Being a disembodied zombie head in a jar, Bill wasn't capable of much movement on his own. "Whazat?"

"Were you sleeping again?" I said.

"Maybe." Bill blinked a few more times, squinting from desk lamp's light. "What are we talking about?"

"Lexie wants to remodel," said Tank. "You've got her back, right?"

"Uh... sure. As long as I get to keep my jar."

"I don't know," I said. "I was thinking about moving you to an aquarium."

"Don't you dare," said Bill. "Having my eyes pecked out by fish is my worst nightmare, followed closely by having my eyes pecked out by birds."

"We wouldn't need to put any fish in there," I said. "Just one of those bubble-activated treasure chests. Come on. You know it would freak out the guests."

Tank snorted. "Like we ever have any of those. Come on. I've got your room mostly cleaned out."

Tank headed up the stairs, and I lugged my suitcase after him. He hooked a left at the top and skirted around a corner into a room above the front door. He gently deposited my boxes in a corner, stood, and smiled at me.

"Well? What do you think?" He waved a hand around the room. It was about ten feet by twelve with a full-sized bed in one corner and a desk and office chair in the other. Other than that it was as empty as the mini-fridge I'd kept in my dorm.

"It's everything an almost twenty-one year old could want," I said. "You even took the plywood off the window."

Tank shot me a pair of finger guns. "And I checked to make sure there wasn't a draft. There is, but it's not bad."

"We can add weather-stripping and caulk to the remodeling list. It'll be fine for now."

Tank hooked his thumb toward the window. "You want me to bring up the rest of your things? It'll take me less time than you."

I deposited my bag next to the bed and had a seat. The mattress wasn't half bad. Better than the ones at the dorms. "I mean, I wouldn't say no."

"You got it." Tank smiled and headed out.

I sat there on the bed, soaking in the ambience as I listened to the stairs creak under Tank's heavy footsteps. It wasn't much. Just a barren rectangle with wood panel walls and beat to death plank flooring, but it was the first room I'd ever had to myself. I'd shared a room with my younger sister growing up, and I'd always had a roommate in the dorms.

It wasn't a sense of ownership that gave me chills, though. It was that this was the first time I'd felt like I was on my own. University dormitories, for all the crazy shenanigans that occurred there, were still supervised. There would be rules here as well, I was sure. Larry and Dawn wouldn't let me get away with everything, like blasting heavy metal at four in the morning or having loud, epic sex—not that I was likely to do either. But I knew them. They treated me as a peer, despite my age. They'd offer me as much independence as I wanted.

The questions was, how much did I want? Larry's spell may have drawn me to the Nyte Patrol in the first place, but I'd stayed for a reason. I liked the excitement and mystery of dealing with the unknown, the thrill of hunting enemies, the sense of pride in solving problems and putting others to justice. I liked learning about the supernatural world, something that a few months ago I would've dismissed as pure fantasy. But there were consequences to my choices. By choosing to spend the summer with the Nyte Patrol, I'd foregone other opportunities. If I'd sent out more applications, I could've gotten an internship with a local engineering firm, just as I'd told my parents. I had the grades for it, but as much as I liked science and technology, the idea of tabulating data paled to that of fighting evil. Was it the right choice? Would I wake up one day to find it was all a dream and I'd squandered the opportunity I'd worked so hard for? My softball scholarship and grades had put me on a path to success, and now I was wandering off it onto a path covered with weeds and coyote scat.

The stairs creaked again, and Tank returned with another impressive stack of boxes. He plopped them in a corner and headed back to the door. He paused there and glanced back at me. I don't think I'd moved.

"Everything all right, Lex?"

"Yeah. It's just... this is a big change. Living here. Doing this full time, even if only for a summer."

"It's a good change, though, right?"

"I think so." I chewed on my lip. "Mind if I ask you something?"

He came back into the room and leaned against the desk. "Shoot."

"Why did you join the Nyte Patrol?"

The big guy snickered. "Not a lot of other career prospects for a werebear."

"Sure there are. You're in control of your turning, at least for the most part. It's not like you don't have skills that are useful in other occupations. You're an expert marksman. You could do military or police work."

"Been there, done that. The hours here are shorter, and I like the people better."

"So is that why you joined? Because of your relationship with Dawn and Larry?"

Tank shrugged. "It's a big reason why I've stuck around, but there's more to it. When you join the military or the police, you do what you're told. Sometimes it helps people. Serve and protect and all that, but sometimes it doesn't. Sometimes you're serving a higher up's interest without regard for what's best for you or anyone else. Here, we take the cases. We decide who to help. We don't always get everything right, but when we do? Doing a job well, making a difference—that's satisfying. It feeds the soul."

I nodded, Tank's words echoing my own feelings. "Thanks. That's what I needed to hear."

Downstairs I heard a knock on the back door, followed by a strong, feminine voice. "Lexie? You here?"

I hopped off the bed and headed to the stairs. "Up here, Dawn. Just arrived."

Dawn strode to the foot of the steps. She'd pulled her long, black hair into a single tight braid. Black mesh capris with a bone white skull design hugged her long, lean legs, and a matching workout bra clung to her chest, showing off the tight muscle in her arms and the slight curve of her traps. If the universe was fair, it would've paired her slender Crossfitter's body with an overly large nose or mismatched eyes or some huge hairy mole on her cheek, but the universe wasn't fair. Dawn was gorgeous in every way.

"Well, what are you waiting for?" said Dawn. "You're late for your training."

3

I grunted as I grappled with Dawn, trying to find purchase on her sweat-slicked arms. She pivoted, ducking under my arm and spinning as she did so. I anticipated the move and pounced, grabbing her around the waist—or at least I tried. She danced back across the mat and I stumbled to my knees, barely managing to keep my face from bouncing off the ground.

"Not bad," said Dawn, her voice even. "You hesitated though, and you need to grip harder. You really have to squeeze with your chest, otherwise your opponent will wiggle out, same as I did."

We stood in the backyard of the house, surrounded by a few stunted trees and overgrown weeds. Dawn had put out the wrestling mats while I'd changed into a tank top and workout shorts. I'd always thought myself in excellent shape, but as I pushed myself to my knees, drawing ragged breaths, I couldn't help but feel my softball trainers were doing something wrong. I felt like I'd been doing burpees for the last half hour while Dawn might as well have gone out for a light jog. At least she was sweating. At this point, I was willing to latch onto any shred of evidence that she was actually human.

I snorted and shook my head, still trying to catch my breath. *"Not bad..."*

Dawn cocked a slender eyebrow at me. "What?"

I held up a finger as I filled my lungs with air. "Look, Dawn... I appreciate you training me ... but I can tell you're going easy on me. I've seen you move in combat. I know your speed, so when you blow smoke up my ass ... it doesn't help me get any better."

Dawn planted her hands on her hips. "I'm not messing with you. Your moves weren't bad. They weren't great either, or even good, but they weren't bad. That's an improvement over a few weeks ago. You weren't even at the ground floor back then. You were in the subbasement."

"Jeez. Twist the knife, will you?"

"Hey, you wanted real talk? This is as real as it gets. You're athletic, but you didn't have a lick of wrestling or martial arts experience when we started. Now you've got six weeks worth. I have about twenty-five years of it under my belt. So don't beat yourself up."

Dawn was doing a good enough job of beating me up on her own. "I know you can't come at me as hard as you're capable of. I get it. I don't want my arms broken any more than you want to break them—"

"I don't know. She might want to. She's got a mean streak." Tank sat on a concrete bench to the side of the mats, eating a bowl of popcorn one kernel at a time.

"—but," I said, annoyed, "you could at least turn up the intensity. Make this more like a real brawl. Just don't patronize me when you slam my ass to the ground, okay?"

Dawn lifted her other eyebrow. "You're sure?"

"If I can walk away and I've learned something, I'll say it was worth it."

"Okay." Dawn hunched into her ready stance. "I'm going to try to choke you. I'm telling you so you know what defense to use. It'll even the playing field a bit. Ready?"

We'd practiced the exercise several times over the past couple weeks when I wasn't training for Regionals. I planted a foot in the ground and mimicked Dawn's stance. "Ready."

Dawn didn't say another word. She sprung at me with unbelievable speed. I knew what to do. I spun away from her and lifted a hand to the side of my face to break the hold she intended to put on me, but Dawn shot a foot into the ground and drove through with her leg. In the blink of an eye, she'd hopped to the side opposite the one I'd expected. As I ducked and reversed my spin, she held out an arm and wrapped it around my neck, using her momentum to catapult onto my back.

As Dawn's legs wrapped around my midsection and she latched a hand onto the wrist of her choking arm, I knew I was screwed, but I didn't give up. I pitched forward, using the extra weight on my back to my advantage. I spun a hundred and eighty degrees through the air and landed flat on my back, or rather on Dawn's.

She didn't so much as grunt. Instead, her arm tightened around my neck, her biceps feeling like braided steel. I clawed at her grip with both hands, trying to rip it free, but I might as well have been trying to fell a tree with my fingernails. My lungs burned as the trickle of oxygen coming through my airway went dry. I rolled around, hoping to loosen Dawn's grip through sheer effort, but her hold on me intensified. Her legs squeezed tight. Every inch of her body pressed against mine from behind, every bubble of air between us squeezed out by the force of her effort. Her chin dug into my clavicle. Her sweat-slicked cheek slipped against the side of my face, and I could feel her hot breath in my ear as I started to lose my vision.

I slapped a hand on the mat, and Dawn's vice-like grip evaporated. I gasped for air, laying on my hands and knees on the ground as Dawn rolled off me.

"Are you okay, Lexie?"

I nodded, blinking away the dark spots in my vision. "Yeah," I croaked. "Fine. I think... that's enough... though."

Dawn grabbed a towel from the side of the mat and wiped her arms and face. "Probably for the best. There's only so long I can press up against someone like that before I get turned on."

"*Dawn!* Christ." I was finally starting to get my breathing under control.

"Hey, you wanted honesty, right? I'm telling it like it is."

"I think she wanted honesty regarding her combat performance, not your libido," said Tank around a mouthful of popcorn.

"It's nothing personal," said Dawn as she wiped the back of her neck. "I'm a sexual person. When I'm physically active, my juices get flowing, and then you throw in that tactile engagement? It's my body's natural response. And I warned you before we started that I get this way. I offered an alternative."

"Yeah," I said, pushing myself to my feet. "You said I could battle Tank instead. I don't think wrestling him is going to be any *less* sexual, never mind that he outweighs me by a hundred and fifty pounds and has supernatural werebear strength."

Dawn threw up her hands. "Hey, it was just a suggestion. Though truth be told, it might not be bad to work you up to a match against him. You're going to need to practice defending yourself against larger targets eventually."

"Or there's another option."

We all turned at the sound of the voice. Larry stood at the back steps of the house, wearing the same leather duster he always did despite the warm weather. His wavy brown hair fell to his cheeks, glossy and wet-looking. I don't think he used gel, rather that his hair naturally absorbed moisture. Still, between that and the perpetual three-day beard he wore, it gave him the look of a homeless person. At least he'd cleaned up a *little* since I first met him. Back then, he'd rocked more of a week-long beard.

"And what option would that be?" said Dawn.

Larry looked me in the eyes. "You could train with me."

I blew a raspberry. "Give me a break. This isn't an opportunity to wrestle the sweaty co-ed, okay? Whatever fantasies you have, keep them to yourself."

Larry blinked. *"What?* No. I meant magical training. You could just as easily use that to defend yourself as martial skills. More easily, depending on the target."

I squinted. "Larry, I'm not a wizard."

"Witch," he said. "Wizards are male. Most of the time, anyway, unless you're a warlock, who's more of a male witch. Magical linguistics is weird and has an undeniably sexist history. Whatever. My point is, how would you know you're not a witch? Have you ever been tested?"

"Tested?"

"You know, like aptitude tests? ACC, SAT, that sort of thing but for magic?"

I glanced at Dawn, then Tank, then back at Larry. "Of course I haven't been tested. I'm a college student and a softball player. There's a reason I go to the University of Texas and not Barfsnoggle Institute of Magic."

"I went to Zephyrburr Academy, thank you very much." Larry shrugged. "Look. I'm just throwing it out there. Nothing wrong with working on your craft. Learning new skills. But hand to hand combat isn't the best way for *everyone* to take on their enemies, much as it works for Dawn and Tank."

Larry took a step back toward the house before stopping. "Wait a second." He spun back toward us. "I *knew* I came out here for a reason. Have any of you heard from Charity Peterson?"

Dawn moaned with pleasure. "Well, now you've done it. If I wasn't turned on before, I sure as hell am now."

Charity was a supernatural sleuth for hire, much like we were, but she also held down a regular job, earning most of her money as an airplane mechanic. She and Dawn had an on-again, off-again relationship, and though she had darker skin than Dawn, had infinitely more tattoos, and happened to be a werehyena, like Dawn she was *insanely* hot. Between the two of them and Tank, you'd think being unnaturally good-looking was a requirement to being a supernatural badass, but then there was Larry, so... yeah.

"Is there a reason we *should've* heard from Charity?" I asked.

"Well," said Larry, "she hired me a few days ago to look into suspicious activities at her house, but I haven't heard from her since. I thought maybe she'd reached out to one of you. Specifically Dawn."

"Wait," I said. "She hired *you?* Not us?"

"All of us. The Nyte Patrol," said Larry. "Look, don't take it as a slight that I didn't mention it. She called the same day as your last final, plus you were focused on your softball tournament this past weekend. I figured you had enough going on."

I know I shouldn't have taken it personally, but it still stung. Larry was right, after all. I wouldn't have had time to investigate anything over the weekend. I hadn't even been in town, but that didn't mean I didn't *want* to be involved.

"Wait," said Dawn. "Charity called? How in the world did you talk to her on the phone?"

Thanks to his magical powers, Larry had the misfortune of turning any piece of electronic equipment that he touched into a smoking heap. He'd never really explained how that worked. "I didn't. She left a message. I followed up by sending ensnared animals to her place for a follow up conversation, but I couldn't find her. I'm starting to get a bad feeling about it."

"Ensnared animals?" I said.

Larry sighed. "Not physically ensnared. I don't need you calling PETA on me. I'm talking about soulcasting. And yes, I know it's inconvenient, but when technology refuses to cooperate, you lean on the old methods. It's quite effective, at least when you cast your soul into birds. Cats are okay, too, but they have the nasty habit of getting run over when they attempt to cross freeways."

Dawn sauntered over to the concrete bench and retrieved her cell phone. "You want me to give her a call?"

"Sure," said Larry. "Wouldn't hurt."

She tapped the screen a few times and held it to her ear. A few seconds later she brought it back down. "Straight to voicemail."

"And you haven't talked to her recently?" asked Larry.

Dawn shook her head. "Not in a few days."

Larry sighed. "I don't like it. Not to mention the soulcast

birds were squeamish anytime I brought them near her house. Something's up."

"We could stop by her place," I said. "Check up on her."

Larry shot a finger at me. "Exactly what I was thinking. Probably would've done it yesterday if it was up to me, but seeing as you're the one with the wheels..."

I grabbed a spare towel from the edge of the mat. "Give me a chance to shower and grab some lunch. Then I'm all over it."

4

I PULLED THE SUBURBAN ONTO A GRAVEL DRIVE ON MOORE Road, a couple miles south of Austin-Bergstrom International Airport. A cute teal cottage with dirty white molding perched next to the drive, surrounded by grass that was starting to look a little thirsty. A trio of outbuildings with aluminum roofs were visible past the end of the gravel—a barn, a garage, and maybe a workshop based on the size—but despite the storage space, Charity hadn't been bothered to keep all her toys inside.

I parked in front of an early 80's open air Jeep CJ that was roughly the same color as the house and hopped out. The beige leather on the CJ's seats was lined with cracks, but the paint was in good shape and I didn't spot any rust. The latter was also true of the station wagon truck hybrid on the grass twenty feet to its left. I'd initially thought it was an El Camino, but there was a Ford logo on the hood and the stylized lettering next to the front door read Ranchero. Beyond that was an even older car, some hulking Plymouth convertible from the 40's that was up on blocks and probably didn't even have an engine in it anymore. I also spotted a small prop plane peeking out from one of the open barn doors in back.

Larry climbed out of the truck. He leaned against the door as he waved toward the Jeep. "I take it this is Charity's car."

Dawn nodded as she hopped out of the back. "One of them, anyway. The one she drives the most often."

"It can't be a good sign that it's still here." Larry slammed his door. A series of barks responded to the sound from inside the home, muffled by the walls but anxious nonetheless.

Dawn's brow furrowed in concern. "That isn't either. Charity wouldn't have left Apollo and Athena behind."

Dawn raced across the pavers and up the front steps to the porch. As she pushed aside a terra cotta pot and dug around behind it, the barking became more frantic. Claws skittered off wood as the dogs pawed at the door, and whines joined the barks.

Larry followed Dawn up the steps. He leaned over to look through the narrow side window. "Dawn, are you sure about these things?"

Dawn pulled back, a key that she'd pulled from underneath one of the pots in hand. "They're frightened and confused, Larry. You said you hadn't heard from Charity in *how* long? Oh my gosh, I can't even imagine..."

"I don't know. They look, ah..."

Larry's uncertain warble was drowned by barking as Dawn turned the key in the lock and pushed the door in. Two squat pit bulls launched themselves out the gap, one a dark brown with a white speckled belly and the other solid white with a chestnut oval over one eye. They tackled Dawn, jumping on her and showering her with kisses.

"Charity has *pitties*?" I said. "Oh, they're adorable!"

I gingerly approached the one with dark fur, holding my hands low where he could sniff them as I read his collar. He gauged me with one quick look before diving into my arms.

"Oh my goodness! Oh, hello! Hello, Apollo! Hello!" The pit bull wrapped his front legs around my neck and licked me mercilessly, his stubby tail turning into a blur as he wagged.

Larry looked at Dawn and me like we'd lost our minds. "You're not concerned these beasts are going to rip your faces off?"

Tank followed us up the front steps. "Pit bulls are one of the most loving breeds there are, Larry. The only reason people fight them is because they're so loyal they'd willingly die for their owners. Well, that and because they have an absurd pain tolerance. But most of them are harmless."

"I don't know about *harmless*," said Dawn, pulling her face out of reach of the white one. "If I'm not careful, I might drown in Athena's affection. Down, girl. Easy."

With Apollo still in my arms, I moved to the front door and took a sniff. Luckily, I didn't recoil. "Doesn't smell like an outhouse. Maybe Charity just stepped out."

Dawn shook her head as she picked Athena up. "There's a doggy door that leads to a fenced yard. Apollo and Athena are well trained, but they're probably starving, not to mention parched."

Dawn led the way inside. As I followed with Apollo in my arms, the home's warmth seeped into me. The place had a rustic feel, with western landscapes hanging from the walls, lots of exposed beams, and wood everywhere, much of it hand hewn. Had Charity built the place herself? Given the fact that she was a mechanic by trade, I couldn't put it past her, much as it rankled me that someone so gorgeous could also be so handy.

Still, not all was idyllic inside. Signs of the dogs' distress were everywhere. Pillows were strewn about the living room floor. Someone had ripped the edge of Charity's couch to ribbons, but as we entered the kitchen, the real damage became apparent. Garbage littered the floor, some of it from a trashcan that had been overturned, but the dogs had clearly contributed as well. As short as they were, it looked like they'd gone counter surfing, pulling down bags of bread and boxes of cereal. Someone had even given a bunch of bananas a good clawing.

Dawn set Athena down and disappeared into the pantry. She exited a moment later with a bowl in hand. "Good news. They knocked over their food bin, so they haven't gone hungry. Their water bowl is bone dry though. I bet they've been drinking out of the toilet. Can't fault them this time."

Larry shook his head as he looked around the kitchen. "I don't like this one bit. Charity called five days ago, I think. Unless these dogs are much bigger hellions than you're making them out to be, there's no way they made this mess in a morning. Charity must've been missing for at least two or three days."

Water gurgled from the kitchen faucet as Dawn refilled the bowl. "Like I said, there's no way Charity would've run off without making sure Apollo and Athena were taken care of. She loves these dogs more than anything."

I detected the faintest hint of jealousy in Dawn's voice. Maybe her relationship with Charity was more than physical. "You said Charity contacted you because of a disturbance, right? Do you remember the exact words she used?"

"Not the exact ones," said Larry. "But she complained about odd noises and said she had a strange suspicion someone or some*thing* was watching her. That's why I sent the animals to talk to her. Maybe better they didn't find her here. They probably would've gotten eaten alive by these dogs if Charity let them inside."

I pried Apollo's tongue from my face as I set him down. "Yeah, they're ferocious killers."

Dawn put the bowl on the ground, and Apollo barreled his way over, slurping at the water greedily. "Well, avian and feline messengers aside, we need to get to the bottom of this. First step is to make sure these pups are taken care of. I know a couple local rescues that can take them in. Hopefully one of them has space. Then we need to find Charity. Something could've happened to her."

"We'll start here," said Larry. "If something showed up to spook her, there should be evidence of it. Let's take a look around. See if we can sort through the chaos, see what was caused by the dogs and what might've been created by something else."

"What do you want us to look for?" said Tank.

"Anything suspicious," said Larry. "Doesn't have to be supernatural in nature. Emptied dresser drawers. Filing cabinets that have been rifled through. Forced doors, busted locks. All that kind of stuff. Although, if you do find glowing runes carved into the walls, that would be something to note, too."

Larry's jacket buzzed. He turned his attention to it, rifling through an interior pocket for his not-a-phone.

I couldn't call it a phone. Larry made it exceedingly clear upon first meeting him that it was *not a phone*. Instead, it was a two way sonic portal device that let him communicate with whoever was in possession of the not-a-phone's matching pair. Basically, it was a magical walkie talkie that didn't blow up anytime Larry laid hands on it, though given its flip capability and dark black casing, it resembled a mobile phone more than anything else.

Larry pulled it out, flipped it open, and put it to his ear. "Larry Stuttgart. What do you need, Frank?"

Frank Connors was the detective in charge of Special Investigation with the APD, a division I didn't know existed until I'd joined the Nyte Patrol and which didn't even sound like it dealt with supernatural phenomena, if I was being honest. Apparently, every police department had one and us normal folk blindly assumed they investigated sex crimes or bank fraud or some such. Frank Connors also happened to be the lucky soul in possession of Larry's paired not-a-phone.

Normally, Frank's gruff voice carried through the magical portal that served as the device's speaker, but perhaps Larry had the not-a-phone pressed more tightly to his head than usual. All I picked up was a tinny mumble and Larry's responses.

"Okay... Is that so? ... Well, look, Frank, I'll give it some thought. I'll pop over if I can. ... Yes, really. We're in the middle of something. ... Yes, something important. One of our clients has gone missing, and we have reason to believe foul play may have been involved. ... Fine, I'll try. Let me at least get things under control here."

While Larry talked, Dawn had wandered off and made a call on her own perfectly normal phone. I could hear her in the other room, speaking to one of the rescue shelters.

"What was that about?" I asked.

Larry tucked the device back into his jacket. "Frank wants us to check out a crime scene at Mt. Bonnell. Says there might be magic involved."

"What sort of magic?" asked Tank.

"How should I know?" said Larry. "Frank isn't a practitioner. Said they found a girl in a coma-like state and that he had a weird feeling about her. Thought it might be a stasis spell."

"And you declined the case?" I said.

"I didn't *decline*. I said I'd think about it. In case you haven't noticed, we have a situation on our hands. Dawn is right. Charity didn't pick up and leave. Something forced her hand. Seeing as she's already a client of ours, her case takes precedence."

I felt a twinge inside, the same as I'd felt when Larry told me he'd taken Charity's phone call and accepted her job without consulting me. Wasn't I supposed to be leading the team? "Larry, no one is saying we should drop Charity's dogs off, dust our hands, and be done with it, but if someone is bewitched, don't you think that's something we should check out? There can't be many other people in town who could help this young woman. Besides, this is our *business*. We get paid by taking jobs." Hell, I'd passed up an engineering internship for this. I needed to make it work.

Dawn returned, phone in hand. "Alright. I've got volunteers on the way. They'll take Apollo and Athena. Won't even have to keep them at a shelter. They have someone willing to board them at their house. I think that'll be better for them. They hate being kept apart." She looked at me, then Larry. "What's up? Did I miss something?"

Larry eyed me. I gave him a confident nod. "It would appear we've taken on more work. Lexie and I are going to meet Frank and see what's going on. Are you and Tank okay staying here and dealing with this mess on your own?"

Tank nodded. "We'll take a look around. See if we find traces of suspicious activity."

"After we get the dogs taken care of, that is." Dawn bent

down and picked up Apollo, who'd been making the rounds smelling our shoes. "Isn't that right, poor baby? Yes it is. *Yes, it is!*"

Larry sighed as Dawn nuzzled the pooch. "Tank, I'm counting on you to make sure those things don't come home with us. Dawn, get it out of your system now. Come on, Lexie."

As we headed down the steps, I gave Larry a sideways glance. "What's your problem with the dogs? Might be nice to have them around the house."

The wizard snorted. "Yeah, until Charity comes back for them, and then she and Dawn have a falling out over it. Trust me, it's not worth it. Besides, you're missing the most important point. Can you imagine if they got ahold of Bill?"

5

I pulled off Mopac onto 35th Street, heading into the nice neighborhoods sandwiched between the expressway and the Colorado River. Larry and I had talked for a while after leaving Charity's about Bill's negative experiences with animals, but eventually the conversation faded and we'd fallen silent behind the steady blare of the radio. Now that we approached Mt. Bonnell, the pups had long since left my train of thought, having instead been replaced by thoughts of the ensorcelled woman Frank Connors had called us about.

As I waited at a red light, I reached out and turned down the volume to Queensrÿche's "Jet City Woman." "Larry? Can I ask you something?"

He broke off from staring at the pedestal-mounted fighter jets at Camp Mabry. "About Charity's place or Frank's call?"

"Neither." I hit the gas as the light turned green. "Did you mean what you said? About teaching me magic."

"Oh." Larry's eyes brightened. "Well, sure. Of course I'd be willing to teach you."

"Okay." I paused for a moment, trying to collect my thoughts. "But... how would that even work?"

"Well, it would take time of course, and lots of practice. There's a reason I spent six years in wizarding school. It's not an easy art to master, but then again I suppose nothing is. Learning is a lifelong affair. That's true of magic as much as it is dentistry or civil engineering. I suppose it would make sense to start you off with the basics. Potions. Incantations. Maybe enchantments, too, though that's getting a little advanced."

"Larry, this all sounds really cool and all, but that isn't what I was getting at. My point is, how in the world would you teach *me* magic? I'm not one of you guys. I'm not a supernatural anything. I'm just a college student. Don't you need innate talent to be a wizard? A magical spark or something?"

"Well, you need *some* innate talent, sure. But it's not as exclusive a thing as you seem to think it is."

"It's not?"

"Not really. I think just about anyone has the potential to be a practitioner of the arts in some capacity, but few have the desire or exhibit the commitment necessary to get anywhere."

I peered at Larry quizzically. "You're not messing with me?"

"Of course not. Magic is everywhere. It's all around us. Why wouldn't anyone be able to access it?"

I drove past Pecos Street and slowed as I reached the bend. "You know I asked you how magic worked once. When we first met, actually. You never answered me."

"I absolutely answered you. I gave about five different plausible explanations as I recall, but they were all a bunch of nonsense. See, *then* I was messing with you."

"So how does it work? For real. No jokes."

Larry sighed. "That's a hard question to answer. It's like

asking a physicist how space works. It's there and there are rules associated with it, but just because I know how to use magic doesn't mean I can explain why it is the way it is."

"Well, explain how to use it then."

Larry looked pensive. "You've seen *Star Wars?*"

I snorted. "Do you even know me?"

"Fair enough. Stupid question. So magic is kind of like the Force. It's all around us. It infuses everything and every one of us. Some of us are closer to it than others and some more adept at touching it, but anyone can use it. You just have to reach out, feel it, grab hold of it, and bend it to your will. Simple as that."

"You're forgetting *Star Wars* explained the Force through the use of microscopic intelligent lifeforms called midichlorians."

Larry blew a raspberry. "Forget that. I'm talking original trilogy *Star Wars. That's* how magic works. The point is, anyone can be a Jedi—or a wizard or witch or sorcerer or warlock or whatever magical equivalent tickles your fancy. You simply have to believe and you have to train, and with time you'll get more adept at it."

I turned onto Mt. Bonnell Road. "But even in *Star Wars,* pretty much all the best Force users show a connection to the Force early on. There was always a moment in each of those movies you could point to and say, yup, that person's got it, whatever *it* is. I'm not that person. I don't have a magical bone in my body."

"You still have that demon tooth in your pocket?"

Larry had enchanted a demon tooth to make it transform into a softball bat and back for me at will. To this day, it was the most badass thing anyone had ever done for me. "These shorts are a little tight for demon teeth. It's in the console, between the seats."

"I saw you punt a nightmarish hell beast two hundred feet through the air with that thing. It must've weighed, what? A hundred and fifty pounds? How far can you bat a softball?"

"That's different," I said. "It's a *magic* bat."

"And *you* were the one wielding it. Seriously, girl, don't sell yourself short. You've got something. I sensed it the first day you walked into our house. Now to be fair, a lot of that was anger and frustration, but some of it was magic. I'd stake my name on it. Remember, my spell chose *you* to lead the Nyte Patrol."

"Yeah, because I'm a competent leader and I have a fundamental understanding of how to run a business."

"*And* because of something else. Something unknowable. Something nebulous. I think it's your ability. You've got the spark."

I saw the police lights as I crested the hill. An officer stood in the middle of the road, directing traffic, while at the side, the parking spots that were normally filled with tourists' and college students' cars were either empty or filled with emergency vehicles.

I pulled into a spot at the far end under the cedars and pulled the key from the ignition. "You really think I might have it?"

Larry didn't smirk. He just nodded. "I do, but we won't know until we try. My promise to you is that I'll work with you as long as you want. I'll include you in everything I do, either until you get a feel for it or you decide you want to give up. Deal?"

"Deal."

Larry held out a hand, and we shook. As we did, one of the

officers crossed from the entrance to the park to our car. He motioned for us to roll down the window.

I did him one better and got out of the truck.

"Turn it around," he said, twirling his finger in the air. "Park's closed. Active investigation going on."

Larry climbed out and puffed himself up, but he still looked as disheveled and untrustworthy as ever. "We know. We're here at Frank Connors' request. You know him?"

The officer blinked. "Yeah, I know him. Who are you?"

"Larry Stuttgart. This is Lexie Rodriguez. We're with the Nyte Patrol. Frank said there was a girl in a coma we needed to take a look at."

The officer shrugged. "Okay, then. If Frank called you, I guess you can go up. Don't step on any toes."

We sauntered past him to the yellow police tape that had been stretched across barriers at the park's entrance. I went under it and Larry over before we put our feet to the mortared limestone steps that would take us to the top of the hill. Neither of us knew exactly where we were going, but it wasn't a big park. Once we reached the top of the stairs, the only choices were to take the path to the right, the left, or to go over the barrier and tumble down the cliff into the million dollar homes at the shores of the Colorado River. A police photographer headed our way from the path to the right, so we took an educated guess and followed his trail. It didn't take us long to find the rest of the officers. A cluster of them gathered past the second scenic overlook, among them a khaki-clad middle aged guy with gray-speckled hair, a Magnum P.I. mustache, and eyebrows so gnarled that baby birds could've nested in them.

Larry called out as we approached. "Frank!"

Connors split off from the group and motioned us over. "There you are. Glad you could fit us into your busy schedule."

"Hey, you have a stiff on your hands, we have a missing persons case. We've each got our problems. Cut me some slack."

"I don't have a stiff," said Connors. "The girl we found is very much alive, just not conscious. Her breathing is shallow but stable. Trust me, if I had another wizard on call who wasn't as much of a thorn in my ass as you are, don't you think I would've called him instead?"

"Well, we're working on that—assuming you don't mind calling a witch instead." Larry gave me a wink.

Connors' brow furrowed as he looked between the two of us. *"What?"*

I didn't want to go into that particular conversation with Connors, not when the most magic I'd thus far exhibited was an ability to swing an enchanted bat. "Larry didn't give me the full rundown on the ride over. You said this girl might be in a magical stasis?"

"It's my guess, but that's why I called Larry," said Connors. "A young couple snuck off into the cedar elms to canoodle. That's when they heard a cell phone ringing. They called out but didn't get a response, so they figured someone might've lost it. When they pushed through some of the underbrush they found her."

"She's in a coma?" said Larry.

"Something like that."

"What makes you think it's a magical one?"

"Well, the glowing crystals that surround her was a good indication."

Larry just about flipped his lid. *"Glowing crystals?* You didn't mention that when we first talked."

"Oh, would that have gotten your attention? Good to know. Next time I need your input, I'll make sure to mention there's a swirling portal threatening my existence as well."

"Just show us the girl, will you?" said Larry.

Connors nodded toward the edge of the path and headed into the woods. The brush thickened quickly, and the hill's slope took a precipitous dip, but as I'd said, it wasn't a big park. Within thirty seconds we spotted a pair of officers and a couple paramedics standing in the shade of a Spanish oak.

Connors swept a low hanging branch out of the way and stepped to the side, gesturing toward a patch of dirt covered with dried leaves and brush. "There she is."

Larry froze. His jaw dropped and his eyes turned into saucers. *"Jesus Christ.* That's not some girl. That's my niece!"

6

THE YOUNG WOMAN WHO LAY ON THE BED OF LEAVES must've been about my age, either in college or high school. She wore a V-neck T-shirt and a pair of distressed jeans with low-tops. She had a bandage around her right arm, just above the elbow, that was slightly darkened with blood, but other than that, she looked okay. She'd either fallen or been arranged into a natural sleeping pose, on her back with her walnut brown hair cascading around her shoulders. Her eyes were closed and she lay perfectly still, like a modern day Snow White except instead of being encased in a glass coffin she'd been surrounded with a few dozen pink crystals. They were geometric and angular, perhaps rose quartz, and each of them pulsed with the faintest of internal glows.

Larry spun to Connors. "This is Madison. My niece! How could you not tell me it was *my niece?*"

Frank looked flabbergasted. "She's related to you? How the hell should I have known that? She didn't have any identification on her, and her phone's locked. I simply called because of the magic angle."

"She didn't have any identification...?" Larry's face hardened. "Wait, did you *search* her?"

Frank frowned. "What do you think? Of course we searched her. We needed to identify her."

"So you *stepped over the circle?* Christ Almighty, everyone step back! STEP BACK!" Larry threw his hands in the air, gesturing frantically to the officers and paramedics already on the scene. They did as he told them, eyeing Larry with distrust as they retreated two paces. One of the police officers even moved a hand to his sidearm.

Frank took a cautious step forward, approaching Larry the same way one might a wild animal. "Larry, calm down. I know it's a shock to find your niece here, but—"

"That's not why I'm upset, damn it! Do you not have eyes? Do you not see the ring of glowing crystals around her?"

"Of course I see them. That's why I called you in the first place."

"*No.* You didn't mention crystals at all. You said you had a suspicion magic was involved. You said *nothing* of crystals, and you certainly didn't mention how they'd been arranged." Larry wiped a hand across his face. He closed his eyes and took a deep breath.

I put a hand to his shoulder. "Larry? Are you okay?"

"I'll be fine." He let his hands drop. "Okay, Frank, listen close. I need to know *exactly* what happened here. Who found her. Who searched her. What happened to them. I need to know about anyone who's broken the circle."

"It was Officers Mendez and Washington who first arrived on the scene. I think Mendez was the one who checked her pulse and searched her for ID. They called it in, and not long after the call rang through to my desk. The paramedics were on the scene before I was. They determined she was unconscious but stable. I arrived soon enough after they did to tell them not to move her because, yes, I *did* notice the crystals. That's when I called you."

"Did anyone else break the circle?"

"You mean walk over to check on the young woman? Yeah, the photographer. The couple who found her might've, too. I don't know. Why? Does it matter?"

"Have you not learned anything in your years on the job, Frank? The circle is the most powerful shape in nature. Add magic to the mix and even the most mundane circle can turn into something dangerous."

Frank shook his head. "I'm not sure about that. I'm pretty sure the triangle is the most powerful shape because it has the fewest degrees of freedom. The Mythbusters did an episode on it."

"Goddamnit, Frank! I'm not talking about engineering or structural mechanics here. I'm talking magic, and in magic, circles and stars are the shapes you need to be worried about. A circle imbued with magic can turn into a potent barrier. It can block things out or keep them in. It can strip magical power or enhance it into something deadly. It can do all sorts of crazy things. Now, think carefully. What happened when you crossed over the circle of crystals? Did anything shift? How did you feel? And most importantly, what happened to Madison?"

To his credit, Frank took the question seriously. He took a slow breath, eyed the girl, and reflected in silence. "I did feel something. Nothing major. Just a prickling on my arms. Goose-bumps. I thought it might've been a breeze or the strangeness of the situation. But Madison didn't react at all. She's been exactly this way since I found her."

Larry turned to the paramedics, a Hispanic man and a middle-aged white lady. "What about you two? Did you feel anything? Has Madison changed as far as you can tell? What's her condition?"

They looked at each other. The woman shook her head. "I might've gotten some goosebumps, too. Hard to remember. But as far as the young lady, she's been stable since we arrived. Heartbeat is slow but strong. Breathing is regular. She seems to have a nagging wound under that bandage on her arm, but otherwise, she's in good shape. We would've already moved her, otherwise."

"*Goosebumps...* Must be the magic." Larry sniffed the air. "Strange. I can't smell anything."

Larry always claimed he could smell magic, which was one more reason to think I didn't have a lick of occult power in me. All I could smell was damp earth and juniper pollen. "That's probably a good thing, right?"

"Maybe. Maybe not." Larry reached into his duster and pulled a fine silver chain from one of the pockets. Charms hung from it at regular intervals, but not the sort you'd find at Pandora. There were items wrought from precious metals to be sure, religious symbols mostly. I spotted a Christian cross, a Star of David, and a Buddhist Dharma Chakra, among others, but there were also less symbolic trinkets attached as well. A shark's tooth. A bleached white bone that had been scavenged from the corpse of a baby bird. A garnet secured with a thin strip of napped leather.

Larry wrapped the chain around his hand, clenching his fist to keep it in place. He swept his eyes across the rest of us before giving me and Connors a nod. "Stay where you are. Don't speak. I'm going to investigate. Hopefully it's not as bad as it looks."

We nodded. Larry stepped to the edge of the crystals. They barely responded to his presence, glowing ever so slightly stronger. The rosy light they emanated reminded me of something, but I didn't have time to give them much thought. Larry spoke, his voice firmer and more confident than I was used to hearing. *"Potestates, quod est, praesidio."*

He took a long step over the edge of the crystals, pausing on the other side. He knelt beside Madison, raking his eyes over the crystals, over the ground beneath her, taking in every element of her positioning. He peered at her fingers, lightly curled with nothing between then. He checked both sides of her neck, then crouched by her head to look down the length of her body. Eventually, he reached out with the hand that clutched the chain and extended his index and middle finger. He pressed them against her throat, his lips moving slightly as he took stock of her pulse. He moved the same hand over her heart, holding it an inch above her chest. He opened his palm fully, the ends of the chain dangling over her V-neck. He closed his eyes, and I could almost see him strain his ears.

A light breeze rustled the leaves above, and I heard a high pitched chirping, maybe a barn swallow. In the distance, cars hummed along Mt. Bonnell Road, the roar of their engines muffled by the trees. Larry had frozen, his arms as still as Michelangelo's *David.*

I tried to wait, but I couldn't. I spoke, my voice barely a whisper. "Larry? Is she okay?"

His eyes opened, and he stood. He turned and took a deliberate step outside the circle. "Yes. I definitely felt something, but

I don't think she's under a spell. Certainly, I couldn't sense one. It's... *odd*." He kept his gaze on Madison, worry in his eyes.

"And the circle?" asked Connors.

Larry shook his head. "I felt some pushback as I stepped over the edge but not that of a magical barrier. Nothing kicked me out or forced me to leave my power at the door."

"So it's okay to move her?"

Larry rubbed his beard scruff. "I suppose so. If we had good reason to."

Connors cocked his head, as if Larry were dense. To be fair, he was. "We can't leave her here. We need to get her to a hospital, get her under supervision."

Larry nodded. "Okay. That's probably for the best. But be careful. No one touch the crystals." Larry pointed at the EMTs for emphasis.

They nodded, though I doubt they did it because they believed they had anything to fear. Probably so they wouldn't trigger the angry hobo who thought he was a wizard.

Someone called for Frank through the trees. "Just a minute." The detective motioned to the paramedics. "You two. Come with me to get a gurney."

As they walked away, I tugged at the sleeve of Larry's coat. "Larry."

He tore his eyes away from Madison. "Yeah? What is it?"

"Can we talk about those crystals?"

"I don't get it either. I could've sworn they'd been placed there as part of a magic circle. They must have another purpose. Was this a ritual of some sort? A cult thing? I don't know, and the fact that it's Madison in there isn't helping me think straight."

I still hadn't totally processed the fact that he had a niece. "Maybe the crystals were placed there as a message."

Larry blinked. "What do you mean?"

"Aren't those the same crystals you procured for Ivan Romanov a few months ago?"

Larry's eyes narrowed. "They're the same color, aren't they? Weren't his larger?"

"Romanov's were raw clusters. These look like they've been cut. They could've come from the same batch, though."

Larry shook his head. "I don't know, Lexie. Those were power focusing crystals, and I've already told you I didn't sense any shield or barrier attached to them. I couldn't smell a whiff of magic on Madison, either. Not to mention you've had Romanov on the brain for months. You need to accept the fact that he's gone. He's not going to bother us anymore."

Larry seemed convinced we'd dealt with Romanov in a permanent matter. To be fair, his body had erupted after I'd driven a stake through his heart, evaporating into a cloud of vaporized flesh and blood from the pressure of the compressed evil inside him. But unlike Larry, I wasn't so sure we'd seen the last of him. I'd sworn something had escaped his body as he died. Something evil. Larry had heard it too, even if he'd since decided to ignore it.

"I don't know," I said. "The fact that it's your niece... This can't be a coincidence, can it?"

Larry's brow furrowed in thought, but Frank's voice brought us back to the present. "Hey." He appeared through the trees, pushing offending branches out of his way. "You know a Carol Flemming?"

"Yeah," said Larry. "That's my sister. Madison's mother. Why?"

"Because she called a few minutes ago on your niece's phone. One of my guys answered. She's on her way."

7

Larry thrust his hands deep into his duster's pockets, his neck tucked into the upturned collar as we descended the steps from the top of Mt. Bonnell. A frown creased his face, and I'm not sure he'd lifted his eyes off the ground since Frank brought the news.

"So... I'm guessing you're not on the best of terms with your family," I said.

Larry snorted. "How'd you guess?"

"Maybe I'm psychic. Could be my area of magical expertise."

Larry didn't so much as smirk.

"So who started it?"

Larry looked up. "What do you mean?"

"Well in my experience, when a relationship falls apart both sides are usually to blame. With that said, there's always someone who instigates and someone who reacts. Were you the one who brought up politics at Thanksgiving dinner or was it your sister?"

Larry flicked a hand dismissively. "It's not like that. We're not on the best of terms, true, but there wasn't one glaring incident where everything went wrong. Our story consists of a long series of falling outs, and with this happening to Madison? It'll be the nail in the coffin. She's going to blame it on me, I know it."

"Why would she do that?"

"Because it was my decision to go into magic. Nobody ever supported me in that. Not my parents and definitely not my sister. She thought I was nuts, same as you did when you met me. She's accepted it, but she's never approved. None of them have."

I blinked, surprised as much by Larry's honesty as by what he said. Here I was, concerned about my parents not approving of my choice to join the Nyte Patrol and it turned out Larry's family felt the same way. I wasn't sure if that made me feel better or not. On the one hand, it was comforting to know my problem wasn't a unique one. On the other, I cherished the relationship with my family. I didn't want to jeopardize that over a job, even if said job did occasionally involve saving the world.

"So your family isn't a bunch of magic users?" I asked.

Larry snorted. "My dad's a dentist, and my mom was a teacher. My sister studied anthropology with a minor in ancient history. The first whiff any of them got of magic was when I accidentally burned down a quarter of our house while goofing around in my room."

I stretched my eyebrows. "How in the world did you do that?"

"I'm not sure. I was screwing around pretending I was a wizard, of all things. I was engaged in an epic battle with an imaginary dragon when the next thing I knew a gout of flame erupted from my fingertips and engulfed the Brittany Spears poster I had on the wall."

"Brittany Spears?"

"I was thirteen years old at the time. We're all allowed a crush at that age, I think."

We reached the bottom of the limestone steps. One of the paramedics was backing the ambulance up to the edge of the stairs. I pulled Larry to the side to get us out of the way. "Is that when your parents shipped you off to magic school?"

"I wish. Instead of accepting the fact that maybe I had supernatural talent, they tried everything they could to sweep it under the rug. I spent three years in counseling in an effort to get me to confess I'd actually set fire to my room as a way of dealing with suppressed feelings of resentment toward my parents. When that failed, my parents found new psychiatrists who tried to convince me I'd suffered a manic episode and set the fire without knowing it. Only when my rage boiled over and I blasted a hole in the side of the psychiatric facility did everyone concede that maybe I hadn't imagined the whole thing."

"Gosh, Larry. I'm sorry you had to deal with that. I always assumed you came from a big family of wizards, like the Weasleys in *Harry Potter*. Either that or you didn't have a family. Honestly, I'm still struggling to picture you as a kid, sitting in the back seat of a van on a road trip to Carlsbad Caverns or waving to your mom after getting third place at a swim meet."

"What, you think I appeared out of the aether as a full grown adult? That a grizzled sorcerer plucked me from the primordial goo while his underlings chanted incantations?"

"Of course not. It's just strange. I didn't expect your origin story to be so... *relatable.*"

"Humble it might be, but it wasn't any fun, I guarantee you. I would've much rather been a Ron Weasley, but I was Harry. The muggle-born. Except muggles don't exist. Like I told you, magic is more like the Force. Everyone can control it, some just do it better than others and with less training."

Wheels clacked off stone as the paramedics wheeled Madison down the stairs on a gurney. Larry looked at her still body, his eyebrows drawn together and his lips pressed into a frown.

"How close are the two of you?" I asked.

He shook his head. "Not close enough, but it's still hard. I'll be honest. I wasn't expecting to find her here, and I'm not entirely sure what's wrong with her."

"Are you going to be okay?"

"Depends on if she is."

An engine revved at the edge of my hearing, but the sound grew louder quickly. In a moment, a tan Buick lurched around the edge of the trees. Tires screeched as the driver slammed on the brakes, pulling the car into a sharp turn a few spots down from the ambulance.

"Speaking of people who aren't going to be okay..." said Larry.

The car door flew open and out jumped a woman who was perhaps a decade Larry's senior. She had dark hair like he did, wavy and with a gloss to it, that fell about a half foot past her clavicle. She had a longer than normal nose, same as Larry, but otherwise she didn't look much like him. Maybe it was because she was actually put together, wearing trim pants, a flowy blouse, and black Kate Spade flats. She did have heavy bags under her eyes, though, and an aura of panic radiated off her.

"Oh my God, Madison!" She raced toward the gurney without bothering to close her car door. "Madison! Can you hear me? Oh God, is she okay? Please tell me she's okay!" She grasped Madison's hand while latching onto one of the poor EMTs.

The Hispanic guy who'd been on the lower half of the gurney was as polite as could be in extracting himself from her grip. "It's alright, ma'am. She's breathing, and her vitals are solid. She's going to get through this, we just need to get her to St. David's for evaluation."

That didn't satisfy her. She stared at Madison with a mixture of disbelief and horror, refusing to let go of her daughter's hand. It wasn't until she looked up that she spotted us.

Her eyes fixed, and her jaw clamped shut so tight I was surprised she was able to get the snarl out. *"Larry."*

"Hey, Carol."

Carol darted around the edge of the gurney and descended upon us. She came swinging—literally. She pelted Larry in the arm and chest with fists as she let out her frustration. *"How could you do this to her?* How could you let it happen?"

Larry turned to the side, shielding himself from her blows. "Christ, Carol! Calm down! I had nothing to do with this. I came to help!"

"Liar! This is your fault. You brought this on her! *You!* With your magic and your supernatural nonsense and gods knows what! God, Madison... I just... I can't even..."

Larry tried to take hold of her. "Carol, please. Hear me out."

He managed to grasp one of her wrists, but by then the anger had left her. She collapsed forward, her weight knocking Larry off balance. She wrapped Larry in a fierce hug and started sobbing uncontrollably. "She didn't come home last night, Larry.

She wouldn't answer her phone. I called so many times. She'd never done that before. Oh, God. I was so worried..."

Larry stiffened, but it only took him a moment to hug her back. "Okay, Carol. It's going to be fine. I promise."

Carol pulled back, tears streaming down her cheeks. "You don't know that. You don't get to make that promise."

"Then how about this? I'm going to do everything I can to make sure Madison comes out of this in one piece. I'm going to figure out what's wrong with her, and if there's *anything* I can do to help, you better believe I'm going to do it. Okay?"

Carol took a deep breath and let it out in a shuddering sigh. She reached up and wiped tears from her face, even though they were still flowing. "Okay." Another deep, body-wracking breath. "What happened to her? What do you know?"

"Not much," said Larry. "Probably no more than you learned over the phone. Physically, she's fine. Mentally, there's some disconnect going on. There might be magic involved. I don't know any more yet, but I will. Soon."

The ambulance clunked as the paramedics loaded Madison's gurney. The Hispanic EMT looked over, uncertain if he should interrupt. "Excuse me? Ma'am? Do you want to ride with us to the hospital?"

"I'll follow you. Give me a second." Carol turned back to Larry. "You promise?"

"I thought I wasn't allowed to make promises."

Carol's face darkened, anger threatening to overtake her again.

Larry hung his head. "I'm sorry. Yes, Sis, I promise. You have my word."

She gave a curt nod, then turned and ran to her car. The back doors on the ambulance clanged as the paramedics shut them from the inside. A moment later, the siren wailed, and the van pulled onto the street. Carol's Buick roared to life, her tires screeching as she pulled behind the ambulance at a closer than advisable distance.

The two vehicles disappeared down the hill. Larry sighed.

I turned to him. "Whoa."

"Don't say anything. I don't want to hear it."

"Hear what? Larry, I'm not going to rip on you for having an emotional moment with your sister. It's more than deserved considering the circumstances. I'm not sure if I should've been here for it, but that's life. It unfolds even when you're not ready for it."

Larry sucked back a sniffle, and I noticed an extra layer of wetness coating his eyes. "Thanks, Lexie. I appreciate it. But I can't let it get to me. I promised Carol I'd fix this, and goddamnit, I'm going to try."

"So what do we do? I've never investigated anything before, much less an actual crime."

"We follow the clues, wherever they take us. And right now, we only have one."

"The crystals?"

Larry nodded. "I think you're right about those being the same ones we found for Romanov. The fact that they were used against my niece can't be a coincidence."

"The last time we saw them was at the vampire rave at Romanov's estate, but when we went back later that same night, Romanov had already moved them."

"Then we need to figure out where he put them—and who might've gotten their hands on them afterwards." Larry nodded toward the Suburban. "Come on. We don't have any time to lose."

8

A LOCKED GATE BARRED ME ENTRY WHEN I PULLED ONTO the driveway to Romanov's estate. The posts at the side of the thing looked like they'd recently been cemented into place. A 'FORECLOSED' sign plastered across the top included instructions to call First Century Realtors or Wells-Fargo Bank for inquiries.

I put the Suburban into park and killed the engine. "This place fell into foreclosure?"

Larry shrugged. "It's not surprising. Romanov was the architect of the vampire academy. Given he was pretending to be his own second-in-command, I suspect he didn't have anyone in waiting to handle things when he blew up into a giblet mist."

Larry hopped out of the car and I followed him around to the gate. "I guess I'm surprised he didn't own the place."

Larry pursed his lips. "Even wealthy folks need loans now and then. Maybe he had all his cash tied up in illiquid investments when he made the purchase. He seemed like the kind of guy who'd have his fingers in all kinds of nasty stuff—illicit arms deals, foreign hotel takeovers, oil and gas rights. You name it."

"Oil and gas?"

"The biggest cartel in the world, kid. Half the wars over the past two centuries have been fought over the stuff, and the companies slinging it haven't kept the world under their thumb by being nice." He flicked the sign. "Come on. Let's see what we can find."

As at Mt. Bonnell, Larry climbed over the gate while I ducked under. We walked along the drive, feeling the warm May sun on our necks and listening to the buzz of insects in the flowers at the side of the road. Eventually, the trees lining the driveway parted, giving us a glimpse of the castle beyond. It didn't have a moat or a portcullis, but it was built of solid stone, and at over four stories tall and with roughly a hundred rooms inside, it was just the sort of place you'd expect to house a coven of murderous vampires. At least, it was in central Texas. There wasn't a lot of Gothic architecture in the Hill Country.

"Any idea what happened to all the vampires who were here when we last visited?" We'd killed a lot of inhuman bat-vampire hybrids during our final tango with Romanov, but the regular vampires who'd stayed at his academy and partaken in meth-fueled dubstep orgies had largely avoided the slaughter.

"I heard they fled to communities in Los Angeles, Las Vegas, and Miami."

"Aren't those places a little sunny for vampires?"

"I don't think they moved there for the weather. You have to remember most of the vampires in Romanov's care were douchebags."

We skirted the house and headed along one of the many gravel paths into the grounds at the back. Despite the fact that the property was in foreclosure, the grass remained green, free of weeds, and trimmed to an acceptable height. The holly bushes and junipers also looked like they'd recently been subjected to the whims of a pair of hedge clippers. Birds chirped in the trees overhead, and water gurgled in a nearby fountain. Given the bucolic nature of it all, it was hard to believe the last time I'd been here a hoard of naked vampires had nearly torn my throat open in a savage bloodlust.

I didn't remember exactly where the vampires had congregated for their party, but the property wasn't so large that you could get lost for long. Larry and I followed the widest path. After a couple false turns, we found our way to the circular plaza. It didn't much resemble the picture I had of it in my mind. The paved area was barely bigger than the backyard on a campus frat house, and with the drugged out vampires, blazing torches, and stake at the center removed, it didn't have the same aura of murderous intent it once had. Someone had repaired the damage we'd done, too. The scorch marks had been sandblasted from the pavers and the grass around the area nursed back to health. Even the spot where Tank had barreled into the trees had been replanted.

Larry stopped at the center of the bricks. He sucked on his teeth as he gazed around him, his hands stuck deep in his pockets.

"Any thoughts?" I said.

"Some. I bet this place would sell faster if they took out the pavers and put in a pool. Not a lot of high end buyers in this neighborhood that would overlook that. This is central Texas after all."

"About the *crystals,* Larry."

Larry lost some of his smile. "Yeah, I know. I'm trying to lighten the mood. When things get too serious, I get stressed, and well, seeing Madison there on the ground..." He sighed.

"Obviously, we need to figure out who could've swiped those crystals. The problem is, we lost track of them two and a half months ago."

"At least we know exactly *when* we lost track of them. And Romanov couldn't have moved them far, not in the few hours between our first trip here and our second to recover the sword."

"I'm not saying you're wrong, but you're already making assumptions. It might've been Romanov who squirreled them away in the wake of our party crashing effort, but it's also possible someone else swiped them in the chaos. If so, that could complicate things."

"Who would've had a motive to do that?" I asked.

"I don't know. Someone who saw an opportunity. Someone who thought they could grab more power for themselves. I'm really not sure. Then again, I also don't know why anyone would've had a motive to come after my niece. Whatever's going on here is part of a puzzle we haven't even begun to piece together."

I frowned. "I think it's more likely Romanov stored them and someone else found them after his death."

"Probably, but that won't help us track them any more than my theory."

"What does it matter whose theory is right? Does it affect the spell you need to use to locate the crystals?"

"Spell?" Larry blinked and shook his head. "You thought I was going to track down the crystals' owner using a *spell?*"

"How else would you do it?"

"The normal way. By snooping around Romanov's house, opening closets and pulling back baseboards and narrowing the field of who might've known about whatever hidey-hole they were squirreled away in. And if that fails by following

Romanov's legal bequeathment or records of sale from the fore-closure of his home. I've told you more than once that tracking magic isn't a thing. I can smell magic, sure, but objects imbued with magical energy smell far less powerfully than spells. I could barely even detect the crystals at the scene of Madison's bewitching, and they were right there."

"So there's nothing your magic can do to help us?"

"I didn't say *that*. I didn't come to this clearing because I thought I'd find a three month old gum wrapper that our crystal thief dropped as he made a desperate escape with the treasure. I'm not Adrian Monk. But I did think I might be able to provide some insight that Tank and Dawn couldn't when they came looking. You see, in addition to magical smell, there's a skill called Listening, and another one called Sight."

"Larry, those aren't skills. You're naming senses."

"No, these are capitalized. That means they're imbued with magical energy and fundamentally different."

I crossed my arms. "I thought we'd gotten past the part of our relationship where you screw with me for shits and giggles."

"I'm not screwing with you!" said Larry. "I'm dead serious. By Listening—with a capital 'L' mind you—I'm able to hear better than a dog or even a mouse. I can parse through frag-ments of conversations from a hundred feet away, and that's not all. Sometimes I can pick up on whispers of the past that linger in the air, kind of like sonic flashbacks that tie themselves to the environment. And with Sight—"

A grumpy voice cut across the expanse. "Hey! What are you doing here?"

Larry and I turned to find an old man in a green jumpsuit heading toward us. A shock of grey hair trailed from behind his baseball cap, and a thick beard engulfed his face. He held a dirt-encrusted shovel toward us menacingly, and the scowl he wore suggested he wouldn't hesitate to swing it if things got out of hand.

"Put down the spade, Pops." Larry held his hands out. "Nobody's making any trouble."

The old guy continued his slow but methodical approach. I noticed the words *AJ's Lawn Care* on his jumper. "Nobody but the two of you. Scram. This is private property."

"We know," I said. "We're from Wells Fargo. We're property assessors." I'm not always the best off the draw, but I have my moments.

The old guy paused, the tip of his shovel dipping. "You're with the bank?"

"Of *course* we're with the bank." Larry shot me a thankful glance. "We're here to determine the outstanding value of the remaining, ah... lawn furniture."

It probably would've helped if Larry picked something that actually existed in the plaza. Then again, the place was barren of anything but brick pavers.

The gardener scowled again. "All that stuff got auctioned off over a month ago."

"And we're here to make sure we got the last of it," I said. "We'll just need to check the house next to make sure—"

"All that got auctioned off a month ago, too." The graybeard clenched his jaw and took another step forward, lifting his shovel. "Now listen here you damn zombie sex fetish weirdos. I've had enough of your kind breaking in here and using this plaza as your personal bedroom. You best leave in ten seconds or I'm calling the cops."

"*Zombies?*" I said. "It was vampires who were here before us. And we're not—"

"NINE! EIGHT!"

Larry and I made like freshmen at a kegger and got scarce. I doubt the old guy could've kept pace with us, but I didn't slow until I reached the house. Larry couldn't keep up either, but he tried. He huffed and puffed as we rounded the corner to the driveway.

He shook his head as he caught his breath. "I can tango with fire-breathing hell beasts and yet I let an old guy with a shovel get the drop on us. How inglorious..."

"We could still break into the house," I offered. "Make sure he was being honest about the estate sale."

"Not worth it. If I had to bet, Groundskeeper Willie over there already called the police, and despite my relationship with Frank, I doubt I could get us out of a B&E. We mostly got what we came for anyway."

I blinked. "We did?"

"Sure. Confirmation that Romanov's stuff was all sold off. I bet you dollars to donuts the crystals were among the items."

"So someone bought the crystals in an auction and used them to come after your niece?"

Larry shrugged as he hoofed it along the drive, sweat beading his brow. "Hey, I didn't say I understood the puzzle any better now than I did a minute ago. But clues are clues. I'll take anything that gets us closer to understanding Madison's condition."

My phone buzzed in my pocket. I pulled it out to see that Dawn was ringing me.

I answered. "Hey, Dawn. What's up?"

"Hey, Lexie. Is Larry with you?"

"Sure. Want to talk to him?"

"Yeah. Put him on speaker."

I did. No way was I letting Larry touch my phone. I didn't have the insurance plan. "Okay. You're on."

Larry paused as we reached the front gate. "What's new, Dawn?"

Her voice warbled. "Oh, you know. Got the dogs picked up. Searched Charity's house. Now we're being haunted by a malevolent spirit. The usual."

"Malevolent spirit?" said Larry.

"Yeah," said Dawn. "And, ah... Well, let's just say some weird stuff is going on over here. You mind coming back and giving us an assist? Because if you don't I'm debating stealing Charity's Jeep and getting the hell out of here."

A shadow crossed Larry's face, and he nodded curtly. "We're on our way, Dawn. You guys hold tight."

9

My door clanged shut as I hopped out of the Suburban. Dawn sat in a faded folding chair that she'd angled toward Charity's house, her eyes fixed on the front door. She didn't even get up as we ran toward her.

"Dawn," said Larry. "Where's Tank? Are you okay?"

"Hey." She cast us a quick glance. "Tank's still inside. I've... been better."

That seemed to be an understatement. She sat there with pursed lips. Her hands gripped the armrests tight, and she refused to keep her eyes off the house for more than a moment or two.

"Is Tank okay?"

"Fine, I think." Dawn gave the house one last wary glance before giving us her full attention. "I guess he's not as skittish as me. I don't like things I can't kill with a piece of sharpened steel."

"What happened?" I asked.

Dawn took a deep breath. "Not much, at first. After you guys left, we cleaned up the kitchen while Apollo and Athena drank another two bowls of water each. Then we looked around the house while we waited for the Madre Santos Pit Bull Rescue to show up. Tank took the first floor, and I headed upstairs to Charity's bedroom. After checking it out, I can say with total certainty Charity didn't leave on her own. Certainly her departure wasn't planned. It might not even have been willing. I found sets of keys to her CJ and her Ranchero." Dawn pulled one of them from her lap and dangled it for emphasis.

"You think she was abducted?" I said.

Dawn shrugged, her eyes becoming less haunted as she got into the story. "I'm not sure. I didn't find any evidence of a struggle, at least nothing I couldn't attribute to the dogs. Charity normally keeps the bedroom door closed, at least she always has when she and I are... you know. It was closed when I got up there, and inside it was mostly in order. I don't think she packed any clothes. Her suitcase was still in the closet. It's almost as if she went out and never came home, but her cars are here, so... I don't know."

The front door squeaked. Dawn's head turned on a swivel. Her eyes widened, but it was just Tank, sandwich in hand. "Hey, guys."

Dawn let her breath out, shaking her head and muttering something under her breath. "God. Don't do that to me."

"Do what?" Tank took a bite from the sandwich as he descended the stairs. "You tell them about the ghost yet?"

"She was getting to it." Larry pointed at the sandwich. "You make that here?"

Tank nodded. "The ham was on its last legs. Figured I'd put it out of its misery."

Larry threw up his hands. "Tank! You can't do that. This

isn't our home, and Charity didn't offer to cover expenses when she hired me. That's an expense."

"It's a ham sandwich."

"Ham that we're going to have to reimburse. You think I want to go to H.E.B. to buy groceries for Charity Peterson? That's not part of the job."

"Guys! Seriously?" I gave the two of them my best reproachful glance. "You were saying, Dawn?"

She gave me a look only women can understand. "Anyway, while I was upstairs checking to make sure Charity's dressers hadn't been emptied, the dogs downstairs *freaked out*. They started barking like crazy. Claws clacking against the hardwood as they accelerated at top speed. Ran straight for the door, I think. You were downstairs, Tank. You should be telling this part."

Tank gestured toward the door with his sandwich. "Dawn's right. Front door was closed. I hadn't heard a darned thing, but the dogs sure did. They took off, barking their heads off like we were under attack by ISIS. I got about ten steps after them before they went dead silent. I mean, not a peep out of them. They froze, too. Stood there for maybe two seconds, quiet as mice, before they turned tail and ran, whimpering and whining, out the doggy door to the backyard. Poor Athena nearly smashed her head into the glass trying to beat Apollo there. As they ran out, a whoosh of air rushed past me, from them running is what I thought at first. But the breeze had a cool bite to it, and it prickled my skin as it went past."

"Like goosebumps?" I said.

Tank nodded, and Dawn kept narrating. "I ran down the stairs to see what was going on. At this point the dogs had already bolted outside. I can't say I felt anything weird passing through the kitchen, but my concern was for the pups. I raced out and tried to get them to calm down, but they'd retreated inside Charity's maintenance shed. I talked to them softly while Tank found treats we could use to coax them out. They didn't help much, if I'm being honest. About twenty minutes into that the Madre Santos folks showed up. Thankfully, they had equipment to help us get Apollo and Athena out, but it was an ordeal, and both of those poor dogs were terrified once we got them into their cages. I almost didn't want to let the rescue take them in that condition. At least, I didn't until I got back into the house."

Tank took his third bite of the sandwich, which was down to little more than a nub. "Once we got the dogs loaded in the rescue van, we headed back inside. As soon as we stepped through the door, we both sensed something was wrong. It was a good eight to ten degrees cooler inside than it had been when we'd left, and there was something else, too. A weird energy in the air. Dawn turned to ask me if I felt it when we heard the moan."

"It was creepy," said Dawn. "Low and pained, like a person on morphine. It was also barely audible, and it died off quickly. I don't know about Tank, but I thought I might be hearing things. Then I heard it again, coming from Charity's room."

"I took point," said Tank, "but we went up the stairs together. The door was closed even though Dawn could've sworn she left it open when she chased after the dogs. Suffice to say we were a little apprehensive when we opened it, but there was no one inside. There were footprints, however. Not from a shoe. From feet."

"Human feet?" asked Larry.

"The same shape, anyway," said Dawn. "But they weren't from mud or dust. They were *burned* into the floor. They led to one of Charity's dressers. As we stood there, we both heard another moan. A clear one. It came from the dresser."

I felt like I was standing around a campfire at night listening to someone with a flashlight held under their chin. The difference was I actually cared about the outcome of this story. "What did you do?"

"We had to check it out," said Tank. "Obviously a person couldn't fit in Charity's dresser. We walked over and pulled out the top drawer only to have the one second from the bottom start shaking violently. Dawn just about jumped out of her capris."

Dawn snorted. "It startled you too, don't act like it didn't. But the rumbling didn't stop. The drawer kept jostling, like there was a rabid possum in it. As it shook out, the eerie moan we'd heard filled the room. Then something exploded from the clothes, scattering underwear and bras everywhere. A force rushed at me. A swirl of wind, surrounded by a whirlwind of lingerie, and it... it..."

"It what?" asked Larry.

Dawn's voice dropped. "It *violated* me. I don't know how else to describe it. I could feel it rippling all over me, pressing against portions of me it shouldn't have, laughing and moaning at the same time. Every pore on my skin prickled. I cried out and slapped at myself to get it off me. I guess that was enough. It shot off, straight through the ceiling, I think. I didn't stay to investigate. I ran out of there as fast as I could and haven't ventured back."

"Christ, Dawn." I grasped her by the shoulder and gave her a friendly squeeze. "Are you okay?"

She smiled and gave a small nod. "I'm fine. Just shook up. It's not an experience I want to go through again."

Tank gulped down the last of the meal. "Not to minimize anything Dawn went through, but I should point out nothing molested me. For the record."

Dawn tipped her head at us. "What about you guys? Were you able to help Connors with that problem of his?"

Larry scratched his neck. "Not really, and it's worse than we thought. The girl they found in the park? It's my niece, Madison."

He might as well have slapped Dawn. She stood, her eyes stretching wide in shock. "Oh my God, Larry! Why didn't you say something? Is she okay?"

"She's in some sort of coma. No one's sure what caused it, but there could be a magical connection. She was surrounded by a magic circle in the forest."

"Oh, Larry..." Dawn pulled him into a hug, which Larry gingerly returned. Tank closed in and gave him a pat on the shoulder as well.

"I appreciate the concern, but it's alright, guys. Madison's stable—for now, anyway. Even if magic isn't to blame, I'm not going to rest until I figure out what's wrong with her."

Dawn released him. "I thought you said you found her in a magic circle."

"One assembled from pieces of the crystals we tracked down for Romanov a few months back, no less," said Larry. "But with that said, I couldn't sense any magic on her."

"So you don't know what's wrong with her?" said Tank.

Larry took a deep breath. "I didn't at first, but taking into account everything you've experienced here: the way Charity's dogs reacted, the temperature fluctuations, the moans, the prickled skin? Pretty obvious we're dealing with a poltergeist. And given the paramedics and police officers broke out in goosebumps entering the magic circle and that I didn't sense any magic on Madison..."

My brow furrowed in thought. "What are you saying, Larry?"

He gave me a worried glance. "Madison may not be bewitched. She might be *possessed*."

10

L<small>ARRY STARED AT ME FROM THE FLOOR, HIS GAZE</small> unwavering and his demeanor dead serious. "Are you *sure* you want to do this, Lexie?"

I sat on Charity's bed, which Tank had pushed into the corner of her bedroom before retreating to hang out with Dawn downstairs. We'd also cleaned up Charity's underwear, returned it to her drawer, and replaced it in the dresser. "I'm sure, Larry. You said you thought I might have some magical ability. The spark, you called it. I don't see any reason to sit around twiddling my thumbs. I want to give it a try, and if I'm going to learn, I might as well start now."

"Fair enough," said Larry. "I said I was willing to teach you, and I meant it. *However*—casting a spell is a different beast than performing a séance. We're talking about entering the spirit realm. The otherworld. The beyond. Whatever you want to call it."

"You might as well be speaking Swahili to me. How is entering the spirit realm not an act of magic?"

"It is, in that crossing over from the mortal realm into the spirit realm requires a spark of magic, but it's not like collecting fire among your fingertips or freezing a pond solid or even slowing time. It's much more akin to summoning a demon than it is to your standard defense magic."

"Swahili, Larry."

Larry sighed. "Okay. Think of it this way. The mortal world, the one in which you and I live, is governed by a set of physical rules. That's the whole basis of physics. To establish the rules that govern matter, motion, space, and time. Technically, chemistry is also a study of the rules that govern our world, but we'll stick with physics. I don't want this to get too complicated. Speaking of which, have you ever read any Stephen Hawking or Neil deGrasse Tyson?"

"I mean, I watched the Cosmos reboot when it came on TV."

"Ok. So you've probably been introduced to the idea that there are more than the four dimensions everyone is capable of grasping: three in space and one in time. The Kaluza–Klein theory postulated in the nineteen-forties that there was a fifth dimension. String theory postulates there are ten dimensions, while M-theory says there are eleven. Some scientists think there are even more. I don't know who's right, but there are certainly more than four. Magic exists on one of those extra dimensions."

The bed squeaked underneath me as I shifted. "So you're saying you can see and feel in more dimensions than most people?"

"Yes," said Larry. "But that's not the point I'm getting at. My point is that like space and time, magic is a physical entity. That's why it's like the Force. It's all around us, even if we can't see it. It's a dimension to the universe in which we live. The spirit realm is not like that. It's an alternate universe, one that's closely tied to our own but alternate all the same. The rules that govern space and time and *magic* are different there than they are here. It's a weird place."

"Hold on," I said. "So if we're planning on visiting the spirit realm, and the spirit realm is an alternate universe, then by performing a séance, we're creating a wormhole?"

Larry nodded. "Precisely. A magical one."

I snorted. "I don't know why I bother. Every time you explain something to me about magic it sounds like you're pulling words out of your ass."

"That's because you never attended Zephyrburr Magical Academy with me. Trust me, everything I'm telling you is well-established Astromagical Physics, and yes, that's the official name of the discipline. But I don't want you getting snared in the specifics of how the wormhole works. What's important is that you learn some of the fundamental rules of the spirit realm so you can protect yourself there."

"Like no speeding in a school zone?"

Larry frowned. "Lexie, this is serious. One unfortunate misstep in the spirit realm can be the difference between life and death, which basically means the ability to come back to the real world or not."

I sighed. "Sorry. I'm listening."

Larry waved at me. "Come down here with me. I feel like I'm talking to a queen."

In moving the bed, we'd found that the ghostly steps burned into the floor had been more soot than actual char. Larry had instructed me to wipe them up with a hand towel while Tank had done the heavy lifting.

I hopped off the bed and joined Larry in the space cleared

by Charity's bed. I sat crosslegged across from him, parroting his stance. "Better?"

"Much." Larry took a slow breath, his elbows resting lightly on his knees. I thought he might start up a yoga session. "Now. The first thing you have to understand about the spirit realm is that it's a parallel universe of our own. *Parallel* is key. It mimics our universe, and by extension, our world. This room exists in the spirit realm. Charity's house does. Austin, Texas does. However, the *dimensions* of the spirit realm differ. Spatial dimensions exist, but they're more fluid than they are here. They tend to stretch and condense without rhyme or reason, and objects are both there and not there. I think it has to do with our perception of space. We're simply not equipped to deal with it. Also, there is no dimension of time. Beings do not age. If you were to construct a clock there from otherworld parts, it wouldn't work. That said, the world is constantly changing because it parallels ours and our world *is* affected by time. So if you were to gaze upon a wall clock that mimics one in our world, the hands would move, if perhaps sporadically."

"Hold on," I said. "If time doesn't pass there but it does here and that world mimics our world to resemble the passage of time, isn't it a semantic difference?"

"In some ways, yes. In others, no. Remember how I said magic is like a fifth dimension? Or twelfth, depending on who you ask? Well any magic that's dependent upon time doesn't function there. I can't cast stasis spells, for example. The whole dimension of magic is different. I probably don't need to go into it because you don't understand magic in our world yet, but trust me, it's a total bear, and I'm not anywhere near as capable there as I am here. Objects imbued with magical energies tend to retain their power though, because again, the spirit realm mimics our own."

"So what you're telling me is that you're as useless as I am over there."

Larry smirked. "A more accurate way of putting it is that *you* may or may not be less useless than I am. You see, there's an additional dimension in the spirit realm, one related to your will."

"I haven't filled out a will. I'm only twenty years old. I don't have any assets."

Larry scowled.

I smiled. "Come on. I'm joking. I know this thing with your niece is weighing on you. I'm trying to make you feel better."

Larry let out a long controlled breath, one longer than I expected him capable of. Maybe he *had* been taking yoga classes. "I appreciate it. I don't like being this tightly wound, trust me. I just need to know you're paying attention."

"Because missteps in the spirit realm are the difference between life and death?"

"Quoting me *is* a good way to prove you're listening, I'll admit. But yes. If you die there, you die here. The parallel nature of the universes goes both ways."

"So the best way to protect myself there is to surround myself with my chi?"

"That's an overly simplistic way of looking at things, but yes. In the spirit realm, the greater your confidence, the greater your ability."

"So if I want to jump over a building or punch through a wall, all I have to do is believe in myself?"

Larry shook his head. "Sort of. The problem is the things you described are wants, and you can't convince yourself you're capable of something. You have to know it going in. That's why people who are extremely righteous in life are extremely powerful there. However, the opposite is also true. Rage. Lust. Greed. Many of the most negative emotions are also the most potent, which means beings that are evil to their core are that much more dangerous there."

I nodded. "Got it. So that's why it's called the *spirit* realm. Because it's all about your strength of spirit."

"No. It's called the spirit realm because that's where the ghosts are. Come on, Lexie."

I rolled my eyes. "Whatever. So is there anything else I should know about this place?"

"Let's see. Different dimensions. Magic. Will." Larry ticked them off on his fingers. "No, I think we've about covered it. The one thing we still need to discuss is how to get there, and for that, we finally get to invoke a little bit of magic. So get your student hat on because it's time to absorb some knowledge."

I didn't know what I'd been doing for the last fifteen minutes if not learning, but the prospect of teaching me magic seemed to be lifting Larry's spirit, so I went along with it. "Teach me, Yoda."

Larry winced. "Wise in the ways of the Force I might be, but I'm not old, wrinkled, and green. I think of myself as more of an Obi Wan figure. Plus out of anyone in *Star Wars*, I think I look the most like Ewan McGregor."

I didn't have the heart to tell him he actually resembled Chewbacca. "So we want to travel to the spirit realm. What's the first step?"

"To create a magic circle. Want to grab that baking soda for me?"

Before heading upstairs, Larry had rummaged around in

Charity's fridge and removed the open box of baking soda in the back. I didn't think we'd be doing any cooking, but I'd learned not to ask too many questions.

The box currently resided on her bed stand. I stood, grabbed it, and held it out. "Here you go."

Larry waved me off. "No. I need you to make it. We're beginning your magical training, remember?"

"Just like that? You want me to dive in? What if I screw something up?"

"Then you'll have dumped a bunch of baking soda on the floor for no reason. I'm sure Charity has a vacuum. It'll be fine. Go on. Make it large. We've got to fit the two of us inside, and I'd rather have extra room if possible."

I shook the box as I judged how much was left in there. "If you say so. Do I need to do anything special while I dump it out?"

"Not at this stage. And you don't need a lot. It's okay if there are gaps in the circle, just as there were gaps in the crystals around Madison. The act of making it is what establishes the magical connection."

I moved slowly, rotating clockwise as I tapped sodium bicarbonate onto the floor. I tried to make the thing six or seven feet in diameter. "Does it matter if it's more of an oval?"

"Some. Try to keep it as symmetric as possible."

No pressure, Larry. "Why am I using baking soda?"

"Because it was readily available, that's why. You can make a magic circle out of anything. You can use chalk. You can draw one in the mud or in the dust or even pee one into the snow if you're in the arctic. However, the circle will be more powerful if you make it out of something that has a connection to you, the user. That's why spells that are difficult to cast, such as summonings, are often performed using circles drawn in blood."

The clumps in the box rattled as I made my way around the room. "Does the strength of the circle make any difference in your ability to travel to the spirit realm?"

Larry shrugged. "It's more important when making magic circles for other purposes, but the stronger it is, the more closely tied your actions in the spirit realm will be to the strength of your will. It supercharges things, more or less."

I closed in on the start of my circle. "Is anything going to happen when I complete this?"

"That's a good question. You won't know until you try."

"You're not inspiring a lot of confidence."

"Just do it, Lexie. Nothing bad will happen. Promise."

I tapped out a last bit of baking soda, coming back to where I started. The good news was that flames didn't erupt from the floor, nor did a portal open underneath Larry spawning a torrent of ferocious, flesh eating ghouls. On the down side *nothing* happened other than my body giving a single shake from a sudden case of the willies.

Larry peered behind him. "You done?"

"Yeah."

"Feel anything?"

"A slight shiver. Does that mean anything?"

"It's better than nothing. Next step is to draw a five-pointed star within the circle. The baking soda will do again."

I hesitated. "Hold on. You want me to draw a *pentagram?* What kind of spell is this?"

"I told you already," said Larry. "Circles and stars are the most powerful shapes in magic. This is just a star inside a circle. If you want to call it a pentagram, call it a pentagram. The shape has gotten a bad rap because of all the nut jobs who've used it to summon demons, but there's nothing inherently demonic about it."

"And it's okay for me to cross over the edge of the circle?"

"You created it. Of course it is."

I stepped inside. I was a little disappointed when I didn't feel any change. "So I'm assuming the star can be drawn with anything as well?"

"The same material should be used as in the circle, ideally."

I worked more quickly now, tapping out a five pointed star with the sodium bicarbonate. "Is there anything else I should know about magic circles?"

"Oh, tons. But as far as séances are concerned, there's not much to learn. Some people say candles and incense can increase the connection to the spirit realm, same as using objects that are personal in the construction of the circle, but I think that's a load of bull. The only other things that affect the strength of the portal are its location—making one where the dead are already close, such as in a graveyard, will result in a much stronger circle, for example—and what I call the *whiff of death*."

"That's different than the graveyard bit?"

"Oh, absolutely. A graveyard is a great place to perform a séance because our world and the spirit realm are closest there. The most parallel. But being close to death *yourself* thins the veil much more strongly. That's why people who are on their deathbeds often see visions from the other side, but it's not a strategy you can really take advantage of. Nearly killing yourself to perform magic isn't recommended."

As I brought the last of the lines to a close, I suffered

another slight shiver. Was I psyching myself out, or was it a reaction to something magical? "Okay. I think that's it."

Larry held his hand out before him. "Have a seat."

I glanced at my work. "Right on top of the lines?"

"You've already established them. Even if you disturb the powder, they'll remain in place."

I sat, figuring baking soda would come off my shorts easier than soot. "Now what?"

"Now we chant the incantation that closes the circle and establishes the connection to the spirit realm. Do you know any of the ancient languages?"

"Like Latin?"

"Latin is one of the newer languages of the world, all things considered, but it does still have a connection to magic. It's the one I've learned and the one most often used, but I've met wizards who speak Aramaic, Greek, archaic Chinese, Egyptian, or even Sumerian. Are you familiar with any of those?"

"I can speak some Spanish."

Larry frowned. "Not old enough, unfortunately. It's fine. We'll work on your linguistic capabilities as we go. For now, listen. I'm going to speak the incantation slowly, without any cadence to avoid having the circle around us pick up on it. Then you'll repeat it in a more syncopated fashion. Okay?"

The hairs on the back of my neck rose. Was it the magic or nerves? "I'll try."

"Alright. Repeat after me. *Vide praeter illam velum. Inferis, aperta.*"

I scrunched my brow, focusing on the pronunciation. "One more time?"

"*Vide praeter illam velum. Inferis, aperta.* All together, fluidly. With conviction."

I took a deep breath. My tongue felt thick, but I gave it a shot anyway. *"Vida pratter illum vellum. Inferno, a person.* Oh, *damn it!* Sorry."

I heard a snap, like a rubber band being plucked against a hard surface. The hairs on my forearms rose the same way the ones on my neck had, and something changed in the air about me. At the same time, Larry doubled over. His palms slapped the floorboards and he curled into a ball. A deep, retching sound forced itself from his throat, and he clutched his stomach. I wiggled back, afraid of breaking the circle but equally eager to keep my legs from being showered with vomit.

Apparently, I overreacted. Larry heaved a few times. His stomach lurched, but nothing came out.

"God! Larry, are you okay?"

Larry opened his mouth to respond, but he broke out in a fit of coughing instead. He held up a finger, fanning his face with his free hand as tears streamed down his cheeks. I sat there, looking like the grimace emoji, hoping I hadn't mauled him by accident.

"I'll... be fine," said Larry after an agonizing wait. "It's... the *smell.* Like the world's worst sauerkraut fart... amplified a thousand times by magic. Good lord, girl!"

"I'm sorry. I told you I don't speak Latin. I tried..."

Larry coughed a few more times, still fanning himself. "It's okay. Gonna be fine. Just need... more air, that's all. Whew. Okay. Officially, the first thing we're doing when we get back to the house is to order you Rosetta Stone."

"Did I screw up the séance?"

Larry shook his head. "I don't think you did a thing other than befoul this room for a week for any seasoned magic user. I think I should do the incantations for the time being, though."

"Agreed."

"And if you don't mind, I'd rather get us to the spirit realm ASAP. I don't know how long I can take this."

I nodded. "Let's do it."

Larry held out his arms. "All I need is for you to take my hands."

I grasped them. Larry closed his eyes and spoke in a commanding voice. *"Vide praeter illam velum. Inferis, aperta."*

And the world shifted around me.

11

IT'S HARD TO DESCRIBE WHAT HAPPENED ONCE LARRY finished his incantation. It was as if the entire world turned upside down around me, but I turned upside down with it. By the laws of relative motion, it should've seemed from my point of view that nothing shifted, but maybe Larry had been right about physics being different in the spirit realm because I sure as hell felt something. It was as if I dove into a pool of ink and came up back on my feet exactly where I'd started, all without moving an inch.

Regardless of how I got there, it was pretty obvious I wasn't in Charity's room anymore. At least, not the version of her room I was familiar with. Charity's bed was there, pushed into the corner, as were her dresser and nightstand, and the pentagram I'd laid out still surrounded me on the floor. However, it was *how* everything looked that made it obvious I wasn't in Kansas anymore.

The world was faded. Dull. Not totally devoid of color, but close, as if someone had gone into Photoshop and played with the color balance sliders. Perhaps they'd messed with the contrast, too, because while the walls were as pale as before the shadows in the corners were several shades darker. I glanced out the window at the sky in the distance. Instead of a pale blue, a heavy gray tinged with purple lingered up high, dotted with yellow-edged clouds.

I stood slowly, making sure my legs would support me. "Whoa."

"Whoa is right," said Larry, standing beside me. "I've crossed over a few dozen times, but this place never fails to impress."

I stepped toward the wall. Even accounting for the differences in color and brightness, there was something else off. Every object, from the bedside lamp to the clock beside it, had a hazy, indistinct quality to it. When I turned my head, they disappeared altogether from my peripheral vision. I turned my head this way and that, watching Charity's clock radio disappear into the shadows only to burst back into existence. I reached out and touched it. The plastic case felt solid, though my fingertips blurred as they met it.

I pulled my hand back, staring at the fingers as they flickered and danced in a chaotic manner. "This is weird, Larry. Am I supposed to feel like I'm in the Matrix?"

"It's nothing to worry about," he said. "Remember, the dimensions in the spirit world are different than those we're used to. What you're experiencing is your mind attempting to process the spirit realm's multidimensional spatial coordinates into the three dimensions you're used to."

"So my spirit is collecting sensory data, warping it back to my brain in our world, and processing it there? How does that work?"

Larry's brow furrowed. *"What?* No, Lexie. We're here. The

entirety of us. Body, mind, and spirit. The whole kit and caboodle."

"Huh?"

"I told you if we die here, we die for good. That's because our bodies are here."

"Are you saying we're not still sitting in Charity's bedroom? That we teleported here? Like in *Star Trek?*"

"Technically, yes, but unlike the transporters you've seen in fiction, I wouldn't recommend popping in and out of the spirit realm as a substitute for normal modes of transportation. It's too risky. Not to mention the whole time not existing thing. Trust me, the shorter our trip here the better."

I nodded, trying to ignore the dark shapes at the corners of my vision. "Okay. So what's the plan?"

"Same as it's been since we started prepping. We find the poltergeist who attacked Dawn and get it to answer some questions for us."

Larry had laid the basics out to me when I told him I wanted in on the action. I'd volunteered, but now that I was here, I realized I probably should've paid more heed to Larry's warnings. "Do you think the thing is still around? It sounds like Dawn scared it off after it fondled her."

"Given what Charity told me over the phone, we have to assume it's been haunting her house for at least a few days. I don't think Dawn's threats scared it off. If anything, us being here might make it more likely to return."

"How so?"

"Ghosts have a way of knowing when other spirits are nearby. It's not a smell thing. More of a sort of energy detection, like hammerhead sharks. I'm not really sure." He nodded toward the door. "Come on. Let's check out the rest of the house. You'll want to stay close to me, for safety's sake."

He didn't have to tell me twice. I closed the gap between us as he cracked the door to the hallway. I peered out at the same time as he did. Dark shadows rippled across the stairwell as if cast by floating algae across the bottom of a moonlit pond. Larry took a step onto the landing, and the stairs groaned in response. They stretched downward, the walls lengthening, the number of steps doubling out of nothing.

I tried to keep my voice calm. "Uh... Larry?"

"I told you the spatial dimensions are weird. Don't worry. The stairs won't eat you."

A couple curtailed yips echoed up the steps, followed by a long, ghostly howl that sent a shiver up my spine. "And what about that?"

"*That* might be something to be more concerned about. Like I said, stay close."

Larry started down the steps, and I had to force myself not to knock him over in my haste not to get left behind. A pair of yips rang through the halls followed by another of the soulful howls. I instinctively checked my pocket for my enchanted demon tooth, but it was still in my car. I really needed to make a habit of keeping it on me.

The stairs condensed as we reached the bottom. I jumped as the howl rang once more. Larry motioned me down the hall. The walls were darker here, more green than the beige I remembered. A darkness crept along them, like black mold across untreated wood. My fists clenched into balls as we turned the corner into the living room. My muscles shook from adrenaline as I gazed across the open space. Heavy drapes cast the room deeper into shadow, and the strange mold-like texture spread onto the ceiling. Of ghosts and spirits, I saw not a trace.

I heard another yip, and my eyes shot to the couch. There I saw it. Curled up in a corner of the sofa lay a bedraggled pooch. Its fur was a faded, near-translucent gray, and its eyes were tightly shut. It yipped again, and one of its legs kicked, as if it were dreaming.

I stepped forward, my fists unclenching. "It's a dog?"

Larry joined me by the couch. He reached out and gently brushed the fur across the dog's back. The pup didn't wake, though it shuddered and kicked again. "Must be one of Charity's previous pets."

"You mean, one that passed away?"

"Look at it," said Larry. "The gray hair. The white across the muzzle. The saggy skin. I'd bet on it."

The dog's slumber grew more restful. It stopped shaking and grew silent. "So after it passed, it stayed at Charity's house, sleeping forever? Sounds like a pretty good afterlife."

"Actually, most ghosts fade over time. It's the natural order of things. It's only those who are angry or unfulfilled who linger, who are able to latch on and keep their spirit whole for long enough to avoid dispersing into the aether. But there are a few who linger due to something else. Love, I guess. I bet this guy refuses to fade because he's so happy here. Probably has a lot of good memories."

I felt a twinge in my heart, and I might've had to blink away a tear or two. I'd lost pets before, like anyone else. "That's so heartwarming."

"They say the purest love comes from animals."

Something crashed behind me, and I spun. "What the hell was that?"

"Sounds like it came from the kitchen." Larry glanced at the pup, who hadn't moved. "Stay behind me. I'm going to check it out."

Larry crept to the edge of the room, slinking around the corner into the hall. A moan undulated through the house, and I knew we weren't dealing with a dreaming puppy anymore. The sound had a muddy, pained quality to it, the sort of thing you'd hear in a burn unit or a war hospital, but there were layers to it. I detected an undertone of amusement or even pleasure in it, too, the sort of moan one might make in a moment of ecstasy—or from watching others take part in the same.

Pots crashed against pans and silverware rattled in trays as Larry and I crept to the edge of the kitchen. Cabinets stood open, some with their contents spilled across the countertops. A flicker of motion caught my eye, the movement of a dark-skinned head as someone knelt underneath the island, digging through drawers.

Larry held me back. When he spoke it was in a commanding voice, one that made every hair on my body stand to attention. "You trespass in another's home, apparition. Stand, face us, and tell us what you seek."

The rustling stopped, and the spirit did as Larry asked. It stood, the sliver of dark skin becoming something far more horrible than I could've expected. The ghostly creature had a human shape, but it wasn't dark-skinned, or at least if it had been there was no way to tell. Rather, its skin had been reduced to a blistered char, crispy and coal black from fire. Cracks laced what was left of it, raw and red and oozing with clear liquid. Not a single hair nor scrap of clothing remained on the being. Its face had been reduced to a scarred mask, its lips mangled but the underlying teeth still bright white.

I gasped and took a step back, my stomach lurching in fear. *"What the..."*

A bright white energy swirled around Larry's hand. He held it out before him, like a guard at a school crosswalk. "I command you to speak. Who are you? What brings you here?"

The spirit placed its hands on the island's countertop and hopped onto it. Fire rippled from its feet, tickling the polished stone beneath. It didn't speak, but it did flash a crooked, cracked smile.

And then it lunged.

12

A SHIELD OF WHITE LIGHT SPRUNG FROM LARRY'S HANDS, stretching from his neck to his knees as the horribly burned spirit leapt though the air. The thing lifted a fist and struck the shield as it descended. Sparks erupted off the face of it with an electrifying crackle. The force of the blow pushed Larry back several feet along the floor. As he slid, a long pole of the same spectral white energy grew from his hands, the end of it coalescing into a point. Larry dug his heels into the ground and skidded to a halt. He swung the shield in front of him and leveled the spear at the spirit, like a Hoplite ready to do battle against the ghosts of Sparta.

The creature rose from its knees. Flames sizzled around its feet, crisping the floorboards as globules of a dark, thick substance dripped from its elbows. Those, too, erupted into flames as they met the wood. The creature moaned again, the pain and desire clear in its voice, but it didn't so much as spare a glance for Larry. It stared past him straight at me.

My voice cracked as I spoke. "Larry..."

"Stay behind me. Whatever you do, don't touch it."

The thing lurched at us. Larry intercepted it in the hall with his shield. More sparks flew from the barrier, and acrid smoke bubbled off, filling the air with a pungent scent that stung my nostrils. Larry grunted in exertion as the thing pushed against his magic, all of his strength going to hold the shield in place rather than jab at it with his javelin.

I desperately looked around for a weapon with which to defend myself, once again kicking myself for leaving my demon tooth in the Suburban. Of course, Larry had said the spirit world was a parallel version of our own. If I ran to the truck, I should be able to grab it, but then again, Larry had said magic worked differently here. Would the bat work? Did I have time to grab it?

The creature seemed to read my mind. It locked eyes with me and moaned louder before redoubling its efforts against Larry's shield. Larry's feet slipped and he skidded back another foot. He pushed with his legs and put his shoulder against the shield, struggling with the long pike.

It gave me an idea. "Larry! Give me the spear!"

Larry didn't look back, his body shaking from exertion. "Are you nuts? You don't know how to use this thing."

"You poke it with the sharp end. I think I've got it."

"That's not what I mean. This is a construct of my mind, not a physical object."

The creature flailed. Bits of the dark substance that stuck to it flew in all directions. I danced to the side as they splattered against the floor, sparking flames before sinking deeper. Magma. It was *magma*.

"Larry. There's no time! I need something. Give it to me!"

Larry grunted. "Ugh. Fine. Here!"

He twisted and tossed the spear. I stretched out to grasp it as it soared through the air, but I wasn't the only one who watched it fly. For once, the spirit's gaze shifted from me to Larry. It cried out in joy and swept an arm at Larry's knees.

My fist closed around the pike. "Larry! Watch out!"

Larry dipped his shield and hopped to keep his legs from being blistered by burning hot flesh, but the poltergeist was too quick. It dipped its shoulder into its attack and heaved, picking Larry up on his shield and launching him into the wall. Drywall cracked and splintered as Larry punched through, disappearing into the powder room beyond.

The creature shifted its gaze to me. It smiled and moaned, and then it touched itself. There was nothing between its legs but a blackened crust, but the way it looked at me, the need and desire plastered across its horribly disfigured face as its hand raked across the bare spot, churned my stomach in revulsion. The creature had been human, had once been a man, and it wanted *me*.

I backed into the living room as he stalked me. The spear of light burned hot in my hands, like a piece of pipe that had been left out in the Texas sun in July. I jabbed with it even though the creature was still a half dozen feet out of reach. "Stay back, you freak! I'm not your property, and neither is Charity. Don't make me shank you!"

The beast hesitated, his eyes flicking to the spear. I smiled, feeling confidence creep back into me now that I had a weapon in my hands. "That's right. Get the hell out of here!"

I took a step forward and jabbed again, but as I did so, the spear grew hotter. I grimaced and loosened my grip, shaking one of my hands. As I did so, the spear flickered and wobbled.

"Oh, no."

Barely had the words left my mouth before the spear disassociated into a mist, like spray from a fountain. The blackened spirit moaned in joy and jumped at me.

I'm not a gymnast, but I might've done a backflip—or, based on the dull pain that punched into my back as I landed and the sharp wooden crack I heard, I simply dove backwards and slammed into Charity's coffee table, crushing it beneath me. The spirit closed on me. I flailed on the floor, trying to force my legs underneath me so I could run while simultaneously scrambling for something with which to protect myself, a chair leg, a pillow, *anything,* but nothing was within reach.

"LARRY!" My voice rang through the air, high-pitched, panicked, and shot through with fear.

He didn't respond, but something else did. A deep, undulating growl filled the air, freezing the spirit in place. I twisted to my side to see Charity's pooch standing on the couch cushions, teeth bared, hackles up, legs splayed, and tail held straight in the air, stiff as a board. Luckily, it wasn't looking at me. It was engaged in a stare down with my attacker.

The ghost growled back, and that was enough for the mutt. It launched itself at him, latching onto his arm with a meaty chomp. The dog shook violently in mid air, ripping and tugging at the beast's arm. I rolled out of the way as droplets of magma fell to the ground, sizzling as they hit couch and floor alike. The hellish rain either didn't affect the pup or the pain didn't register. He kept growling and pulling, nearly knocking the spirit off his feet.

The spirit moaned, the sick pleasure in his voice replaced by pain. He knocked the pup to the ground with his free arm, but the pooch had barely hit the floor before he launched himself back into the fray, snapping at the thing's legs before retreating and placing himself between us.

The dog growled, the beast growled back, and a resounding boom split the air. The room's lights and darks inverted. The windows turned into brilliant squares while darkness enveloped the walls. The magma beast took one look toward them before turning tail and running. He didn't even bother with the halls, instead evaporating into mist as he disappeared through what had previously been a solid wall.

The pooch slumped on the ground next to me, licking an arm whose fur looked a little singed. I sat up. "Holy cow. You saved my life."

The dog looked at me with old eyes that somehow remained bright. He stretched his neck and gave me a couple quick licks to the chin.

I smiled and scratched him on the head. "Yeah. You're a good boy. I'll bet Charity loved you a hell of a lot. No wonder you've stuck around."

I heard a thump, then a curse. A moment later, Larry burst around the corner into the room, covered in plaster dust. He surveyed the broken coffee table, me, and the dog all in a glance. "Thank God. You're alive."

"No thanks to your spear. The thing disassociated in my hands when I took that beast on head to head."

"Hey, don't blame me. I told you it wouldn't work. You don't even know how to use regular magic yet, much less spirit realm magic."

"Well, it's okay," I said. "Thankfully Charity's pooch drove that thing off, whoever he was."

Another crack of lightning split the air, sending bright white shadows racing around the room. Larry looked at the windows, concern etched in his face. "Yeah. As much as that pup seems to have taken a shine to you, I don't think it scared the spirit off." Larry waved a hand at me. "Come on. Time to go."

I gave the pooch a good scratch behind the ears. "Thanks, buddy. I won't forget this." I stood, brushing bits of the coffee table from my shirt. "I assume there's something about spirit lightning I should know?"

"Well, seeing as it wasn't thundering when we left, that means this particular storm probably isn't reflective of Earth. That means something here is creating its own lightning."

"*Creating* lightning?"

Larry waved me over. "Come on."

He walked to the kitchen and threw open the sliding glass door. He took a step onto the back porch and pointed. "There."

The sky had turned from the grayish purple color I'd first noticed upon arriving to a much angrier fuchsia. A ball of matte black clouds clustered in the distance, perhaps a dozen miles to the east, crackling with lightning. Another flash inverted the world around me, followed by a reverberating crash.

"You're saying something is responsible for that?"

"In my experience, yes," said Larry. "And trust me, there are things in this universe that are a lot nastier than the spirit we just tangoed with. We need to get out of here."

"But we didn't learn anything."

"Oh, we learned something all right. We learned that someone who died a horrible death in a fire is haunting Charity for some reason. We learned that whoever it is is *way* stronger than a normal ghost, and we learned that despite that, it's scared of whatever is at the center of that maelstrom. For now, that'll have to be enough."

I eyed the storm. It was still far away, but was it moving

toward us? "Fair enough. Let's get out of here. Back to the pentagram?"

"No need. There's an easier way out of the spirit realm." He nodded toward the sliding glass doors.

I frowned. "Being?"

"Your reflection, Lexie. Find it anywhere. In a mirror, the back of a spoon, or a pane of glass. Doesn't matter which. Just stare at yourself and dive on through."

"Really?" I lifted an eyebrow. "How come you have to perform a séance to get here but all it takes to get back is gazing at a reflection of yourself?"

Larry sighed. "It has something to do with the reflection being another portal. Look, I don't know why it works, but it does, okay? Now can we get out of here before anything else nasty shows up?"

I nodded. "Sure. So I just... walk on through?"

"It works better if you jump, believe it or not." He took my hand and faced the glass. "Ready?"

I tilted my head to find a glimpse of my reflection. "As I'll ever be."

Larry squeezed my hand, and together we jumped.

Once again the world turned around me, but instead of diving into a pool of ink, it was as if I'd jumped into a rainbow. Colors brightened and surfaces solidified as my feet hit the ground—and Dawn appeared out of mid air in the middle of the kitchen.

She jumped and shrieked as we materialized in front of her, reaching for one of the knives in a block on the counter. *"Jesus Christ!* Don't *do* that."

Larry let go of my hand. "Sorry. We had no way of knowing you'd be in the house. I figured you'd still be on the front lawn."

Tank was in the kitchen, too. He waved nonchalantly, as if we hadn't coalesced out of nothing. "We heard more moans and thumping. Figured we'd investigate. I'm guessing the ghost came back?"

"Sure did," I said. "And apparently he doesn't just have a thing for Charity or you, Dawn. He came after me, too, though I'm not entirely sure if he wanted to molest me or kill me. Maybe both."

Dawn sneered. "Sick bastard. Were you able to identify him? Figure out what he wants?"

"Unfortunately, no," said Larry. "He'd been horribly burned in a fire. He attacked us before we had a chance to question him, but I'm not sure we could've gotten anything out of him even if we'd managed to immobilize him. Ghosts may love to moan, but in the spirit realm, he should've been capable of speech. I think the fire wrecked his vocal cords."

"So Charity's being haunted by someone who burned to death?" said Dawn.

"Looks like it," said Larry. "Though that doesn't explain why she fled without a trace, or why she won't answer her phone. Something bigger than ghosts is at play here."

I shook my head, trying to banish the nightmarish image of the spirit from my mind. "Larry... do you think the spirit we found is responsible for your niece's coma?"

He shrugged. "I don't know, but I intend to find out. Come on. We've done what we can here, and I need you to drop me off at the hospital."

13

I closed my laptop with a heavy sigh and leaned back in my chair. I stretched my arms overhead and leaned my head as far as I could to the side. At the moment that my neck popped and I felt a satisfying release of tension from my spine, someone knocked.

I swiveled in my chair to find Tank standing outside my room. His knuckles hovered over the door that I'd intentionally left open. In one hand, he held a tray covered with a lid, while tucked under his other arm was Bill's jar. "Is that for me?"

Tank gave me a nod. "Figured you'd be hungry by now. For the record, when I'm cooking I try to have dinner ready by seven-thirty."

"*Seven-thirty?*" I glanced at the window to find the sky had darkened. "What time is it?"

"Quarter past eight." Tank walked into my room and placed the tray on my desk. He grabbed a stool and pulled it up next to my office chair. He set Bill and his jar down past the end of the tray.

Delectable scents tickled my nose. Cracked pepper, saffron,

onion, and garlic among others. My stomach rumbled, and I realized I'd barely eaten all day. "Tank, I don't know what this is, but it smell delicious."

"Yeah," said Bill. "Now that I can get a whiff of it over the stink of your armpit, I'd have to agree."

Tank snorted and flicked Bill's jar. "Be glad I brought you up at all." He lifted the lid off the tray, revealing a platter piled high with yellow rice, chunks of chicken, peppers, onions, and peas. "It's called *arroz con pollo*. Ever had it?"

I cocked an eyebrow at the big guy. "Are you kidding? My mom is Mexican and my dad is Puerto Rican. The question isn't whether I've had it but which kind. Did you braise the chicken in beer and use anatto oil?"

"Uh... no. Should I have?"

"Nope. Just means you made Spanish *arroz con pollo* instead of Puerto Rican. Either way, it smells amazing. You cooked this?"

"Bill didn't, that's for sure. Go on, dig in. No sense letting it get any colder."

"Hey," said Bill. "I resent that. I bet I could cook a great meal if our kitchen wasn't so flagrantly set up for the able-bodied. Give me a pulley system, a Roomba, and a mouthguard with an attachment for kitchen utensils and wait and see what I can do."

I grabbed a fork and shoveled a bite into my mouth. I almost melted. *"Oh my gosh.* This is ridiculously good, Tank."

"Glad you like it. Cooking you a nice meal is the least I can do on your first night here. You want some, Bill?" He gestured toward the jar with a heaping spoon.

"I wouldn't even need knives. I could chop celery and carrots just fine with my teeth."

"*Bill...*"

"Alright. Fine. Dump it in," he said.

Tank tilted his spoon. A lump of sticky rice dotted with diced vegetables and a bite sized chunk of chicken plopped into Bill's jar. The zombie rolled a little, tilting his head downward so he could get within range of the rice, which he brought into his mouth one grain at a time with deft flicks of his tongue.

I was past being horrified by Bill's table manners and far too hungry to care. I devoured half my plate before I realized Tank had yet to touch his. "Oh. Uh. Sorry."

"You don't have to apologize for being hungry. I tasted as I cooked. Besides, you're talking to a werebear, remember? I can put it down when I want to, trust me."

I nodded and kept eating, thankful there wasn't anyone within eyeshot I was trying to impress. Not that I'd ever cared much about looking dainty.

Tank gathered his fork and nodded to my laptop. "You make any progress?"

I'd finally gotten enough in my belly to soothe its protests. "I mean... sort of? I found the auction service Wells Fargo used to sell Romanov's stuff. I even found a cached version of the page listing the property for sale. So the good news is I was able to confirm the magic crystals were among the items sold. The bad news is I have no way to figure out who bought them. That information wasn't listed online. I called the auction company to ask, but they wouldn't give me the time of day. I even tried being sneaky, telling them I wanted to purchase one of the items directly from the buyer, but they said client confidentiality was of their utmost concern and they couldn't help me. Since then I've tried to see if I could find anything sold at that auction on third-party sites, thinking maybe whoever bought them resold them and I could pick up the trail elsewhere, but that's been a gigantic waste of time. Do you have any idea what sort of junk comes up when you search for magic crystals on Google?"

Tank grabbed a Shiner Bock off the tray. It fizzed as he twisted the cap off. "I can guess."

"You have any better luck?"

Tank shrugged. "Worse. I talked to five different informants, but none of them knew Charity was missing, much less where she is. When I asked if they'd heard any rumblings about evil spirits, hauntings, or possessions, they either thought I was making a joke or they wanted to know what I'd uncovered and if they needed to get out of town."

"What about Dawn?"

"She was on her phone most of the afternoon, but I don't think she got any further than I did. She's still out and about, trying to find anyone who might have a bead on Charity. I think she's really worried about her, Lexie."

"I don't blame her. I'm worried, too, and I barely know her." I took another bite. "You think her and Dawn are... I mean, is there anything there more than the physical stuff?"

"I'm not sure," said Tank. "All I know is Dawn's more on edge than normal. Might be nothing, but then again, having someone taken away from you can make you realize you had feelings for them. Or it can intensify the feelings you had all along."

"Sounds like you're speaking from personal experience."

Bill froze, his tongue a centimeter out of his mouth. "Uh, oh. Careful, Lexie."

"What do you mean, *uh oh?*" Tank might've stiffened a little at my mention of personal experience, but that was it. "Did I step in something?"

Tank scooped some rice onto his fork. "It's okay. You're one of us. I don't mind talking about it. I'm divorced. Have been for years."

I blinked. "Really? What happened?"

"If you're asking what led to her leaving me, there are probably a hundred different reasons. The simplest explanation is I wasn't there enough. You know I was in the Marines, right?"

"I didn't know it for a fact, but given that you know how to use every firearm ever built and you look like you could crank out two hundred pull-ups in succession, I figured you served in some branch of the military."

Tank nodded. "I was deployed in Afghanistan. Spent three years there, plus another two in different spots around the world. Iraq. Thailand. Burkina Faso. I was married the entire time, or so I thought."

"So you thought? Your wife divorced you while you were deployed?"

"No, but she might as well have. When I returned after my third tour, I found out my home was no longer mine. Literally. I knocked on the door to my apartment to find another family living there. My wife had moved out eight months prior."

I lay my fork on my plate. "Christ, Tank. I had no idea."

He shrugged. "It wasn't a good moment in my life, but like I said, I wasn't blameless. I played a role in the relationship falling apart, same as she did. The things I'd done. Who I'd become. By the time Kiara left me, I wasn't the man she'd fallen in love with anymore."

"So it happened while you were deployed?" I said. "You becoming a werebear?"

Tank surprised me by laughing. "No, Lex. I'm talking about the emotional toll war takes on you. The arkoúdathropy occurred afterwards. Since my personal life was in shambles and I'd more or less lost the will to live, I signed up for the craziest mission with the Marines that I could. Turned out it wasn't so much of a mission and more of a secret government program to turn regular humans into super soldiers, kind of like Wolverine without the adamantium."

"Sorry. Back up. *Arkoúdathropy?*"

"I'm guessing you're not prolific in Greek. It's like lycanthropy, but for bears instead of wolves."

I shook my head. "What's with everyone wanting me to learn Greek? First Larry and now you."

"Speaking of, how's your magical training going? Is that really a thing now?"

I still had a lot of questions about Tank's past, but the eager look he gave me said he was desperate to change the subject. Maybe he hadn't been as at ease with his divorce as he'd claimed. "Other than showing me how to enter the spirit realm, we haven't had a chance to go over much, and given how badly I botched the incantation, I'm not sure how much time Larry's going to want to waste on me."

Bill snorted in laughter, and a grain of rice flew from his nose, sticking to the side of the jar. "You realize Larry nearly burned down his house the first time he used magic, right? I think you're on a better trajectory than he was."

I stared at the slimy grain, thankful I'd finished eating. "Yeah, he told me about that earlier today."

"But I bet he didn't tell you about the time he accidentally transported one of his teachers at Zephyrburr Academy into low Earth orbit or that the polar vortex in twenty fourteen was partially his fault. Trust me, if Charity's house is still standing and you're all alive, then your first experience with magic was a success." Bill tapped his forehead against his jar. "Hey, Tank! Are you going to bogart that beer all night?"

Tank frowned. "You want me to pour it over what's left of your *arroz con pollo?*"

"You act like I'm picky. Come on. It's all going to the same place."

"Yeah. The bottom of your jar."

Tank poured the last of his beer into Bill's jar, leaving a soup of malted barley and rice swimming around Bill's neck. Whatever Bill lapped up would all come out his neck hole anyway. Actually, I think some of the alcohol absorbed directly into his muscle tissue, as the guy had a habit of getting really drunk really fast.

Watching the severed zombie head suck up beer and rice probably should've turned my stomach, but I was used to it. What I wasn't used to was Bill sticking up for me so readily. Tank, too.

I smiled. "Thanks for the dinner, Tank, and the conversation. I needed both."

Tank lifted his empty bottle. "Want a beer? I won't call the cops. Promise."

I stuffed a fist into my mouth to stifle a yawn. "I'd better not. I'm fading fast, and it's barely dark out. There's no way I'm getting more work done tipsy."

"You're planning on getting back on your laptop?"

"Dawn's still out there, and Larry's at the hospital. I know I can't do much on my own, but I'm not a quitter. People we care about are counting on us. Maybe I'll find a clue that can give us some direction."

Tank gathered the utensils and his bottle on the tray. "I

understand completely. Maybe I'll give Dawn a call. If you need anything, don't hesitate to holler."

"You bet. Good having dinner with you, Bill."

Bill hiccuped. His eyes had already gone glassy. "What's that? Oh, yeah. Good... *hic*... talk."

I BLINKED, my eyelids heavy. Night suffused my room, but the red numerals on my bedside clock burned through the darkness. 4:47. I closed my eyes, willing myself back to sleep.

I lay there, breathing deeply, my heartbeat slow and steady. Sleep should soon take me, but something niggled at the back of my mind. Had there been something I'd needed to do before I went to bed? Someone I had to call? Had I scheduled something I'd forgotten about?

I didn't think so, but the nagging sensation wouldn't leave me. I knew I wouldn't be able to sleep if I ignored it, so I cracked my eyes and reached for my phone. I blinked a few times at the screen's bright light as I brought up my calendar. Nope. Nothing.

I turned the phone off and set it back on my nightstand. I closed my eyes again only for them to snap back open as the image of the room processed in my brain.

My door was open. I hadn't left it that way before going to sleep.

I tossed the covers off me and hopped out of bed, my body suddenly infused with adrenaline. I checked the room's corners as I moved, but I was the only one there. A bit of the sudden panic bled from me as I realized nothing had been touched, but I nonetheless paused as I reached the door frame.

I couldn't put my finger on it, but something felt odd. A shiver ran down my spine, but not from a cool breeze. The loose T-shirt I wore hung lifeless against my otherwise bare flesh, and my window was shut tight, with nothing but the pale yellow cone of a distant streetlight visible in the darkness.

I poked my head into the hall and perked my ears. Again, I couldn't hear a thing.

It worried me. Shouldn't I hear *something*? The hum of a refrigerator. A ragged snore. The creak of a bed. The rumble of cars along Guadalupe.

"Tank?" I called out quietly, so as to not wake anyone. "Dawn? You guys up?"

Nothing.

I crept around the hall to the top of the stairs. A pale glow flickered across the thick shag carpet at the bottom from the transom window over the back door.

I headed down the steps, gripping the banister harder than I needed to. The boards in the stairs creaked in response to the touch of my feet.

When I reached the bottom, I leaned over, peering into the living room. "Bill?"

His jar was gone. Larry's office chair sat cold and empty behind his desk. The couch was similarly devoid of life, though someone had left the TV on. It displayed nothing but static, a red mute symbol showing in the bottom left corner. My feet sunk into the carpet as I walked to the coffee table. I grasped the remote and hit the power button.

The TV died with an electric bloop. At the same time, I heard a distant crackle. The hairs on the back of my neck lifted, and I spun. "Hello? Someone there?"

The flickering glow over the carpet had intensified. I took a few steps into the hall and peered toward the back door. The trees in the backyard obscured my view of the sky, but there was more color and light than there should've been given the hour.

I should've gone back to bed, or at the very least woken Tank or Dawn, assuming she'd come back after I'd gone to sleep, but something drew me to the door. With trembling legs, I crept down the hall, put a hand on the handle, and cranked.

The door swung open with a creak. A wall of warm air swept over me, bringing with it a latent electric crackle that prickled the hairs on my arms. I took a step onto the porch and turned my eyes to the sky. It flickered with a yellow essence similar to the shadows I'd seen dancing in the entryway. Was it a tornado? The only other time I'd seen any similar colors in the night sky had been when one of the destructive vortices had touched down a few miles from my parent's home in San Antonio, but then there had been accompanying wind, rain, and ferocious lightning.

Now there was nothing—or was there? I followed the pulsing yellow light to the east. There, over the tips of the condominiums that had grown next to the University, I saw another flicker, this one more purple than yellow. Another crackle lit the sky but without an associated rumble, and my world inverted in color. Just like it had in the spirit realm.

I took a step back, but a whoosh of air pushed against me. It caught the door, slamming it closed with a thud, leaving me trapped on the porch in nothing but a T-shirt and boy shorts. I grasped the handle and twisted, but it was locked. "Tank? Dawn! Is anyone in there?"

A deep, low voice called to me, undulating through the warm air. "*Lexiiiieeee...*"

It hadn't come from within the house. I turned, my heart

hammering in my chest, to find the purple and yellow storm had crested the top of the nearest condominium. A dark energy swirled within the clouds, bolts of black lightning firing through the morass with little more than an electric hiss. The system moved through the sky quickly, quietly, and with purpose.

It was headed toward me.

My eyes widened. My breath caught in my throat, and I felt beads of sweat sprout from my pores. As I stared at the storm, I heard the voice again. *"Lexiiiieeee..."* The clouds moved in conjunction with the sound, a crease forming among the black mist. Dark pools formed above the lips, backlit with yellow fire.

My tongue could barely move. "Wha... *What?"*

The face in the sky smiled, a thin, cruel line that stretched past the edge of the eyes. The yellow pools grew as the smile did, swallowing the edge of the condo building, then the moon, then a quarter of the sky.

The wind gusted, bringing with it another howl. *"Lexii-ieee!"* The face screamed, but it wasn't growing. It was rushing at me with incredible speed.

The eyes turned to balls of flame, the mouth to a pool of midnight. It stretched, swallowing the sky, the trees, and the fence, and I shrieked as it swallowed me, too.

14

I shot up in bed, a scream reverberating in my ears and my heart hammering in my chest. My sheets clung to my sweat-slicked arms. I batted at them, trying to get them off me, but they clung to me like nooses, squeezing tighter the more I struggled.

With a desperate cry I ripped myself free and tumbled to the floor. I stayed there a moment on all fours, sucking air greedily, willing my heart back to a state of relative calm. I closed my eyes, squeezing them tight, focusing on the air flowing through my nostrils, on the thump in my chest, on the worn smooth wood beneath my fingers and the distant mumble of activity, the rumble of cars, and yes, the hum of a refrigerator.

I opened my eyes and glanced at the door. It was closed, as it should've been. The bright red numerals on my bedside clock read two minutes to five. Thirteen minutes past when I'd gazed at them in my dream—and it *had* to have been a dream, even if so many parts of it felt so real. Maybe I'd cracked my eyes while asleep, absorbed the time without processing it consciously, thus allowing my mind to create a fiction that more closely resembled reality.

But I didn't believe that.

As my breathing returned to normal, I stumbled to my feet and grabbed my phone. I pulled up my browser and searched for Saint David's. Once the page loaded, I scrolled to the bottom, clicked on the phone number, and brought the phone to my ear.

The phone rang a few times before someone picked up. "Saint David's Hospital. How may I direct your call?"

"Yes. Madison Flemming's room, please."

"One moment."

I heard an electronic click, and then the phone rang again. It only sounded twice before someone picked up. "Hello?"

I could heard the strain and fear in the voice, but it was nonetheless familiar. "Hi. Carol Flemming? This is Lexie Rodriguez, from the Nyte Patrol."

"What? Yes. What do you want?"

"Is Larry there?"

I heard a rustling, as well as the beep of a medical instrument. Several voices spoke in the background. "Just a moment."

She spoke Larry's name. Someone in the room was having a heated discussion. There was a shuffle of feet and a swish of fabric before Larry came on the phone. "Hello?"

"Hey, Larry. It's me."

"Lexie, what's going on? It's five in the morning."

"I don't know, exactly. I just had the weirdest dream."

Larry voice crackled over the line. "Lexie, I'm sorry, but I don't have time for this. Madison took a turn for the worse, we've got nurses and orderlies coming out of the woodwork, and

I'm doing all I can to make sure this phone doesn't explode into a rain of molten plastic."

I heard another swish of fabric. Larry must've been holding the receiver with a towel. "Okay. I'm sorry, but... Look, this dream felt *real*, Larry. I didn't even realize I was dreaming until the very end. I think it might've meant something."

Larry sighed. "How so?"

"You know the storm we saw in the spirit realm? With the purple clouds and the lightning? It was in my dream, except there was a darkness about it, too. It saw me, Larry. Something in the storm gazed right at me, spoke my name, and came at me."

Larry didn't say a word. I would've thought the phone might've blown if not for the steady din of commotion in the background.

"Hello? Larry, are you still there?"

"I'm here," he said. "When did this happen?"

"I woke up right before I called you."

"I mean when you saw that spirit. When it attacked you. What time was it?"

"I don't know exactly. Maybe two or three minutes ago? It's what scared me awake."

Larry muttered under his breath. *"Damnit.* This is bad."

"Why? What's bad?"

"Lexie, that's precisely when Madison's vitals dipped. I think you should get to the hospital. We need to talk."

I SAT in the lobby at Saint David's, nursing a travel mug full of coffee. Tank paced along the stretch of empty space in front of the information desk while Dawn sat in one of the sofa chairs next to me, container of java also in hand. She looked the most tired of us by far, but then again, I wasn't awake when she came home. For all I knew, she'd only gotten a couple hours of sleep.

The elevators at the far side of the lobby dinged, and out popped Larry. He scanned the seating area, but I caught his eye with a wave.

Tank closed in, and Larry gave us a nod as he joined our circle. "Hey, guys. Thanks for coming."

Dawn gestured at him with her coffee mug. "How's your niece?"

Larry sighed. "Not great. As I told Lexie over the phone, her vitals dipped precipitously earlier this morning. The nurses got her stable within fifteen minutes, or perhaps I should say Madison stabilized. I'm not sure the medical staff had any impact on her condition, much as they tried." Larry gave me a nod. "You didn't bring Bill?"

"He's hard to hide, Larry. He doesn't like being stuffed into a purse, and I don't like carrying one anyway."

Larry gave a dismissive wave. "Fair enough. I figured the more heads we have to brainstorm the better."

"Brainstorm what?" said Tank. "Have you found a lead on what's going on with Madison? Or with Charity for that matter?"

Larry nodded. "Sort of. Given what we found at Charity's, I figured Madison's condition might be one of the spirit rather than the body, so I entered the spirit realm again to see what I could find. Carol didn't want me to. She's inherently distrustful of anything even remotely occult, and since I'd already told her I didn't think magic was responsible for Madison's condition, she was against it from the start. I had to make the magic circle in the bathroom. She wasn't happy when I appeared out of thin air in Madison's room seven hours later."

"*Seven hours?*" I said.

"Yeah," said Larry. "Remember how I said time doesn't exist in the spirit realm? It makes it extremely tricky to figure out how long you've spent there. Apparently, I got carried away. The point is, I crossed over to check on Madison's spirit. The good news is I wasn't attacked by any hideous burned spirits during my time there. The bad news is Madison's spirit, while present, was as unresponsive as her body is here in our realm."

"I'm assuming that's not normal," I said.

"Folks who are alive don't normally have their souls in the spirit realm *at all,*" said Larry. "The fact that I was able to find her there means she's on the brink of death. As likely to tilt in one direction as another. But the news gets worse, I'm afraid. I found an artifact on her."

"An *artifact?*" asked Dawn.

"A pendant on a leather thong around her neck. A cross made of wood and red twine, about the size of my fist. I've never seen anything like it."

"Hold on," I said. "You found an artifact on her in the spirit realm, but she's not wearing anything of the sort now?"

Larry shook his head. "Trust me, I understand your confusion. The spirit realm is supposed to be a parallel version of our own. Objects present in our world exist in that one and vice versa. However, the *actions* of spirits in the otherworld only manifest in this one on rare occasion and in a limited fashion, as you can confirm based on your interactions with that magma spirit versus Dawn's. It stands to reason then that the object I found around Madison's neck is something fashioned from pure spirit energy."

"That's a thing?" said Tank.

"Let me put it this way," said Larry. "When I found it around Madison's neck, my first instinct was remove it. Only problem was I couldn't."

"Why not?" I asked. "Did Madison go into shock when you tried to pull it off?"

"Nothing so dramatic," said Larry. "I quite simply *couldn't*. The air around her solidified as I reached toward her, getting denser the further I stretched. At first it felt like I was sticking my arm into molasses, but soon enough, I might as well have been reaching into stone."

"Only when you reached toward the pendant or toward Madison in general?" asked Dawn.

Larry tapped the side of his nose. "Aha. I see you've been paying attention during my rants on magical theory."

Dawn shrugged. "It's hard to spend as much time around you as we do and not pick up *something*."

"The effect was more pronounced near the pendant than with the rest of her, so I'm guessing whatever's keeping her trapped in the spirit realm is tied to that thing."

"So how did it get there?" I asked. "Did someone put it on her without her knowing?"

"I don't know," said Larry. "It's something I'd like to figure out, but for the time being, the important thing is to figure out how to get it off her. For that, I need your help."

"You're the one with the magical know-how," said Tank. "What do you expect us to do?"

"The research," said Larry. "I've already told you I've never encountered something of this nature before. I need to know how to get it off Madison, and *safely*."

"Larry, you know we're always willing to help," I said. "But you're making it sound like there's a reason you can't do this yourself, and it's freaking me out."

Larry wiped a hand across his face. "It's nothing to get concerned about. Mostly it's because I haven't slept in over a day. I told you I was in the spirit realm longer than I expected. It takes a toll on you, even if you can't feel the passage of time." He took a deep breath and let it out slowly. His voice lowered, and I could hear the strain in it. "Also because Carol isn't doing well. She needs someone with her, and even though we've had our issues, I'm the person best suited to help her through this. Her husband Dan is on a work trip in Shanghai. She got hold of him, but even if he gets on the first flight out, he won't be here for over twenty-four hours."

"Larry..." Dawn stood and hugging him. "We've got your back. Take care of your sister."

I felt like a heel for even asking Larry why he needed our help. I should've realized how much stress he was under. "Is there anything else you can tell us about the pendant?"

Larry shook his head. "Nothing that'll make any sense to someone without extensive magical training. But I could sketch it for you. That might help."

Larry grabbed a pad of paper and the cheap pen that accompanied it from a side table and started scribbling. He spent about twenty seconds on his drawing before he ripped it free and held it to Dawn. "There. I never went to art school, but it's better than nothing."

Dawn accepted it. "We'll do everything we can."

"Thanks." Larry stood. He gave me a nod. "You get that coffee here?"

"No, but there's a bistro here somewhere," I said. "You can take mine if you want."

Larry held up a hand. "It's alright. I'll find my own."

He turned toward the elevators, but I stopped him before he'd taken more than a step. "Wait. Larry. About my dream. You never told me what any of it meant."

Larry looked me in the eyes. "It means the spirit realm and the dream realms are crossing over, multiple parallel universes approaching a singularity right here at this point in time. In case you're wondering, that's probably a bad thing."

"Should I even ask why it's happening?"

The lines in Larry's brow deepened. "Could be chance. Or it could be something is drawing them together."

15

I SHIFTED IN MY SEAT, FIDDLING WITH THE DEMON TOOTH in my pocket. Honestly, I should've chosen a different pair of shorts before I left the house, a pair that reached past mid-thigh and had more than four cubic inches of pocket space, but since the Texas summer heat had already descended on us, I wasn't about to sacrifice comfort for a few extra inches of pocket. Besides, I'd forgotten I intended to carry my demon tooth bat with me when I'd first gotten into the Suburban. Luckily, I'd remembered as I'd parked, though it didn't seem as if I'd need the thing anytime soon.

As I nudged the tip of the tooth into an orientation where it wasn't poking me in my privates, I caught Dawn approaching. Instead of the skin tight leather pants and tank top she usually wore, she'd thrown on a pair of cut-off shorts and a plain black V-neck. Maybe it was because she'd also been in a rush to leave the house. For all I knew it was what she'd slept in, though I'd always assumed she was the type to sleep nude. Her current outfit made her look less intimidating than normal, though.

She set my mug down on the table in front of me. "Got you a refill."

After Larry had returned to his sister, Dawn and I moved to the cafe on the ground floor of the hospital. We hadn't had a chance to grab breakfast before leaving, so we'd ordered a few things before getting to work. Considering how the day was shaping up, continued doses of caffeine would be the most important portion of the meal.

I pushed my phone to the side. "Thanks." I took a sip of the coffee and grimaced. I'm not sure what I expected from a hospital café, but something better than dishwater would've been appreciated. "Well... At least it's hot."

"Sadly, that's the best thing you can say about it." Dawn sat down beside me. "You know, in the Philippines we have a type of coffee known as *kapeng barako*. Most coffee consumed around the planet is from one of two species, *arabica* and *robusta*, but *barako* is distinct. It has a very strong flavor, a lot like anise. I like it a lot, although some find it off-putting. I wish you could get it around here, but the trees don't grow as well as the more popular varieties. They're also too large to harvest the beans from easily, which is another reason most farmers don't bother with them."

"Well, I'm not the biggest fan of licorice, but I have to imagine just about anything is better than *this*." I lifted my cup.

"It is. Much better. And there are more benefits to it than flavor, or so the traditional healers would have you believe. In Filipino, the word *barako* translates to 'stud.' You can imagine men have been drinking it for centuries with hopes of increasing their *performance*. I don't think it does anything of the sort for women, but consuming it produces the pleasurable side effect of making any men who notice us drinking it angry that a woman would dare consume such a masculine drink." Dawn smiled, tipped back her mug, and took a long draught of her coffee. She set it down and made a face. "Then again, perhaps drinking American coffee is the real test of a woman's mettle. Yuck." She shook her head, as if doing so would rid her mouth of the taste. "So. Any luck with the research?"

I shrugged. "I don't know. Maybe? It's hard to tell because the stuff I'm coming across online is either two page snippets from Google Books or total unsourced BS someone slapped on their blog. I mean, I understand Larry needed help with this, but I don't feel qualified making life and death decisions about his niece based on random internet searches. I wish he could've spared us a half hour to get us on the right track."

Dawn snorted. "First of all, let me point out that Larry *hates* doing research. Perhaps he wouldn't despise it so much if he was a fourteenth century monk, but since we live in the internet age and *everything* is online, research is pretty hard for him to perform on his own given his technological impairments. Which isn't to say he didn't need to get back to his sister or catch up on shut eye. I'm just saying there might've been a subconscious inclination to push this onto us even if he hadn't been so stressed. With that said, I'm going to let you in on a little secret. When it comes to the paranormal, information posted on random blogs is some of the most accurate stuff you can find, especially if the site still has one of those pixelated under construction GIFs and looks like it hasn't been updated since the early nineties."

"Really? Why?"

"Because the folks who are in the know about supernatural stuff tend to be a lot like Larry. They're either literally hundreds of years old and don't know a coffee machine from a smartphone or they can't be trusted to move their site off GeoCities for fear of the workstation they're using exploding." Dawn scooted her chair in. "Show me what you've found. The crazier the site the better."

"If you insist." I turned my phone back on and opened up the tabs on my browser. I flicked through until I found the one I thought was the most off the wall. "Might as well start with this one. Mind you, I have no idea how to perform a reverse image search, and I wasn't getting anything but religious mumbo jumbo when I used a search string of 'wooden cross with red twine,' so instead I switched strategies and searched for 'how do you trap a spirit?' This is one of the first results that came up."

The site was nearly as outdated as the ones Dawn had joked about. It didn't automatically resize on my phone, so I had to zoom and scroll so Dawn could see. "This is some Scottish woman's blog. Maggie Megan Moore. I guess her parents liked alliteration. In this one post she's talking about creating what she calls a spirit trap. She claims it's for capturing evil spirits, not immobilizing a person's soul, but there were enough similarities with what Larry told us that it piqued my interest. For one thing, she says the trap can be fashioned into several forms, either a cage called a *breuddwydiwr*, which I guess is like a Scottish dreamcatcher, or an amulet. All of them are made of wood. Specifically, the heartwood of a Rowan tree, whatever that is."

Dawn nodded. "It's a kind of tree that grows in Northern Europe. It's well established in Norse mythology, and it's known as the portal tree to the druids. They consider it a threshold to the otherworld that you travelled to with Larry. Honestly, making a trap out of it would make sense, especially if you used the heartwood. That's the tree's core, which is of a darker hue than the rest. It's supposedly where the portal lies, protected by the rest of the tree."

I blinked. "How do you know so much about druidism and British trees?"

"You think this is the first time we've dealt with ghosts? Like I said, Larry hates doing research. Bill doesn't have fingers with which to type, and I love him to death, but Tank lacks the requisite focus to dive into most deep learning projects. You can figure out who the task falls to. Does it describe what these things look like?"

"Beyond the general shape of the traps? No. But there's a clue that suggests it might be what Larry found. The post goes on to explain how you're supposed to trap the evil spirit. For that, you need something that *belongs* to the spirit. A piece of clothing, a favored talisman, or a piece of the spirit itself. Hair, flesh, blood. Don't ask me how you're supposed to get any of this stuff. Anyway, it says whatever you obtain has to be incorporated into the trap. A strip of the clothing can be wrapped around it, the talisman can be tied to it, as can the hair, but in the case of blood, it should be soaked into the Rowan wood or into something that can be wrapped around it. Larry said the pendant he saw was wrapped in red twine."

Dawn's face tightened. "It could've been soaked in blood, but Larry said the pendant only existed in the spirit realm. How would something have gotten Madison's blood there? Aren't flesh and blood real world constructs?"

"Beats the heck out of me," I said. "Larry said you can die as easily in the spirit realm as you can here, but he didn't go into specifics. Probably didn't want to freak me out with detailed explanations of spiritual disembowelments. However, Madison does have a nagging wound on her arm. It was still bleeding a little when we found her."

Dawn leaned in close and nodded at my phone. "So what does it say about actually trapping the spirit?"

"I didn't bother reading that far, honestly." I scrolled down on my phone. "Let's see. Attach the item obtained from the spirit to the trap. Already covered that. Then it says to place the trap in a spot the spirit frequents in the case of the cage or *breuddwydiwr,* or if using the amulet, wear it for protection when frequenting areas within the spirit's territory. The spirit should be attracted to the trap, and if it gets close enough, it should be drawn inside."

"Then what? You keep the spirit trapped in a heartwood cage forever?"

I scrolled some more. "Uh... it says you can banish the spirit from the face of the Earth by burning the cage."

"Banish?"

I showed Dawn the phone. "That's the language."

She leaned back and frowned. "So does that kill the spirit or return it to the otherworld?"

I shrugged. "Your guess is as good as mine. This is all based on a blog post, after all."

I heard heavy footsteps and someone cried out in indignation. I looked up to find Tank barreling toward us, the elderly couple who'd barely avoided his onrush staring at him in disapproval.

Tank skidded to a halt in front of our table. "Hey. You guys need to come up right away. Larry needs our help."

"Why? What happened?" I asked.

"I don't know," said Tank. "But Madison just went into convulsions. It looks bad."

16

I RUSHED DOWN THE HALLWAY, DAWN AT MY SIDE AND Tank only a few paces behind. Larry stood next to a sign touting the benefits of thorough hand washing, his hands stuffed deep into the pockets of his duster and his shoulders slumped. Nurses rushed in and out of the room past him, calling instructions to each other as they did so.

I slowed as I reached the commotion, my heart beating quickly from the rush up the stairs. "Larry. What's going on?"

"Excuse me!" A nurse nearly collided with Tank as she rushed past, a sealed plastic tub contained a syringe and a vial in her hands.

Larry took me by the arm and ushered us closer to the wall, a few paces from the action. "It's not good. Madison was doing okay until five minutes ago. Then out of the blue her heart rate spiked. A nurse came in to check on her, found her pupils had dilated. While she was checking her IVs, Madison started to shake. Only a little at first, but it spread fast, from her arms to her shoulders to her whole body. Big, wracking convulsions. Madison's room filled with nurses in about twenty seconds. They kicked me out. Tried to do the same to Carol, but she wasn't having any of it. She's still in there. God, this is bad..."

Larry's face was drawn. I don't think I'd ever seen him so worried. Part of me wanted to reach out, to give him a hug and tell him everything was going to be okay, but I didn't know that. The facts suggested the opposite.

"Can the doctors do anything?" asked Dawn.

"Maybe. The nurses said they needed a drug to counteract the seizures. Someone mentioned something called Phenobarb, someone else mentioned... Dilantin? I don't know."

"Is it going to work?" I asked.

"How the hell should I know?" said Larry. "I'm not a doctor."

"That's not what I mean, Larry. Will the drugs keep her under control if her spirit isn't here. Tied to her body, in our realm."

Larry sighed. "I don't know. I assume they'll stop the convulsions. That's a physical response to a psychological strain. But the drugs won't keep her spirit tied to her body. If something's happening to her in the spirit realm, it could kill her. Christ. I need to get back there. Now."

Larry wiped a hand across his face. His scruff was thicker than I was used to, and bags had grown under his eyes.

"Did you get any sleep at all?" I asked.

Larry shook his head. "Maybe half an hour. There wasn't any time. I'll be fine. It's Madison who won't be if I can't push through. Something might be attacking her. I need to get over there. Even if I can't figure out what's going on with that talisman around her neck, maybe I can do something. I just need a spot to lay down a circle..." Larry gazed around the hall in a haze as if he planned on whipping out a stick of chalk and performing a séance then and there.

"Wait," said Dawn. "We might've uncovered something. Lexie found a website that described something similar to what you sketched. It's called a spirit trap. It might be holding Madison hostage."

Larry blinked the film from his eyes. *"What?* Why didn't you say so? How does it work? How do I get it off her?"

"We don't know exactly, but it might not be that easy," said Dawn. "It might be made of Rowan wood."

Larry's mouth fell open. *"Son of a...* That's why I couldn't touch it!"

Another nurse rushed by with a bag of saline. I tried to focus on the conversation. "Sorry, but I'm missing something. Dawn said Rowan wood was magical. That druids thought the trees acted as portals to the spirit realm."

"They can be used for that, yes," said Larry. "And they *are* magical, but their magic lies in their ability to ward off evil spirits."

"So," I said. "Sometimes you make questionable decisions, but you're not evil and you're sure as hell not a spirit."

"How nice of you to think so," said Larry, "but in this case I'm using the term as the druids who discovered the power of the Rowan trees in the seventh century did. For them, an evil spirit was any magical being. Any being that used magic rather than the latent power of nature, specifically witches, and as far as a Rowan tree is concerned a wizard is just a male witch. *Damnit!"*

Larry turned and slammed his palm against the wall, startling a nurse who ran past toward Madison's room.

Tank held out a cautious hand. "Larry. It's okay. Calm down."

Angry tears sparkled in his eyes as he spun toward us. "I will *not* calm down. Don't you see? That pendant was specifically constructed so *I* wouldn't be able to remove it. *Christ.* Carol was right. Someone targeted Madison because of *me.* This is *my* fault."

"*No.*" The word came out more forcefully than I'd intended. "You didn't come after her. You didn't involve her in this. Heck, I didn't even know you *had* a niece until yesterday morning. So don't blame yourself when there's clearly something evil out there pulling the strings. And don't give up, either. You may not be able to remove that pendant from your niece, but the last time I checked there are four of us here and only one wizard."

Larry shook his head. "Tank can't leave this world, Lexie. He's half man, half bear. The two souls coexist, but if he entered the spirit realm, they'd battle for superiority. It would tear him apart. Dawn's deathly afraid of going, and as for you? Trust me, it wouldn't be a great idea."

"Why not?" I said. "Look, I know you believe in me and that you think I can be a great sorceress one day, but there's no denying I'm not one yet. I could retrieve the pendant."

"For the record," said Dawn, "I'd do it, too. For your family, Larry. You know I would."

Dawn trembled as she said it, and her face had paled. I hadn't realized Dawn was scared of anything, but now I understood why the attack at Charity's place had traumatized her so, beyond simply the invasion of her privacy.

"It's not that," said Larry. "I suspect you could push through and retrieve the spirit trap, Lexie, but we're not at Charity's anymore. This is a hospital. People have died here. *A lot* of people. We wouldn't be alone. Not by a long shot."

Dawn took a half step back, and she swallowed hard.

"I don't care," I said. "I'll do it. Same as Dawn. I'm not going to let any harm come to you or your family if I can prevent it."

Larry blew air from between his lips. "Okay. We'll just be careful, that's all, and we'll stick together."

Dawn grasped me by the arm gently. I barely heard her, but I could read her lips. "Thank you."

One of the nurses from Madison's room poked her head from the room. "Suzi! Call ICU. We're transferring!"

Larry's eyes widened, and the furrows in his brow deepened. "We don't have a lot of time. Tank, Dawn? Keep an eye on Carol for me. Lexie? Time to move."

17

The door slammed against the backstop as Larry barreled through. I peered through the inset window as it clanged shut behind us, checking to see if any of the orderlies had spotted us, but they all seemed too consumed with what was going on in Madison's room.

"Quit gawking and get over here." Larry burst from the bathroom with a jar of tongue depressors in one hand and one of cotton balls in the other.

"What's all that for?" I asked.

"We need to make the magic circle out of something, and I didn't bring a permanent marker with me. Quick. Push that hospital bed to the side."

I did as Larry asked. Thankfully, the thing was on wheels, so it didn't take a lot of strength to move. By the time I got it wheeled into the corner, Larry had already spread a collection of tongue depressors into a half circle, even if he wasn't doing a terribly precise job of it. Parts of the arc consisted of a single depressor while others were piles of four to five. Some of them stuck haphazardly to the side, making right angles to what should've been the circle's surface.

"It's a little sloppy, don't you think?"

"Don't lecture me on magic right now," said Larry. "A circle's a circle. So long as we complete it, it'll work. Here." He tossed me the cotton balls. "You do the star."

I did as I was told. I tossed the lid to the side and dumped a bunch of cotton balls into my hand, tossing them into lines within the circle Larry was constructing, not worrying about their thickness or even how straight they were. Larry didn't chastise me, so either precision really didn't matter or he was so distraught at the prospect of his niece being tortured that he wasn't making smart decisions anymore. Hopefully the latter wouldn't lead to anything worse than the stink I was responsible for when I flubbed the incantation as opposed to, say, the séance teleporting us into a universe that lacked air and heat and was full of flesh-eating spiders.

Larry finished before I did. He grabbed some of the remaining cotton balls from the jar and tossed them into place along the last line himself. He didn't hesitate as he hopped into the middle of the circle.

He paused as he took a good look at me. "You're sure you want to do this? I can't guarantee it'll be safe."

I met his gaze without flinching. "It wasn't safe when we transported at Charity's either. I'm helping you Larry, like it or not, and don't question my commitment again. When I say I'm doing something, I follow through."

Larry nodded. "Okay then. Give me your hands."

I held them out. Larry grasped them and closed his eyes. "*Vide praeter illam velum. Inferis, aperta.*"

Once again, the world turned upside down around me. I

plunged through the invisible ink and came up standing exactly where I'd been the moment Larry started speaking except the colors had faded from the room. Every surface had the same indistinct, fuzzy quality to it Charity's house had, and certain surfaces flickered chaotically, trying to maintain a connection with their associated pairs in the real world.

"Alright," I said. "The first thing we need to—*AAHHH!*"

I jumped as I spotted the woman in the padded chair in the corner. Blood covered the side of her face, soaking through her pale blonde hair. It streamed down her neck, staining her shirt a deep crimson, a shirt that sunk into her chest cavity at an unnatural angle and clung to ribs that bent the wrong way. She stared at the hospital bed I'd wheeled into the corner, eyes glazed.

I jumped as Larry touched me on the shoulder. He spoke quietly in my ear. "I told you there'd be spirits everywhere, but the ones who remain are here because they feel their purposes in life went unfulfilled. They're angry and confused, but they don't care about us. Most of them won't even notice us. So don't interact with them. Don't talk to them. Don't even look at them if you can avoid it. Understood?"

I nodded and took a step toward the door. The woman in the chair didn't look my way. "Got it. Let's find Madison."

Larry opened the door and we stepped into the hallway. Despite the warning he'd given me, I paused.

When Larry said we wouldn't be alone in the hospital, he wasn't kidding. The corridor outside our room was like a scene from *The Walking Dead*. Individuals stumbled back and forth along the hall, some of them covered in blood, others pale and ghostly. Some were missing limbs, others had faces and arms covered in pock marks or boils, while others still had giant scars that stretched across the skin exposed by their hospital gowns.

True to Larry's word, though, none of them paid us any more attention than they would've flies on a horse's ass.

"Follow me." Larry wove through the stumbling masses, taking care not to bump into anyone as he headed down the hall. I followed him just as carefully. We needed to get to Madison as quickly as possible, and getting into a fight with a dead person wouldn't help.

Larry pushed through into Madison's room. I almost barreled into him as he came to a sudden stop.

"Hey! What's—" The matter, was what I was going to say, but my eyes told me the story. Madison's bed was missing, as was she.

Larry sighed heavily. "We're too late. She's gone."

"Don't get all fatalistic on me, Larry. The nurses said they were moving her to the ICU. Let's check there."

Larry perked. "You're right. Or rather, they were probably *on their way* to the ICU when we passed through the portal. Chances are we'll find Madison along the way."

"Just hanging out in the hall?" I said.

"I'm sure the nurses are still moving her in our world," said Larry, "but remember, time doesn't exist here. The state is locked when we pass through the portal."

"These rules are getting hard to remember, man."

"Trust me. Come on."

We headed back into the hall. Neither one of us knew how to get to the ICU, but luckily, hospitals have signs. We found the closest map and oriented ourselves.

Larry jabbed a finger into it. "There. That's where we are. ICU's above us. Elevators to our left."

We took off, avoiding the ghosts with ease. As much as their presence disturbed me, I brimmed with confidence. Perhaps I'd watched too many zombie shows and lost all respect for creatures that shambled, but I figured if any of them did confront us, I'd be able to handle myself. I might not be able to tango with a spirit with boiling hot magma for skin, but I figured I could fight off the ghost of a middle-aged woman who'd died from esophageal cancer.

We turned a corner, and Larry pointed. "There!"

Madison lay on her hospital bed fifty feet shy of the elevators. Despite the corridor being as full of ghosts as the last, not a soul approached within eight feet of her bed, as if she was protected by an invisible bubble. Perhaps it had something to do with the amulet that had been placed over her.

Larry ran forth, skidding to a halt at Madison's side. He waved me in and pointed to her neck. "There is it. See if you can touch it."

Larry's artistic skills wouldn't win him any prizes, but he'd sketched the thing accurately enough. It was a cross of dark wood, four inches by six, liberally tied together with crimson twine. More of the twine had been wrapped around the perimeter, making the thing look more like a kite than a religious symbol. It lay motionless against Madison's chest, which didn't appear to be moving either.

"Shouldn't she be breathing?" I asked.

"One more reason to get it off her," said Larry. "Go. Give it a try."

I reach out tentatively, half expecting to be slapped away by an invisible force, but I didn't feel the same wall of molasses Larry had described. The hairs on my arm prickled, but that was it. Nonetheless, I hesitated. My hand hovered over the pendant like Indiana Jones about to swap a bag of sand for an idol, except I didn't have anything to swap it for. Hopefully, it wouldn't make a difference.

My hand closed around the pendant. Black magic didn't burst from between my fingers, nor did a burning fire sear my palm. I simply felt the rough scrape of wood and the soft bristles of the twine. I pulled the thing carefully off of Madison, lifting her head with my free hand to get it from behind her head.

Larry watched Madison. "Nothing happened." He pressed a couple fingers against her neck. "She's barely clinging to life. Why didn't anything happen?"

"About that," I said. "The website I found said spirit traps can be made in different forms. Some of them are actual traps. Amulets are shaped that way for portability. I'd imagine whether or not you're wearing it has no impact on the spirit trapped within."

Larry's face darkened. *"Now you tell me.* Don't you think this is something that should've come up before we raced off into the spirit realm?"

"There was never a good moment, but the site explained how to destroy the trap."

"Thereby freeing the trapped spirit?"

"The website used the word *banish,* actually."

"Banish? Lexie, that sounds like how you'd send a spirit *to* the spirit realm, not vice versa."

"Yeah, well these things are supposed to be used against evil witches, not harmless teenagers. All I'm basing this on is a website, okay? I don't have all the answers."

Stress lined Larry's face. His eyes had adopted a crystalline quality, looking like they might break at any moment. "Okay. So how do we destroy the trap?"

"All we have to do is burn it."

"Burn it? Oh, is that all?"

A nearby ghost turned toward us in response to Larry's outburst. I closed on Larry and lowered my voice. "Why is that a problem? I've seen you summon fire from your hands a hundred times."

"Yes. In the real world. I've told you, magic works differently here. Perhaps you noticed the spear and shield of light I fabricated at Charity's. Not exactly my usual fare."

"Well, you weren't going to have a lot of luck beating back a magma monster with a fireball."

"The point is, Lexie, I can't summon fire in the spirit realm! It's not possible! *Jesus Christ!"* Another ghost turned our way. "Don't you get it? Not only did someone make this trap out of a material I wouldn't be able to touch, they placed it in the spirit realm where they knew I wouldn't be able to destroy it! And they left it around Madison's neck to taunt me! They're attacking me through her!"

As Larry's outburst grew, more pairs of eyeballs landed on us. A few of the ghosts had even stopped shuffling to stare. "Larry, calm down. You've said everything on Earth has a parallel, right? All we need to do is locate a fire that's burning there, and its pair should be present here."

Larry didn't lower his voice. "And where are we supposed to find that? Last time I checked the Olympics weren't being held in Austin. There's no eternal flame burning merrily down the hallway. Let me remind you, we're in a *hospital.* There are fire suppression systems everywhere. You can't even smoke within a hundred feet of these things."

One of the ghosts took a step forward, past the invisible barrier provided by the pendant, but that didn't stop a sudden thought from popping into my mind. "That's not true. This is a religious hospital. It has a chapel. And if there's a chapel, there will be votive candles. *Especially* in a hospital."

Larry blinked. "Holy fire. If there's anything that would free Madison while keeping her safe, that would be it. Lexie, you're a *genius!*"

Another of the ghosts stepped toward us, reaching out a hand while uttering a pained moan. I pulled Larry out of the way, hissing at him. "Watch out! And keep it down!"

"Sorry." Larry looked around us, finally noticing the attention he'd drawn. "The chapel is on the main floor, right? We need to get to the elevators."

The ghosts bunched around us, their focus now fully shifted. "How do you propose we do that?"

"You ever push sleds as one of your softball workouts?"

I tucked the wooden pendant into my back pocket. "Once or twice."

Larry nudged me toward Madison's bed. "Do you remember how I told you to leave the ghosts alone and they'd leave us alone?"

"I remember."

"Well, they're not going to leave us alone anymore, so no point in being nice. Grab those handles on the side of the bed and PUSH!"

Larry grabbed ahold of the left side of the bed and threw his weight behind it. I did the same with my side, getting low and driving my feet into the floor. Madison's hospital bed lurched forward, straight into the nearest group of the formerly living. Ghosts they might've been, but they felt real enough as the bed slammed into them. The thing shuddered and rattled as we knocked a half dozen souls to the sides and ran over half as many more. The guard rails at the side of the bed kept Madison from being knocked off as we rushed down the hall, leaving the cluster of ghosts behind us.

"The button!" said Larry. "Quick! Before they catch us."

I jabbed the down button on the elevators. The button lit up, but my heart nonetheless sank. "Wait, do these things work in the spirit realm? You said this place is static, right? Locked into place, everything the same as it is in the real world when we left. Oh, God, no. How the hell are we going to get Madison to the first floor? We can't push her bed down the stairs. Now those ghosts are going to catch us and—"

The elevator dinged, and the doors slid open.

"Stop being so dramatic and help me push this thing in," said Larry.

I pushed. We wheeled the bed inside. I took a position on the right side of the cab and Larry on the left.

I pushed the button for the ground floor. My heart beat hard in my chest, first from the sprint down the hall, then from fright at the thought of the ghosts catching us. "Sorry. For a second there I thought we were going to have to battle that herd of angry spirits."

"Relax," said Larry as the doors closed. "We made it out. Besides, you don't have to worry about normal ghosts. It's the aggravated and evil ones that are dangerous."

Something clacked, and the elevator dinged angrily—probably because the doors hadn't closed all the way. It wasn't any part of the hospital bed that blocked them. Rather, it was a cone of burnished metal, about the size of a pen but smooth all around. I think it was the tip of an umbrella.

It poked through the gap between the doors at chest height. It clacked again as something twisted on the umbrella, and the doors opened back up.

18

THE UMBRELLA LOWERED AS THE ELEVATOR DOORS SLID back into their pockets, and a man stepped forward into the gap. In some ways, he looked a lot like Larry. He was his equal in height, with long, matted grey hair and a rat's nest of a beard that hung to his sternum. He wore an artichoke green trench coat that dangled to his feet, and he gripped the steel-tipped, crook-handled umbrella in a vein-laced hand. A hat that looked like it was from the Confederate War sat atop his head. Two frayed tassels hung off the end of it, a feather stuck from the top, and there was even an insignia of a bugle sewn onto the front in gold brocade.

Unlike Larry, however, the man was completely and totally soaked. Water dripped from the rim of his hat, from his beard, from the tips of his gnarled eyebrows, from the wrists of his jacket, and from the bottom hem. In fact, it veritably *poured* off. It pooled around his feet, the *drip drip drip* of the droplets turning into a burble as the pool overran the lip of the elevator and fell through the gap into the shaft below.

The man lifted his head and cocked a cold, grey eye at

Larry. A thick film covered it, as if he suffered from bad cataracts. He opened his mouth, and his voice seeped out, watery and distant and uncertain. "*Stuttgart...?*"

I took a step back in the elevator. "Larry? Who is this?"

Larry spoke quietly without taking his eyes off the water-drenched intruder. "His name is Günter Wahreflamme. He's a fellow wizard. I fought him in a brawl at the Colorado River shores a few years ago. He looks like he *drowned*... Honestly, I had no idea he'd died. He must've been treated at the hospital."

Wahreflamme frowned, as if he was having a hard time following the conversation. His lips turned down into a frown.

My heart, which only recently decided it was safe to slow its beating, now began to hammer away again. "Are you saying you *killed* him?"

"Not on purpose."

Günter's frown deepened, and his rheumy eye began to glow. I didn't even get a chance to remind Larry about his insistence that angry ghosts were the most dangerous before Günter flicked his arm into motion. His umbrella blurred as he whipped the steel tip at Larry's head. Bright white light erupted from Larry's forearm as he parried the blow, sending the tip of the umbrella streaking across the back of the elevator car. I cried out as sparks few from the metal cab, and I ducked just in time to avoid the sharp cut of the tip. A cruel orange-tinged line spread across the wall, the metal peeling like strips of paper in a fire.

Günter pulled the umbrella back and lunged into the car, stabbing with the tip as if it were a fencing foil.

"Larry, watch out!" I cried.

Larry batted it aside with his magical bracer, sending it flying into the wall. The tip popped through the metal as if it were butter. "Don't worry about me. Protect Madison!"

I tugged on the hospital bed, slamming it against the back of the elevator car as Wahreflamme's umbrella whipped back, slicing off a chunk of the plastic baseboard. "How?"

A sword of light grew from Larry's hand in time to parry another blow. "I don't know. Think of something!"

Sparks of light mingled with the regular kind as Larry's magical sword clanged against Wahreflamme's umbrella. Larry grunted as he pushed Günter's weapon to the side, slicing a gouge in Madison's mattress. I grabbed Madison's legs and pulled on them, tucking them to the side. "Christ, Larry, you almost took her foot off. Push him out!"

The sword cut a wide arc, more sparks spraying as it slashed through the button panel. The entire elevator car shook violently. The panel sputtered and blinked out. "Don't you think I'm trying?"

I looked on Madison's bed, but it didn't appear anyone had squirreled away a knife among the sheets. Desperate, I snatched one of the pillows from under her and chucked it at Günter.

The thing bounced off his coat, spiraling into the hallway amid a crowd of approaching ghosts. I thought Larry might use the opportunity to stab Wahreflamme in the throat, but the once drowned wizard was too quick. He batted Larry back before casting his gaze in my direction.

His eye still glowed. In fact, it glowed much stronger than before.

"Oh, shit." I dove into the side of the hospital bed as a beam of white hot light shot out of Günter's eye. Pain blossomed in my shoulder as the bed slammed against the far side of the elevator. Larry yelped. I caught the blur of his feet as he dove out of the cab and into the hallway, narrowly avoiding getting crushed by the bed. As I tumbled to the ground, something sharp jabbed my inner thigh.

"Christ!" Larry rolled to a stop. "Lexie, are you okay?"

I reached into my shorts pockets and pulled out what was stabbing me. My enchanted demon tooth. "Yeah. I'm good."

My heart soared as I squeezed on the tooth, but it didn't stretch and transform into the thirty inches of brain-splatting death I was used to. Nothing happened at all. "Larry. It's not transforming!"

Larry rolled across the hallway as Wahreflamme's umbrella cut a cruel gash across the tile. "What isn't?"

"My demon tooth. It's not transforming into a bat!"

Larry danced out of the way of another swipe. "How many times do I have to tell you? Magic works different in the spirit realm. Just because something works in our world doesn't mean the same thing is true here."

"But you said every object exists as a parallel version of the one back home!"

"Yes, the *object*." Larry parried another blow, sending a shower of white sparks over Günter's coat. "Not the magic imbued to it. That's hit or miss."

Wahreflamme growled, and a spout of boiling water shot out of his sleeve. Larry dove to the side, barely avoiding the hissing steam and searing hot liquid. As he rolled to his feet he waved a frantic hand at me. "Go! Get out of here! Get Madison to the chapel!"

"Right!" I punched the button for the ground floor on the elevator panel, but other than sparking angrily, it didn't respond. I could see the electronics within through the gaping wound Larry's sword had left in it.

"It's not responding," I said. "I think you busted it!"

Larry swore. He spun and kicked an approaching ghost in the chest with his boot. "Can you hot wire it?"

I didn't get a chance to tell him I'd never learned how to hot wire elevators in my undergraduate engineering program because a man who was missing an eye and had blood pouring down his face lurched into the open elevator doors. I cried out and slashed with my demon tooth. I caught him across the cheek on the side that still had an eye. The half-blind ghost man howled and clutched his face as black swirling mists spewed from the wound. He stumbled and fell to the floor, hissing as his face melted into vapor.

"Holy Jesus," I said. "I guess I don't need the bat after all."

Another blast of white hot light from Günter's eye drew my attention to Larry's fight. My partner bobbed and weaved, parrying blows and performing acrobatics I had no idea he was capable of. "What are you waiting for, Lexie? Get Madison to the chapel! Take the stairs if you have to."

"Right." I grabbed the handles on Madison's bed and tugged, but as soon as the thing lurched into motion, another pair of angry ghosts shambled into the open elevator doors.

I cursed and slashed at one with my tooth. I caught him across the chest. He shrieked and stumbled back, but the other grabbed me by the arm. I didn't break out in blistering boils or anything of the sort, but the ghost sure had a solid grip.

I grunted, twisted, and kicked, knocking the ghost back. She stumbled to the floor only for another three to step over her and her buddy to take their place.

"Larry, I can't!" I cried. "I'm trapped. Can't you use your magic? Blast them back, just for a moment. Long enough for me to get Madison out of here."

"For the last time, I can't." Larry spun around another of

Wahreflamme's slashes. "It just..." He parried the attack, sparks flying. "Doesn't..." He cocked his sword back and unleashed a wild blow. *"Work that way!"*

I heard a metallic clang, and the umbrella flew from Günter's hand. It spun through the air, spinning wildly in my direction. I shrieked and dove to the floor, once again pushing Madison's bed to the side. The umbrella chopped through two of the ghosts in front of me, slicing them as easily as it had metal and plastic before slamming point first into the back of the elevator cab, a bare six inches above my head.

I swallowed. Hard.

Larry's voice cut through the fear. "Lexie. The umbrella!"

More ghosts closed in to fill the gap. I stood and ripped the umbrella from the wall with my free hand. "What do I do with it?"

"Use it to get Madison to the chapel, that's what!" Larry kicked another ghost to the side as he closed in on him.

"How the heck am I supposed to do that?" I cried.

Larry spared me a frantic glance. "For starters, make sure you open it. I'll be right behind you."

He flicked his hand, and the floor fell out from underneath me.

19

I SCREAMED AS GRAVITY GRABBED HOLD OF ME AND PULLED me into the yawning abyss of the elevator shaft. The floor of the elevator flickered as I passed through it, suddenly providing as little resistance as a cloud. Madison and her bed tumbled into the void beside me. My hair lifted past my face, and as we fell below the level of the elevator floor, darkness swallowed us.

My heart beat like a drum inside my chest as air whistled past me. Snippets of thought darted through my mind at lightning speed. The rate of acceleration of gravity was nine point eight meters per second squared. From a height of five stories, that gave me fifty some feet to fall, unless the hospital had high ceilings. How long did that give me? Shit, I didn't know. Goddamned English to metric unit conversions. Did it even matter? Larry had said death was permanent in the spirit world, but I'd just passed through a floor as solid as mist, so could a fall really kill me? Maybe I'd land light as a feather, maybe not. Maybe I'd turn into a bloody pancake. Even then, what would happen? Would my spirit linger? Would it walk away, with only my body broken behind? *God, I was going to die!*

Fear screamed at me as I fell, the air whipping past. Despite the flurry of thoughts that bombarded me, adrenaline kept my body functional. My left hand squeezed the umbrella handle with vice-grip force while my thumb probed the smooth wood for any lump, any nodule, any raise in elevation. I don't know enough about physiology to understand how it worked, but when my thumb touched that raised piece of plastic nestled among the worn wood, the signal shot along the nerve endings in my fingertips, rocketed up my arm, and blasted through the wall of fear into the center of my panicked thoughts. Right as the sensory information coalesced in my mind as that of a button, a name burst through the bullshit, taking precedence.

"Madison!"

I let go of the demon tooth and stretched across the edge of the bed as my mind sent the signal back into my left arm to act. I felt flesh, thin digits, the fingers of Madison's hand and squeezed, right as my thumb flicked the button on the umbrella.

A *whump* of air and a mechanical *twang* sounded as the umbrella expanded to full size. The rush of air in my ears died with a whimper. The arm with which I held the umbrella jerked in my socket, pulling me up, but Madison kept falling. I clamped my teeth as my other arm jerked downward, pulled toward the bottom of the shaft by Madison's weight. Pain stabbed me in the shoulder, but I squeezed with all my might. The hospital bed smashed against the bottom of the shaft with a splintering crash, and still I held on, using every ounce of strength to keep Madison from falling. I ignored the pain, my arms stretched taut between the umbrella and Madison's limp body like a cross between Mary Poppins and one of those Hercules Hold strength events. My teeth ground against each other. Needles pricked me along the arms, the shoulders, and the neck. My entire body shook with effort, but just when I thought I couldn't hold on any longer, Madison's weight lessened. I shifted in the air, and a moment later, my feet landed gently against a mattress.

I slumped against the wall of the shaft behind me, breathing hard as the pain receded from my shoulders. A slice of light crept into the shaft, slowly revealing my surroundings as my eyes adjusted. The hospital bed had fallen on its side and the mattress over it, but Madison lay atop it, sleeping as peacefully as if she'd never left her room. I lifted the umbrella and took a look at it. The tip no longer glowed orange, and the internal ribs looked no worse for wear. Either the thing was made of vibranium or the umbrella's magic was useful for activities other than killing people.

Nonetheless, I planned on having words with Larry after he made it down the shaft. I folded the umbrella and clasped it shut. *"Make sure you open it.* Maybe I'll open your ass with it, Larry. Could've given me a damn warning."

I looked up toward the elevator. I couldn't make out anything but darkness. "Larry? Any day now, pal." He did say he was going to be right after me, didn't he?

I waited twenty seconds and called out again. Larry didn't respond, but a moment later, I heard a loud clang and a screech of metal on metal.

I still couldn't see a thing above me, but it suddenly occurred to me that being at the bottom of an elevator shaft underneath a cab that had been rendered structurally unsound by slashes with magical swords and umbrellas and might now be filling with dozens of ghostly bodies might not be such a great idea.

I stepped over Madison to the elevator doors and pawed at

them, trying to find a latch or lever that would open them. There had to be one for safety purposes, right?

Another clang and an ear-piercing screech sounded from above. A shiver ran down my spine. "Oh, crap."

I dug my fingernails into the thin gap between the doors, but the crease was too small and my fingers too weak to pry them apart. I needed a crowbar, something I could use to leverage them apart.

The umbrella. Duh. I grabbed it and slammed the tip in the gap between the doors. The strip wasn't big enough to allow entry to the umbrella's tip, but some of the magic in the thing must've lingered, because the tip punched through the metal doors as easily as it had the back of the elevator cab. I took hold of the handle and wrenched on it sideways. The elevator doors groaned and opened four inches.

I stuck the umbrella further into the gap and again pulled on the handle. This time, the doors slid open to a width of about two feet. I tossed the umbrella into the hall, hopped between the doors, put my back to one end and my feet to the other, and pushed. They groaned in protest, but they slid the rest of the way apart.

The elevator above clanged again, and an image formed of it in my mind, breaking from its cable and screaming down the shaft in an uncontrolled rage. I hopped back inside the shaft and dug my arms underneath Madison's limp body. I tugged her toward the door, but her weight threw me off balance. I re-gripped and tried to scramble over the lip of the door with her in hand, but I stumbled and fell. How the hell did mobsters make moving bodies look so easy?

Another clang. Another metallic screech. This one sounded closer. *Shit.*

If I couldn't carry Madison out, I'd have to try something else. Gathering up what strength I had left, I hefted Madison's body up and over the lip so that her arms flopped through the open doors. I jumped into the hall and grabbed hold of them, driving my feet against the floor as I pulled.

I tugged. She moved a few inches before her weight pulled her back into the elevator shaft. I tried again, harder this time, and she moved another foot. Not good enough.

I squatted down low and looped my arms underneath Madison's armpits. I envisioned my softball strength and conditioning coach yelling at me, drove my legs against the ground, and *pulled*.

Madison shot out of the shaft, and I went flying onto my ass. I tumbled to the floor with a thud. I heard a crack. At first I thought it might've been one of Madison's bones. Then I remembered what I had in my back pocket.

I pulled the spirit trap from underneath my butt and looked at it. One of the pieces of Rowan wood bent to the side, but the twine kept the thing together. I looked at Madison, eyeing her chest carefully. It still rose and fell, albeit slowly.

Crisis averted. I tucked the talisman back into my back pocket only to realize my front pocket was empty.

The demon tooth. I'd dropped it to grab Madison.

I hesitated for a fraction of a second, but I couldn't leave it behind, not knowing how powerful it was. I hopped back through the elevator doors and tossed the mattress to the side, scanning the bottom of the shaft for the tooth. My eyes had already acclimated to the lights in the hall, so I couldn't see as clearly as I would've liked. I saw plenty of trash. A crushed Whataburger cup. A set of car keys with a Pikachu key chain. Someone's belt. No tooth, though. *Damn*. Where was it?

The elevator shaft shuddered and groaned, and the whole thing shook.

I shoved the remains of the hospital bed to the side as I cursed my luck. "Where is it? *Where is it?*"

I tossed garbage to the sides. An empty bag of Doritos. A crumpled billing invoice. Someone's wallet. And then, as I picked up the wrecked guardrail from Madison's bed, I saw a flash of white. The demon tooth.

I dove on it. The instant my fingers wrapped around it, I heard a resounding *crack*.

I looked up to see a glimmer of motion in the darkness. I didn't hesitate. I leapfrogged the broken bed and dove out the doors, sliding as I hit the floor. A piercing whistle followed me as I rolled onto Madison, and I brought an arm up to shield my face as well as hers. A fraction of a second later, an explosion rocked my ears. Cymbals crashed. Metal tore. A concussive wave blasted over me. Flying debris stung my skin as if it were a swarm of angry bees while other pieces clanged and ricocheted off polished surfaces.

My ears rang as I sat up. I blinked and waved my arm, trying to clear a cloud of dust from the air in front of me. Through the open doors, I saw the jagged bones of what had once been the elevator. Sharp pieces of metal stuck up at all angles. What I didn't see were the remains of ghostly bodies, or god forbid, Larry's broken corpse.

As much as the latter was a relief, it struck me that he wasn't coming down the shaft after me any time soon.

I stood and oriented myself. I wasn't familiar with the part of the hospital I was in, but if I could get back to the lobby I was sure I could find my way to the chapel. Luckily for me, a stack of folding wheel chairs lined the hall twenty feet from me. I rushed over, popped one open, and wheeled it back to Madison. I had to channel my inner powerlifter to get her in the seat, but once I had her elbows on the armrests and her feet on the paddles at the bottom, she became effortless to move.

I set off down the hall. Thankfully, no ghosts packed the corridor as they did above. I quickened my pace. I'd just passed a set of double doors when I heard a boom.

It wasn't like the crash of the elevator. This boom was distant, and it held a bit of a crackle. The rumble of thunder.

I slowed as I reached a set of windows. A storm crackled overhead, one with deep purple clouds that choked the sky as far as I could see. Dark mists swirled among the clouds, tendrils of darkness undulating around them, caressing them, flowing through them. As I watched, a bolt of yellow lightning ripped free from the mist-shrouded clouds. The world around me briefly inverted before returning to normal a moment later.

A lump rose in my throat. Perhaps there was a reason ghosts didn't roam the ground floor corridors. The magma beast had fled when it heard the thunder. *Where are you, Larry?*

I swallowed down the fear that rose within me and took off down the hall at a jog. The wheels on Madison's chair squeaked as I rolled from the tile in the hall to the carpet in the reception area. Purple energy cascaded through the windows, sending dark shadows skittered across the floor. Not a soul occupied a seat in the lobby, and no one sat at the welcome desk. My vision inverted momentarily as another booming crash reverberated through the hospital, this one louder than the last. I picked up the pace, scanning the signs above for mention of my quarry. As I skirted the bistro, I spotted a sign for the gift shop, and below that, the chapel.

The lightning flashed again, warping the world around me,

and the hairs on my arms rose. I broke into a run. Madison jostled in the wheelchair with each of my footfalls, but I couldn't slow. Something nudged me, some deep-seated response in my core that told me I didn't have much time.

The wheels squealed as I sprinted around a corner. I spotted the lettering for the chapel over a pair of broad double doors. I screeched to a halt, maneuvering the wheelchair sideways as I kicked them open. Inside, the space was empty. Three rows of pews lined a central isle that led to a lectern in front of a wooden crucifix affixed to the wall. A water-filled font stood on one side of the room, though I couldn't imagine it was used for baptisms. Stained glass windows featuring a scene of Jesus en route to Calvary lined the wall along that same side, but little light shone through them. Likewise, the lights within the room were off, but a warm, flickering glow cascaded across the space thanks to a rack of votive candles to the left of the lectern.

At least a half dozen were lit. I hurried down the aisle, pushing Madison's chair in front of me. I hooked a left at the end and pushed Madison to the side. A spark of fear grabbed me at the thought of having lost the spirit trap in my mad dash through the lobby, but when I reached back, I found it there, tucked tightly against my rear.

I held it out, staring at it in the candlelight. The flickering, yellow light gave the blood red twine an eerie hue. The website had said burning the trap would banish the spirit, but would that save Madison? Larry seemed to think it wouldn't harm her, that holy fire couldn't hurt an innocent soul, but was Madison innocent? I didn't know anything about her. For all I knew, she'd engaged in premarital sex, taken drugs without her parents knowing, cheated on exams, hell, maybe even killed someone in a car accident. What if she wasn't as innocent as Larry thought?

What if the website was wrong? What would happen to her if I burned the trap?

I glanced at the crucifix. In the shadowed room, it seemed as if Jesus looked down at me, his face gaunt but peaceful. I'd never been particularly religious, but my parents were. Despite the more black and white interpretations of Catholicism I'd been exposed to by my grandmother, my parents always stressed that no matter what, Jesus loved me. He would always forgive.

In my heart, I had to believe they were right. He wouldn't hurt anyone, and he wouldn't let harm come to Madison.

I took a deep breath, said a silent prayer, and held the spirit trap toward the nearest candle. The flame flickered and danced, licking the underside of the twine, and I saw the faintest spark appear among the twisted fibers.

Suddenly, a fierce wind blasted the chapel doors wide open. It swept through the room, fluttering the cloth over the lectern and flattening the flames of the candles. In unison, the half dozen votive offerings extinguished, the flames disappearing in tiny puffs of smoke. As they died, shadows swept into the room, and with them, a voice.

"Hello, Lexie..."

20

I SPUN, SCANNING THE ROOM. DARKNESS SURROUNDED ME, but a bit of purple-tinged light crept through the stained glass windows. Shadows lingered in the corners, thick and dark, but I didn't think anyone could be hiding in them.

"Who's there?" My voice only shook a little.

"Don't you recognize me, Lexie?"

The voice was deep, dry as dust, and vaguely familiar. It echoed around the room, but it drew me toward the open doors. Beyond them, the darkness was all consuming, like staring into a moonless night sky from underneath a thousand feet of ocean. Only two points of light flickered within the inky morass. Yellow orbs that sparkled like eyes.

I took a step back, stumbling as my feet caught on the edge of the dais. I fell, landing on my butt a foot shy of the lectern. "Who are you?"

"Lexie. How could you possibly forget me?"

A jagged line appeared in the darkness underneath the eyes. It yawned open and rushed me. Air blasted me into the wall at my back as the mouth turned into a malice-filled sun. The lectern wobbled and shook, and the crucifix clattered to the floor with a sharp crack. The creature of darkness shrieked, just as the face in my dream had, but before the mouth swallowed me, it darted to the side, sweeping around the room with a dry, wracking laugh.

It was a laugh I remembered. I'd heard it once before as it shot into the sky, cackling with glee. *"Romanov?"*

The creature darted from one corner to another, melding into the pitch black spaces regardless of the size. The entire room pulsed with a dark energy, but the yellow eyes and cruel mouth always remained. They burned with a dangerous fire. *"Ivan Romanov is dead, Lexie. Only I remain."*

The creature cackled with glee and rushed me once more, black-outlined teeth appearing amid the gaping yellow maw. The mouth snapped, sending a sharp *crack* through the chapel, but again it veered off at the last possible second, sending a rush of wind swirling around the room. The doors slammed shut. The lectern toppled and crashed as the rusty laugh raked like claws across the chalkboard of my mind.

My chest rose and fell rapidly, my heart beating hard under my ribs as I stared at the face in the darkness. What was it if not the spirit of Ivan Romanov? Something older, darker, more evil? And more importantly, what did it want with me? Revenge? Why else would it be taunting me, rushing at me over and over only to pull back and smile?

I scrabbled backward on all fours, but one of my hands slipped upon the smooth wood of the crucifix. I glanced at it, suddenly wondering if there was a reason the nightmarish creature hadn't attacked me yet.

I had to believe. I didn't have any other choice.

I jammed the spirit trap in my pocket and picked up the

crucifix in both hands. I scrambled to my feet, my back against the wall, and held the carving of Jesus on the cross before me. "Stay back, you filthy nightmare! You don't scare me."

The spirit laughed, the dry cackle echoing off the walls. It darted from corner to corner, trails of dark mist following it. Shadows danced, and the darkness in the corners of my eyes pulsed as it spoke. *"You don't have to be as old as I am to recognize a lie as brazen as that."*

I skirted around the chapel, trying to keep the creature as far away from me as possible. I held the crucifix before me like a shield, my fingernails digging into the wood. "It's not a lie. I've dealt with worse than you."

Another booming chuckle. *"What do you think me? A vampire?"*

Something clacked as I bumped it from behind, and a cool splash of water sprayed my legs. *The font.* With my right hand still gripping the crucifix, I scooped water with my left and flung it across the room in the direction of the yellow eyes. "I think you're as scared of me as I am of you. Prove me wrong."

The yellow eyes crinkled around the edges, and the thing's laugh adopted a joyous tinge. *"Is that so? How are you so self-assure, Lexie? You're no woman of faith."*

The creature flicked to the corner above the votive candles, and it occurred to me I'd left Madison alone in her chair, utterly defenseless. How stupid could I have been? "I may not have an unyielding faith in God, but I have faith in myself. I have faith in my friends, and I have faith that this isn't the end of the road for me. I don't know who you are or what you want with me, but I guarantee you, I have no intention of rolling over and dying."

The mirth left the creature's cackle as it skittered out of its corner, tendrils of dark mist clattering across the ceiling like spider legs. *"Oh, Lexie. I love nothing more than to see faith so misplaced."*

I wrapped both hands tight around the crucifix and my teeth ground together with enough force to snap bone. Adrenaline surged through my muscles. I prepared to leap, to slash with the cross, to do something.

Instead, I merely jumped as the doors to the chapel crashed open. Blinding light shot through the room as Larry darted inside, an undulating white energy rippling over his hands and arms. The evil spirit paused as it turned its gaze away from me for the first time. It growled, a deep crackling sound like a tiger emptying its lungs into a dying PA system.

Larry extended a hand toward the center of the dark mass. *"Valeo, daemonium!"* A bolt of condensed light, similar to what had blasted from Wahreflamme's eye, shot across the room. The evil spirit retreated to the corner with mind-numbing speed as Larry's spell seared the ceiling, leaving a bright white mark amid a sea of creeping darkness.

I took the opportunity to right a wrong. I dove across the chapel, skidding to a stop next to Madison's wheelchair. I lifted the crucifix back up, calling to Larry without taking my eyes off the demonic spirit. "Larry! It's the thing that shot out of Romanov's corpse when we killed him. I told you he wasn't dead!"

"Not the time for I told you sos, Lexie." Larry shot another bolt of light toward the evil spirit, but it darted away before Larry's arms finished moving. "Now's the time to kill this thing."

"Well, what are you waiting for?" I said.

Larry collected energy between his hands. "Don't you think I'm trying?"

"Not hard enough," said the evil spirit. It bolted from its

patch of darkness as Larry fired another bolt of energy toward it, flying right at me instead of to another corner. It didn't open its mouth this time, didn't howl or cackle, and it sure as hell didn't swerve to avoid the crucifix I held in front of me. It barreled into me, knocking me back into Madison's wheelchair. She fell to the ground, as did I on top of her. The crucifix flew from my hand, cracking in half as it smashed against the wall.

Larry cried out. "Lexie!"

The spirit rebounded off the wall and coiled, its eyes fixed on me. I scrabbled back on all fours as the spirit launched itself at me. As it flew through the air, I reached into my pocket and slashed with the only thing I had left, my enchanted demon tooth.

The spirit hissed and darted back, the black mists parting around the arc of my slash. It growled and spun, air whipping along behind it. Larry rushed to me. As the ball of darkness coalesced in the far corner, Larry threw up a shield of white light between us.

The yellow eyes grew larger. Veins of black grew into them like roots. *"You have more tricks than I expected, but they won't save you."*

Larry planted his feet, and the shield in front of him thickened. "Leave Lexie out of this, beast. Your beef is with me."

"Is it?" The room pulsed with dark energy.

"Why else would you come after Madison if not to get to me? I'm the one you want. Come at me."

The spirit laughed again, the dry crackle like autumn leaves scraping against cold concrete. *"You presume I'd be sated with revenge on you alone. My hunger is much greater."*

Larry spoke over his shoulder. "Lexie, get Madison out of

here. Find another fire to destroy the spirit trap. I can hold this thing."

"What other fire?" I said. "You said it yourself. We're in a hospital."

"Find something. There's nothing here. You need to go!"

"I'm not leaving you, Larry. We can beat this together!"

The edges of the nightmare spirit's mouth tipped into a ragged grin. *"Once again, your faith is misplaced. Yours in your friends, Lexie, and yours—"* The thing stared at Larry. *"—in yourself."*

A shiver ran through me. At the same time, a flicker of orange light cut through the darkness, reflecting off the back of Larry's magical shield. I turned to find one of the votive candles had rekindled. As I watched, two more flames joined the first, small dancing beacons of hope in a room devoid of it.

Larry's eyes grew as he noticed them. "Lexie!"

I didn't need his encouragement. I ripped the spirit trap from my pocket and thrust it into the heart of the nearest flame.

The nightmare spirit's voice burst through the air. *"NOOO!"*

A burst of air shot toward me again, but this time, Larry's shield blocked it. It flowed around us, barely lifting my hair as the candle's flame licked the twine. The twine brightened and caught, and the entire thing erupted in fire, nearly engulfing my hand.

"Yah!" I dropped the flaming mess into the rack of candles, but the fire burned hot and bright. Smoke puffed and ashes fluttered to the ground as the trap evaporated. As the flames died, Madison's body flickered, becoming oddly translucent. A moment later, it disappeared, whisked away as if it had never existed.

The spirit's mouth widened, and a roar shook the room. *"GRRAAAHHHHHHH!"* The pews clattered and danced. The lights overhead swung wildly. The stained glass shattered into a thousand pieces, and the font clattered to the floor, cracking in half as the water within spread across the tile.

Larry grabbed me by the arm. "Time to go!"

"Where?" I had to shout over the howl of rage.

"Home!"

Larry lurched into motion, pulling me toward the growing pool. The spirit's eyes widened as it realized what we were doing. Larry dove through the air, pulling me with him as the spirit shot toward us from its perch. Its angry shriek cut through the air. My face raced toward the hard floor, and it was only at the last moment that I saw my reflection in the rippling water.

21

THE WORLD FLIPPED UPSIDE DOWN AROUND ME. THE FLOOR that had rushed toward me reversed course, and I hovered for a second above the marble before flopping back down with a thump. The tiles felt cool and dry underneath me, but I could still hear the spirit's evil shriek. It rang in my ears, and though the surfaces around me seemed solid enough and back to their normal colors, the air flickered with latent darkness. A rush of air swirled over me, flipping my hair down the aisle as it rushed out the chapel doors. The wail died with the rush of air, but it left the doors swinging in its wake. They banged as they bounced off their doorstops, friction and a squeak of hinges slowly bringing them to a stop.

Dawn's voice startled me. "What the *hell* was that?"

I looked up to find Dawn and Tank standing over us. Carol sat on a pew behind them, her forehead creased with worry and tears streaking her cheeks. Behind them, three of the two dozen candles on the votive rack flickered merrily.

I pushed myself to my feet, dusting off my shirt. "Dawn. Tank. Did you hear that?"

"You mean the weird wailing and the wind that slammed the doors open?" said Dawn. "Yeah. We heard it. What the heck is going on? Where did you come from?"

Larry grunted as he lurched to his feet. "There was a puddle on the ground and we needed to get out quick. Any port in a storm, right?" He flicked a hand at the candles. "Did you light those?"

Tank cast a quick glance at Carol and spoke in a low voice. "Madison stopped breathing. The doctors had to put her on a respirator. Her heart rate also dropped. It... wasn't looking good. Carol came down to pray. We all did. The candles were out, so we each lit one."

"They'd barely caught before the two of you body slammed the floor and we heard that shriek and the gust of wind," said Dawn. "Seriously, what just happened?"

"What happened is the three of you saved our asses," I said. "We wouldn't have gotten out if not for those candles. Certainly not Madison."

"*What?*" Carol turned at the mention of her daughter. She blinked and focused on us from whichever far off place she'd been visiting.

Larry put a hand on Dawn's shoulder. "I'll explain everything soon enough." He stepped past her and approached his sister. "Carol? I don't want to get your hopes up, but I think we might've been able to help Madison."

Carol blinked again. She shook her head almost imperceptibly. "What do you mean? How?"

"We found her spirit. Someone trapped it in a realm where it couldn't be accessed. I think we freed her."

Carol sat there for a moment, frozen by the news, but her reaction didn't last. She burst out of her seat, pushed Larry out of the way, and bolted for the door. Larry, Tank, Dawn, and I all shared a brief glance before tearing off after her.

Carol headed for the elevators, skidding to a stop outside their shiny metal doors as she jammed the call button. She swore when they didn't open immediately, instead bolting for the nearest stairwell. The door clanged against the wall as she crashed through, and we all followed her, trying to keep up with her adrenaline-fueled burst. Up several flights, through another door, down the hall toward the ICU, then past a nurse who held open the doors to the ward and shouted at us to slow down. Carol raced forward, knowing exactly where to go as she careened around a corner and through an open door. The disgruntled nurse's cries followed us as we burst through the gap after her.

I skidded to a halt, pulling Larry to the side with me to avoid steamrolling Carol, who'd frozen a few feet from the foot of the room's hospital bed.

Madison lay there, sitting on a pair of pillows with a nurse to one side, checking her vitals. She blinked as she caught sight of Carol, and a nervous smile spread across her face. "Mom?"

Carol stumbled forward, falling into Madison. She wrapped her in a hug and burst into tears. "Oh, God, Madison. My sweet baby. Are you okay? You have no idea how happy I am to see you!"

Madison hugged her mom back though not as tightly and without the tears. "Mom, calm down. Everything's fine. I'm okay... I think."

"You think? Madison, ten minutes ago you were barely breathing. Nurse, how is she? Really?"

The nurse looked up from the patient monitor beside Madison's bed. She shrugged. "Honestly, everything looks fine. Heart rate's normal. ECG doesn't show anything of concern. I'm going to get the doctor. Now that she's awake, he'll want to check for signs of a concussion. Maybe run an EEG or a CT scan."

Madison blinked as the nurse headed for the door. *"Concussion?* When would I have gotten a concussion? Mom, why am I here? Nobody's explained anything to me, and—" Madison squinted as she took stock of the rest of us. "Uncle Larry?"

Larry stepped forth, leaning over the footboard to pat Madison on the shin. "Hey, Maddie. Been a while. You gave us all a scare."

"What do you mean? Seriously, what happened? Did I fall and hit my head?"

Carol's grip on her daughter loosened, but she hadn't let go. "Do you not know? Madison, you went out two night ago and never came home. The police found you in the woods yesterday morning, and... God, I can't even say it."

Madison cocked her head. "Say what?"

"That there was reason to believe someone cast a spell on you," said Larry. "That's why I'm here. Not that I wouldn't have come if your mom called to tell me you were in the hospital for any other reason, but you know what I mean."

Madison's eyes widened. "Someone bewitched me?"

"No," said Larry. "At least I don't think so. Someone, or perhaps some*thing,* trapped your spirit outside your body using an enchanted talisman. We were only now able to free you."

"An enchanted talisman?" said Carol. "Oh, for God's sake, Larry, that's a spell. Call it what it is."

"It's *not* a spell," said Larry, "and the last time I checked, *I'm* the wizard here. *I'm* the one who knows how magic works, and if you want to know what happened to Madison, I suggest you stop dismissing my talents and start *listening* instead."

Carol took a step back, a look of hurt spreading across her face. Meanwhile, I questioned if being in a room with Larry and his family was the right place to be at the moment.

Madison lifted an eyebrow. "Are you okay, Uncle Larry?"

Larry sighed. "I'm sorry. I haven't slept in over a day. It's not an excuse for being short-tempered, but being worried sick about you is. Madison, we need to know how you came to be trapped in the spirit realm. What's the last thing you remember?"

"Um... I don't know," said Madison. "You said I went out, Mom?"

"Yes. Two nights ago," said Carol. "You said you were headed out with Macey and Esmeralda. They were the first ones I called when you didn't come home, but they said you weren't with them. That you didn't even have plans together."

Madison shook her head. "I don't remember calling or texting them."

"Is there anything you do remember?" asked Larry.

Madison blinked, her eyes focusing on something distant. "I... remember a dream I had. At least I think it was a dream. I don't remember going to bed, but I remember getting up. Everything around me was fuzzy and dull. It was like watching an old black and white movie, except there was color to certain things and not to others. I heard a crash of thunder, and I remember walking to my window. The skies were dark and angry."

"With purple clouds?" asked Larry.

Madison nodded. "Yeah. Now that you mention it, I think so. There was lightning, and I remember laughter. Not happy laughter, but evil laughter, like a Disney villain but deeper and scarier. It was coming from outside, and I got the impression something was staring at me through the window. And then..."

Larry gave her a moment, but she didn't finish the thought. "Then what?"

"That's it. The next thing I remember is waking up here a few minutes ago."

"The voice that laughed," said Larry. "Did it speak? Did it mention anyone?"

"I don't think so. Not that I remember."

"Did you see a face in the clouds? Yellow eyes? A yawning mouth?"

Madison shook her head. "No."

"Did you see anyone else? A person who'd been very badly burned, so badly burned that their skin was black and crusty?"

"God, no." Madison's face contorted in disgust. "What's this about, Larry? What's going on?"

Larry cast me a worried glance, as if wondering how much he should say. Ultimately, he just patted Madison's leg. "I'm not sure, but I'm going to get to the bottom of it. You should rest. Have some time alone with your mom, but I've got to ask one more question. Do you remember any suspicious activities going on around you over the last few days? Strange sounds, objects moving on their own, ghostly faces appearing from thin air?"

"Are you serious, Uncle? I'm not being haunted, if that's what you're asking."

"That's good to hear, Maddie. Very good." Larry gave us a nod. "Come on, guys. Let's give them some privacy."

Dawn touched me on the shoulder, and we headed toward the exit. Larry followed us, but Carol's voice stopped him. "Larry? Wait. You can stay if you like. You're family. You saved her."

Larry dipped his head in acknowledgement. "You have no idea how much I appreciate that, Sis, but there's still work to be done. Maddie? Take care of your mom for me. We'll talk soon, okay?"

Carol and Madison both nodded and smiled, and we headed out.

THE SUBURBAN RUMBLED as I pulled off MLK Boulevard onto Pearl Street. It was only a couple miles from St. David's to the house, but Larry had been silent for the full eight minutes it took us to drive them.

I killed the engine as I parked in the driveway. Dawn and Tank hopped out the back, but Larry lingered in the front seat.

I lingered with him. "Something on your mind, or did you fall asleep?"

Larry blinked and looked up. "What?"

I snorted. "A little of both then. Seriously, what's up? I've never seen someone who saved their niece's soul look so morose."

Larry cocked an eyebrow at me. "Implying you've been around *other* people who've saved a sibling's daughter's soul?"

"Touché." I hopped out of the truck and closed the door behind me, following Tank and Dawn toward the back.

Larry merged beside me. "It's Madison, if you have to know. I'm still worried about her."

I figured the quip was all he was going to offer. Guess I was wrong. "You think the spirit that came after us is going to attack her again?"

Larry shrugged. "I have no idea. I can only say two things with total certainty. We didn't kill the spirit who attacked us in the chapel, and we didn't prevent Madison from becoming a target again. The bigger problem is I don't understand what's driving the last couple days' events. That makes it impossible to predict what'll happen next."

"Well, we have a better idea of what's going on than we did a few hours ago," I said. "The spirit who came after us is the same one who possessed Ivan Romanov and turned him evil. At least that's what it told me. I suppose it could've been lying, but I don't think it had any reason to, not about that. And it makes sense. It's angry we defeated Romanov and it lost its mortal vessel. Now it's coming after us for revenge."

"That part makes sense," said Larry. "But it doesn't explain half of what's going on."

"Such as?"

"Why the thing came after Madison, for one. Think about it. This evil spirit—let's call him, I don't know... Benedict."

"Benedict?"

"Why not? It has an evil ring to it, don't you think? It's more intimidating than Fred, less so than Nightsbane or Bloodreign. Just go with it. So Benedict possesses Romanov. Romanov was probably a nasty dude to begin with, but Benedict makes him an order of magnitude more evil. Gets him to seek out items of power—a magic sword, *Gwyriad,* crystals of power, the *Librum de Virtute*—so that he can take over the world. We stop Romanov and foil Benedict's plans. Now Benedict wants revenge. Sure. Makes sense. But why did he go after my niece? Clearly he was able to infiltrate Madison's dreams. He did the same to you last night, so why not come after us directly? Trap *our* souls, torment *us*. Why go after a third party?

"And that's not all. Benedict may have used Romanov to acquire those pink crystals in the first place, but he didn't arrange them around Madison at Mt. Bonnell. He's a spirit, presumably trapped in the otherworld. A person, a physical vessel of some sort, put those around Madison. Who? And what about the beast that attacked us at Charity's house? I have no idea who that was, but he sure as heck wasn't Benedict."

I ascended the back porch steps. "I figured that was a random spirit creature. You think its presence at Charity's is related to *Benedict?*" I felt stupid even saying the name.

Larry tipped his head and lifted an eyebrow. "Come on, Lexie. If there's anything you should've learned by now it's that there are no coincidences in this biz. Charity's and Madison's attacks are undoubtedly connected, the only question is *how.*"

Tank and Dawn had already passed through the back door. Larry and I followed them in. As we reached the stairwell, Bill's voice echoed from his jar. "There you are! I was starting to get worried."

I filed into the living room alongside the others. "We weren't gone *that* long, Bill."

"It's not how long you were gone," he said. "It's that we got three calls in the last ten minutes. I thought it might be Frank trying to get ahold of you, or worse still, you guys trying to get ahold of me. Not that I can answer the phone. Speaking of which, you should buy me a bluetooth headset, Larry. If I'm going to be stuck in my jar most of the day, the least I can do is answer calls."

Dawn ignored Bill's blathering and moved to the corded, black phone on the corner of Larry's desk. "Three calls? I wonder if it was Charity."

She pushed the voicemail button, and a tinny, computerized phone spoke through the desktop unit's speaker. "You have... *three*... calls. First call. From 5-1-2-5-5-5-8-6-4-4—"

The computer voice hadn't finished speaking the last two

digits before Tank pushed his way forward. "Hold on. That's Kiara's house number."

"Your ex-wife?" I said.

He didn't have a chance to respond. The desktop unit beeped, and a frantic voice sounded through the speakerphone. "Oh my God. Tank. Larry. You guys, we need your help. You need to get over here *right now*. There's something here. In the house. It's... oh, *Jesus Christ*."

The call ended abruptly. Tank stared at the phone in shock, his mouth open. "That was Zane. Kiara's husband."

The phone beeped, and the computerized voice sounded again, reading the number of the second call, same as the first.

Tank smashed buttons, trying to get the thing to skip them. "Come on, you piece of junk. Give us the next message."

The thing beeped again, and Zane's voice screamed through the speaker. "It's here! It's breaking through the front door. *God, it's coming for us. You've got to help us. You've got to...* oh. Oh no. *AAAHHH! HELLLP!!!*"

Tank didn't wait to hear the third message. He bolted out of the living room and burst through the back door. I was only a pace or two behind him.

22

Tank's fingers dug into my shoulder. He pointed past the windshield to a stop sign ahead. "There! Take a right."

I ignored the sign, barely laying off the gas as I cranked on the steering wheel. The Suburban's tires screeched as I rounded the corner, the entire car shaking as the uneven weight bounced off the shocks.

Beside me in the front seat, Larry spoke angrily into his not-a-phone. "For the last time, Frank, I don't know what the hell it is. You think Zane went into detail as the thing tried to tear them to pieces?"

I glanced into the rear-view mirror, noting the grimace on Tank's face, the veins bulging in his neck, the cold fury in his eyes. He leaned forward, practically in the console. His fingers gripped me like a vice, causing part of my shoulder to go numb, but I didn't dare tell him to calm down. I feared it would only make matters worse.

Larry shouted over the roar of the engine. "Send patrol cars if you like, but you'd better lend us more backup than that. The guys who've trained for the crazy shit, Frank. I *do not* know what we're dealing with, but chances are it's bad, okay?"

Tank's grip tightened, and I thought my clavicle might snap. His finger swung to the left side of the dash. "Eighty-nine forty-five. On the left, with the terracotta roof tiles."

Larry followed Tank's finger, too. "I've got to go, Frank. Send everything you've got!"

I pumped the brakes and yanked on the wheel. The car shuddered as I pulled into the driveway of a large Spanish colonial home with white stucco walls and a bunch of cactuses and shrubs in lieu of a lawn. I hadn't even come to a stop before Tank threw open the door and jumped out.

By the time I put the Suburban in park, Larry and Dawn had exited the car, too. Larry's cry reached my ears as I popped my door. "Tank! Wait! We don't know what's in there."

Tank didn't listen. He burst across the gravel, racing up the steps to the front of the house. I think he would've kicked the front door in if it wasn't already open. Dawn and Larry shot in after him, and I wasn't far behind.

I skidded to a stop over polished wooden floors in the foyer. A wrought iron chandelier hung from the ceiling high overhead, flanked on both sides by exposed beams stained a dark coffee color. Similarly styled iron railings lined the steps along the staircase leading to the second floor. The walls were the same white as the stucco outdoors, but sections of it had been stained with dark streaks, as if a fire had swept through and left angry soot in its wake. Deep gouges marred the floor, revealing the pale, unstained wood beneath, and sections of the railing looked as if they'd been struck with sledgehammers.

Tank spun, his eyes wild. "Kiara? *Kiara!*"

His voice echoed off the ceiling, but no one responded. It

didn't take a detective to see where the trail of destruction led, though. The scratches, dents, and burnt walls followed the steps to the second level.

The evidence struck Tank at the same time it did me. He took off up the stairs, rounding the corner at the top as he followed the blackened sections of wall. Larry was second in line behind him, lightning crackling among his fingers, and Dawn third, her sheathed katana in hand. I pulled my demon tooth from my pocket and squeezed on it. Only after it stretched and popped into a bat did I follow them up. I'd learned my lesson about running into fights unprepared.

I chased after the pack, watching as Dawn padded around a corner. Tank had disappeared as I reached the end of the hall, but Larry was there, kneeling before a white guy in his mid-thirties who sat against the wall. His dress shirt was half-tucked into his khakis, he wore a single shoe, his glasses were askance, and the hairs at the front of his head stood on end. Black marks similar to those along the walls covered his forehead and cheeks, and he mumbled something incomprehensible as he stared into the distance.

"Zane? Buddy?" Electricity popped as Larry snapped his fingers in front of the guy's face. "Can you hear me?"

Before he had an opportunity to respond, Tank's shout shook the house. "NOOO!"

Dawn had paused at Zane, same as Larry had, but she sprinted another ten feet down the hall into an open door. I followed her, scanning the remains of the master bedroom at a glance.

If anything, the room was in worse shape than the hallway. A canopy bed tilted to one side, two of the posts that held it up broken and the entire footboard smashed to splinters. Shards of glass surrounded a lamp that had tumbled to the ground, and the flooring looked like it had been abused by wild dogs. Worse still were the walls which had been overtaken by a virulent black mold-like substance. It crept across the paint and onto the ceiling in undulating tendrils.

In the center of the carnage, Tank knelt over a petite, dark-skinned woman. She wore a yellow summer dress, but the thing had seen better days. Even from a distance, I could see the tears in the fabric, not to mention the bruises that covered her arms and the cuts on her face. More importantly, she wasn't moving.

Tank shook her with one hand and cupped the side of her face with another. "No. Kiara. *No no no.* Please. Don't die. *Don't die.*"

Tank's arm shook, and his fingers bounced as he pressed them against her carotid artery. He took a deep breath, his body stilled, and for a second I thought he might've felt a pulse, but the moment didn't last. Tank leaned his head back and bellowed. *"NOOOOOO!!!"*

Somewhere in the distance, I heard sirens. Dawn slipped her katana into her belt and took a cautious step forward. "Tank... I'm so sorry."

Tank surged to his feet and roared with bearlike ferocity. His muscles bulged, veins popping as fur sprouted from his skin. He spun and smashed the already savaged bed with an over-hand blow, breaking the thing's back and collapsing it to the floor.

Dawn didn't back down. "Tank, I know you're hurting right now."

Tank grew a foot before my eyes. His shirt and pants tore as his body expanded, fur erupting from his skin as if it had been sped up in a nature documentary. He bellowed and slammed a half-fist, half-paw into the wall, smashing a hole in it. He lashed out again and again, knocking chucks of plaster to the floor.

The sirens grew louder and stopped. A car door slammed and shouts rang outside. Red and blue lights flickered across the window.

Dawn took another step forward, both her hands outstretched. "Tank, please. Listen to me."

Tank's head brushed the ceiling as he turned on her, his clothes hanging off him in tatters and his body that of a mature Kodiak. He opened his maw and roared, his teeth flashing red in the light of the police cruisers.

I heard more shouts in the hall. Larry burst into the room. "Hey, we've got—*oh, crap!*"

A half dozen police officers surged into the room in Larry's wake with guns drawn, pointed at the floor. The one in front shouted. "Everybody, on the ground. Now! Get—" His eyes widened as he took notice of Tank. *"Holy shit!"*

The officer lifted his sidearm and pointed it directly at Tank while the others swore and fanned out to his sides, each of them lifting their pistols in kind. Everyone started shouting.

"Get down! Get down!"

"Holy Jesus, what is that thing?"

"Calm down, everyone! Please!"

"He's a werebear. Don't shoot him!"

I don't think anyone heard more than a collective chorus of yells. Tank certainly didn't. He let out another roar and slammed his front paws on the floor, shaking the room.

That was enough for the officers. Someone opened fire, and the others followed. I dropped to the ground, covering my ears as explosive cracks split the air. Larry and Dawn lurched to the side of the room, out of the line of fire. The bullets screamed at

Tank, faster than I could follow, but rather than ripping through his flesh, they bounced off him and clattered to the ground with a melodic tinkle. Tank bounded forward and slapped the foremost officer with a giant paw. He connected with a meaty thud, and the poor guy went flying, bouncing off the wall with a crunch.

The officer groaned as he hit the floor. The others shouted in fear and fired faster. Bullets tore through the air, the cracks of the pistols and the click of empty clips joining the cacophony of cries.

Larry jumped forward. "Everyone stop! For the love of God, STOP!"

He extended his arms, and a sonic boom blasted through the room. It lifted me and tossed me to the side, along with everyone else. One of the officers flew out the door, the bedside table soared out the window with a crash, and I slammed into a wall.

I barely had time to put my hands up, but they didn't soften the blow. A wave of pain rippled through me, my body crumpled as I fell to the floor, and everything went dark.

23

I sat on the curb, my eyes turned toward the skies. A thick wall of clouds shrouded the horizon. Lightning didn't flash among them, and they didn't have that angry, dark grey tint that usually indicated an oncoming downpour, but the cool breeze that wafted past me suggested they might change their minds as they got closer. Texas thunderstorms were as fickle as sorority girls and could be far fiercer.

I had an umbrella in my truck, but I'd survive if I got wet. I'd been caught in rainstorms before. Thunderstorms, too, including one where the sky turned a sickly shade of green and I was sure a tornado wouldn't be far behind. But despite the fact that the clouds in the distance had yet to flash and fill the air with the boom of thunder, something told me they weren't entirely natural in origin. I told myself as long as a face didn't form among the suspended mists, I'd be fine...

I heard footsteps, then a familiar voice. "Hey. Mind if I sit?"

I looked over my shoulder. Larry stood there, hands thrust deep into his pockets. "Help yourself."

Larry groaned as he squatted and seated himself beside me.

I looked behind him at the hive of activity outside Kiara and Zane's home. A pair of officers stood by the patrol car they'd parked behind my Suburban, chatting and occasionally responding to their walkie talkies. A plainclothes cop—a detective, I guess—exited the house and headed down the street toward another pair of cops parked on the curb. A third car was parked behind that one. Frank Connor's police issue Impala.

"Look, Lexie," said Larry. "I wanted to apologize..."

"For dropping a magic bomb and blasting me into the wall?"

Larry grimaced. "Yeah. Are you sure you're feeling okay? You were out for a minute."

"Pretty sure I'm not concussed, if that's what you're asking. I got a mild concussion once after getting hit in the helmet with a fastball, so I've got an idea of what it's like. Seeing as I haven't dry heaved or had trouble remembering where I am, I think I'm okay."

"Still, you have my apology. I didn't plan on putting a stop to the fight that way. Sometimes I react to situations and the magic just... comes out."

"They have adult diapers for that, you know."

Larry snorted. "Yeah. You're feeling just fine, aren't you?"

I cracked a smile. I wasn't feeling merry, but sometimes if you faked it, your body reacted as if it were the real thing. "Don't sweat it, Larry. If knocking everybody out was what it took to put a stop to the shooting, so be it. Nobody got seriously hurt. Well, except for the officer Tank batted, but that wasn't your fault." The ambulance had already come and gone with him in the back. Broke three ribs, the medics suspected.

"Hopefully Frank can smooth that out. He feels bad about rerouting the nearest patrols without warning them about what they'd find. Not that they ran into a demonic nightmare like we expected, but your average cop isn't prepared to find a Kodiak bear inside an Austin home, either."

I heard the rumble of an engine. I looked down the street to see another ambulance approaching. The living had already been attended to, leaving only the home's lone deceased to be taken care of.

I sighed. "I suppose I should apologize, too."

Larry looked at me askance. "For what?"

"For not staying inside with you. To help with Zane... or with Tank."

Larry glanced at the ambulance as the medics hopped out and removed a gurney from the back. "There's no need to apologize for that. There's nothing you could've done for Zane. Trust me. I tried my best, and I couldn't get anything but gibberish out of him. I hate to say it, but he's going to need serious psychotherapeutic help. He probably would've even if his wife died from something normal like a car accident or a heart attack, but this..." Larry shook his head. "It's rough. It's going to be hard enough for Tank to deal with it, and he lost Kiara years ago."

"You think he wants company?"

Larry peered toward the backyard. "Dawn's with him. That's probably what he needs. I know the two of you have formed a strong connection, but he's known Dawn the longest, even longer than he's known me. She has a way of calming him that the rest of us don't."

"So she's the Black Widow to his Hulk is what you're saying?"

Larry snorted. "Something like that."

The gurney clattered as the EMTs pulled it over the lip of the sidewalk and up the path toward the house. My heart hurt just thinking about what Tank was going through. His skin might be able to deflect bullets, but he was as brittle as the rest of us on the inside. "Did you talk to Frank about Kiara?"

"You don't have to be a detective to guess what happened to her, even lacking coherent testimony from her husband. A concentrated bundle of evil came after her. Given we all felt something come through the portal from the spirit world back to Earth with us, it's not hard to guess what it was. Benedict came after Madison first. He didn't kill her because he wanted me to suffer while she wasted away. He didn't make the same mistake with Kiara."

I frowned. I still had a hard time referring to the evil disembodied soul as Benedict, but Larry seemed determined to stick with it. "You're probably right, but it would be nice to know for a fact what came after her. Not for curiosity's sake but so we can protect ourselves when it comes back for the rest of us."

"I can assure you we're dealing with Benedict here," said Larry. "His stink is all over the house."

"You can smell him?"

Larry nodded. "His magical aroma. I picked up on it in the spirit realm, though it was only mildly offensive there. Something to do with our senses being different in that universe. But here? His stink infuses every surface in the home. That's why I came out here, besides wanting to apologize. I couldn't take it anymore."

Gravel crunched, and I turned to find Frank Connors heading our way. "Stuttgart." He flicked his hand at Larry. "We need to talk."

Larry grunted as he pushed himself to his feet. "What about? You spot something I missed?"

"Probably, though it would be impossible to know without comparing notes. None of which you took, I might add."

Connors lowered his voice. "But that's not why I'm here. We need to talk about your friend Tank."

I stood and joined the party. "How's he doing?"

Frank's mustache bristled. "That's none of my concern. What is is that he attacked one of my officers."

"To be fair, Frank, those weren't *your* officers," said Larry. "They were simply the closest ones on patrol."

Frank planted his hands on his hips. "Are you *trying* to piss me off, Stuttgart? You think this is a joke? Your associate turned in broad daylight and attacked a police officer. He broke three of his ribs!"

"First of all, he was indoors. The only ones who saw him were your men. And yes, I'm aware he batted one of them into a wall. We already went over this. You told the other officers the situation was under control and you were going to handle it."

"It's called displaying confidence, Stuttgart," said Connors. "If you don't grab a situation by the scruff of the neck and wrestle it into submission, it can blow up real quick. And I *am* handling it, right now. So consider this your only warning. Unless you want to find out what it's like to be a target of the APD instead of a consultant, you need to get your team under control, ASAP."

"Look, Frank, I'm sorry," said Larry. "Tank was out of line, but you have to understand he found his ex-wife murdered on the floor a minute before your officers arrived. You know enough about transformations to understand how it works. What did you think was going to happen? And then your men show up and start yelling and screaming and shooting indiscriminately? If he hadn't been in bear form already, we wouldn't be talking about me getting my team under control. We'd be discussing how the hell your department was going to deal with the fallout of pumping thirty-seven rounds into an unarmed black man."

Connors pinched the bridge of his nose. "Point taken. But here's a counterpoint. Unlike at the scene of your niece's incapacitation, I didn't ask you to provide assistance. You called me, and when I arrived, I found myself at the scene of a murder and a police assault. Don't get me wrong, Larry. I understand who the victim is. I see the parallels between your niece being targeted and Tank's ex-wife being killed. But this is a *murder* investigation. Regardless of who the victim is, *my* people are the ones charged with finding the killer and bringing them to justice, not yours. Even if I wanted your help, your team has become too emotionally involved to be of use here, which means I need you to vacate the premises immediately. Out of respect for you and in an attempt to avoid another incident, I'll give you five minutes. Make sure Tank doesn't hurt himself or anyone else on the way out."

Frank turned and headed back into the house. Larry sighed. "Guess there's not much we can do here anyway." He nodded at me and headed around the back.

We found Dawn and Tank on a concrete bench at the edge of a circular patio, shaded by a Monterrey oak. Tank had long since transformed back into human form and was wearing a pair of sweats and an AC/DC T-shirt I kept in the truck for just such occasions. He leaned forward, his head hanging low and his shoulders hunched. Dawn had a hand on his back, speaking to him in a hushed voice. As I got closer, I noticed a tremble in Tank's legs and spotted the tight muscles of his forearm. He gripped a picture frame at his knee. I didn't need to see the photo to know who it was of.

Larry and I stopped a few feet from him on the pavers. From that vantage, I could see Tank's eyes were closed.

Larry swallowed. "Uh... hey guys."

Dawn acknowledged us with a glance. She made a gesture with her hand, a sort of pushing down motion like teachers would when they wanted kids to quiet down. Tank didn't look up.

Larry tried again. "Tank, I don't want to rush you, but—"

Tank's eyes snapped open. He surged to his feet. I took a step back as he stepped forward, his shadow falling over us. Moist trails streaked his cheeks, and red cracks ringed his eyes. "We need to find whatever did this, Larry. *Now.*"

"Look, Tank, I'm not going to pretend to understand how you feel, even having just gone through what I did with Madison. But I talked to Frank and—"

Tank reached out and grabbed Larry's jacket. He pulled him close. The picture frame in his hand snapped, shards of glass and splintered wood falling to the stone. *"It killed Kiara, Larry.* No buts. We find it. We end it."

To his credit, Larry barely flinched. "You didn't let me finish. Frank told us to leave the investigation to him, but I don't take kindly to evil spirits threatening and murdering our family. I'm with you a hundred percent. We need to find this thing and kill it, for good this time, before it can harm anyone else."

Tank had started to lift Larry off the ground, but his grip loosened and he nodded. "Point me in the right direction and I'll do the rest."

"Settle down, big guy," said Larry. "We'll do it together. But pointing us in the right direction may not be any easier than killing what we're trying to find. So far this thing's done a much better job of finding us than we have of it."

A thought struck me. "Yeah. But thus far it's been relegated to the spirit realm. That doesn't seem to be the case anymore."

Larry cocked an eyebrow at me. "True, but unless there's a spy satellite you have access to, I don't see how that helps us."

"There are ways to track things besides sight. Stick your nose back inside that house if you don't believe me."

Larry shook his head. "Lexie, I've told you, I'm not a bloodhound. Benedict's stench might infuse that home, but as far as tracking it? I can't turn smells into directional inputs. My mind doesn't work that way."

Dawn frowned. *"Benedict?"*

I held up a hand to ward her off. It wasn't the time. "There's got to be a way, Larry. We don't have a lot of time."

As if in response to my claim, a droplet fell on my shoulder. Hopefully the rain would hold off a little longer.

Larry's brow furrowed, but then his eyes brightened. "Actually, there might be a way, if we *all* work together..."

24

HEAVY DROPLETS SPLASHED ACROSS MY WINDSHIELD, turning the stretch of asphalt in front of me into an undulating mirage. I flicked the wipers on the Suburban to high, accelerating their steady wave into a frantic jive, but the rain had started to pour in earnest now. I let a little off the gas as the visibility dropped. At least I didn't have to read the street signs to know where I was going.

"I'm still smelling it more to the east, maybe a bit to the south as well," said Bill. "Take the next cross street."

Bill sat in Larry's lap in the front seat. He couldn't see out the windshield from his vantage point, but I suppose it didn't matter, same as it didn't that I had the windows up thus obscuring the smells around us. Magical scents were their own beast. Good thing, too, because even cracking the windows would turn my Suburban into an aquarium.

I pumped the brakes, slowing the truck as I reached the turn off. We were somewhere south of Austin, east of I-35. The last sign I'd seen said we were five miles outside of Lockhart. There wasn't any street sign on the road to my left, however. It looked like it wasn't even paved, though it was hard to be sure given the heavy rain and the fading light in the evening sky.

"Looks like dirt," I said. "How close do you think we are?"

Bill's nostrils flared, and his brow wrinkled. "Hell of a lot closer than we were the last time, that's for sure. Hard to say. I'm still getting used to this whole smelling evil thing."

Larry may not have been able to track a magical scent on his own, but he didn't have to. Before he'd died, turned into a zombie, and had his head separated from his body by the sword of a Spanish privateer in Bermuda, Bill had been the navigator aboard an English barque. By methods I wasn't clear on, that made it so he was able to find his way around darkened mazes the rest of us would fly blind in. Unlike Larry, he didn't have any magical sensibilities to speak of, but while the rest of us had prepared ourselves for a fight, Larry had conjured magic that had lent Bill his own sense of magical smell.

Nonetheless, the severed head suffered a learning curve with the new ability. "Are you *sure,* Bill? The last time you sent me on a dirt road I ended up halfway in a gravel pit with an agitated bull mastiff barking his head off at me."

"Take the turn, Lexie," said Larry. "We're close. Even I can smell it now."

Larry stared at the turnoff, his eyes distant. He hadn't changed like the rest of us—I'd slipped into a pair of jeans and a raincoat, Dawn had pulled her hair into a French braid and yanked on a pair of cargo pants and laced boots that made her look like Lara Croft, and Tank had shrugged into a black tactical vest that I think he stole from Arnold Schwarzenegger in *Commando.* Larry had merely donned a black oilskin cowboy hat with flared edges that was as worn as his trench coat, but between it, his bedraggled hair, and the cold, dead look in his eyes, he managed to look the most dangerous of us all.

I didn't question him. I gave the truck some gas and pulled onto the drive. The Suburban bounced as the tires left smooth pavement and hit the dirt. I'd already turned on the headlights, but I flicked the high beams on as I ventured onto the forest-lined path in front of me. The yellow cones from the lights blurred as they struggled to cut through the sheets of rain coming down through the overhanging branches.

Larry's nose wrinkled as we bounced along the pothole ridden path. "Oh, we're close all right. That *stink*. It's the scent of liars and mass murderers and politicians all rolled into one. It's coating the inside of my nose." Larry hacked out a short cough. "Can you smell it, Lexie?"

I didn't have to remind him I wasn't a witch. His hopes about my abilities were higher than my own, but I gave it a shot anyway. Lacking any idea how to activate my magical sense, I instead filled my lungs with air. I picked up on the expected things. The smell of rain, of damp soil, the earthy scent of decay you always got in a forest in spring, all tinged with a hint of gas fumes as the air passed through the Suburban's engine block and through the vents on the dash. But there was something else there, too. A sebaceous sensation that hit me along with the rest. Not the scent of spilled oil, more like the feeling of dragging a finger through the stuff but instead of a finger it was the back of my tongue and my sinuses.

I shuddered and shook it off. "Yeah. Maybe I do smell something."

"I think we're getting close, too," said Bill. "That scent is getting... *overpowering* to say the least."

I curved around a bend. The sky opened up as the path spit

us out of the trees into a broad open swath of land. The Suburban's headlight's wavered in the pouring rain, showcasing an endless field of corn in front of us. Off in the distance, two porch lights gleamed on the front of an old farmhouse. A tall barn stood to the side of it, perhaps red with white trim though it was hard to tell in the rain and deepening gloom. A tractor was parked inside the barn's open doors, and there appeared to be more outbuildings surrounding the house, but the only lights were those on the home.

I braked to a stop. A shiver ran down my spine at the prospect of coming face to face with Benedict again. "You want me to pull up to the house?"

Bill frowned. "I... don't know. The smell's everywhere now. Seems as strong in front as behind. Maybe it's saturated my nostrils or magical receptors or whatever."

"Larry?"

He shook his head. "I'm in the same boat. It's all around us. Might as well pull up. The lights are on, and we don't know whose land this is. We should probably introduce ourselves before we go monster hunting."

Tank's rough bass rumbled over the seat back. "Assuming anyone inside is alive."

I glanced in the rearview mirror as I gave the truck some gas. Since leaving Kiara's home, Tank had reverted to the silent, stoic demeanor he'd had when I'd first met him. He'd barely uttered a word, but every action he took was deliberate. Even now, sitting in the back next to Dawn, his eyes were trained out the front windshield. His muscles were taut, and the veins in his neck stuck out. I could almost hear his teeth grinding together.

I parked the Suburban on a patch of gravel some fifty feet from the house and killed the engine. As the rumble died, I didn't hear any barking dogs. No hum of a generator, no mooing cows. Just the steady roar of raindrops on steel.

Tank's duffel bag clunked as he pulled it out of the back. He unzipped the thing and pulled an assortment of firearms out. He slipped a single-action, semi-automatic Browning Hi-Power into the holster at his side before setting a SIG Sauer tactical patrol rifle against the back seat and pulling out his favorite, a Mossberg 500 pump action shotgun. He turned the weapon upside down and pushed shells into the magazine port, each of them clicking as they went in.

Beside me, Larry removed a mesh shoulder bag from inside his duster, pulled open the top, and slipped Bill inside.

"What happened to your baby carrier?" I asked.

"It's emasculating, is what happened," said Bill. "Larry? Cinch me."

Larry tightened the top and looped the bag's strap over his shoulder. "Not to mention the carrier kept getting in the way during fights." He pushed his oilskin hat further onto his head, opened the door, and stepped into the rain.

"Lexie."

I turned at the touch of Dawn's hand on my shoulder. "Yeah?"

"Take this." She held out a holstered pistol, a Glock based on the lettering machined into the grip.

I patted my pocket. "I've got my demon tooth."

Dawn lifted a thin, curved eyebrow. "When I'm expecting a fight, I carry my katana and my wakizashi, and I've got another four knives on me that aren't immediately obvious. Larry has unlimited magic at his disposal. Tank is strapping a half-dozen firearms to his body, and he's a *werebear*. If you don't take it, you're not getting out of this car."

Dawn's fierce amber eyes burned into me. Apparently, Tank's demeanor had rubbed off on everyone but me. "Got it."

I took the pistol and stared at it. Though I'd trained with Dawn in hand to hand combat, I'd never done the same with Tank at a gun range. Although I'd put in time shooting all manner of weapons on my Xbox, the only real gun I'd fired was my uncle's .22 Ruger. I lifted the edge of my raincoat and stared at the waistband of my jeans.

"So... if I'm not wearing a belt...?"

Tank leaned over the seat and grabbed the pistol from my hand. He flipped up some flap on the backside of the holster, tugged on the side of my jeans, and clipped the thing straight onto them. He reached back, grabbed a pair of magazines, and held them toward me. "You know how to reload, right?"

I grabbed the magazines and slipped them into my coat pocket. "I think so."

Tank unlatched the holster and pulled the gun from my waist with a smooth motion. He pointed with his finger. "Magazine eject button, by the trigger." He flipped it to the back. "Safety." He jammed the gun back into the holster and latched it back. "Come on."

He looped his tactical rifle over his shoulders, grabbed his shotgun, and popped open the door. Dawn headed out her side. The rain cascaded down, splattering against the inside of the doors and over the floor mats, but if the rest of the gang could ignore the weather, so could I.

I opened my door and hopped into the rain. My sneakers splashed in a puddle, and I immediately wished I'd put on galoshes—not that they'd keep me dry long in this downpour.

Larry stood there, the rain wicking off the edges of his hat and falling to the earth in a steady stream. His nose wrinkled as he swiveled his head back and forth, first staring at the farm-house, then the barn, then the field of neck high corn beyond.

Tank stepped forward. His shotgun clicked as he pumped it. "Well? Where is it?" His meaty growl carried over the patter of rain.

Larry shook his head. "I don't know. The smell's everywhere."

Tank's assault rifle bounced off his hip as he closed the gap. His rain-slicked fingers gripped his shotgun tight. "Tell me where to find it, Larry. We didn't come out here for a fucking bath."

"It's nearby, Tank. You've got to understand, this thing doesn't have a cell phone. It doesn't leave a trail of breadcrumbs behind it. We're dealing with a spirit creature that's manifested itself in our world. It's always found us, not the other way around."

A flash of lightning tore through the sky, and a half-second later the boom rolled in. It slammed me in the chest, harder than it had any right to. As the sound echoed and died, I heard something else alongside it. A deep-throated laugh, dry and rusty, same as I'd heard at the chapel.

My hand slid to check on my pistol and tooth. "Anyone else hear that?"

"You bet I did." Tank turned toward the corn field, brandishing his shotgun in the air. *"Show yourself you demonic piece of shit!"* His shotgun cracked as he fired a shot into the air.

"Jesus, Tank," said Dawn. "What are you doing? This is someone's property!"

"I already told you, they're either dead or they will be if we don't stop whatever's out there." Tank took another step toward the corn and raised his voice. "What's wrong? Too scared to show yourself now that we're prepared? It's easy to kill an unarmed woman, but when we show up you run and hide?"

Tank fired his shotgun into the air again. I covered my ears and glanced toward the farmhouse, but none of the interior lights had lit up.

Another flash of lightning seared the sky, followed by an earth-shaking boom that sent a ripple through my chest. Two points of light shone deep within the corn, forming into distinct yellow orbs. The same voice spoke, this time after the thunder had faded. *"Do you want to know how much pain she was in, Tank? How hard she cried for mercy?"*

Tank cried out with a guttural bellow of rage that rivaled the thunder and took off into the corn at a sprint.

"Tank! Wait! Don't!" Dawn sprinted after him.

Larry lurched into motion, and before I knew what I was doing, I was running into the field after them.

25

Rain lashed against my face. Corn stalks slapped me as I ran. I dipped my head and shielded myself with my arm, but doing so only slowed me, and the sound of Tank's mad rush into the corn was already being drowned by the relentless patter of rain.

"Tank! Slow down! *Larry!*"

I could still see him through the corn in front of me. He paused long enough to look over his shoulder and wave me forward. "I can't slow! Tank certainly won't. We can't let him get lost in there. Same for Dawn!" He cupped his hands around his mouth. *"Dawn!"* He bolted again, but Bill kept the shout up for him. "Tank! Dawn!"

I churned my legs to keep up. A sharp crack from Tank's shotgun ripped the air, further away than before given the blast of sound didn't punch me in the eardrums. A yellow glow zipped across in the distance, and I thought I heard more laughing.

"Tank... Your compassion is weakness."

Another bolt of lightning split the sky, and by the flash I

spotted something ahead. An undulating dark mass through which the bright light couldn't penetrate. Something whipped through the air around it, tentacles maybe, or perhaps it was just rain and my brain was creating terrors out of thin air.

The yellow orbs appeared again, this time accompanied by the yawning mouth I'd seen in the spirit realm, and I knew it wasn't my imagination. It was a nightmare come to life.

Tank roared, somewhere in the direction of the barn. Larry veered toward the sound, as did I, but as we ran the roar turned deeper, more raw, more guttural. I'd only heard it a few times, but I knew what it meant. Tank was turning again.

I dug deep and pushed, driving what energy reserves I had into my legs, same as I might when I raced for home plate after my teammate hit a double.

I caught up to Larry and grabbed him by the sleeve. He nearly dragged me into the mud before he'd realized I was attached. "Lexie, what are you doing?"

"We can't get separated," I shouted. "Can't you see? He's trying to pull us apart!"

"Too late. We're already separated. Dawn? *Dawn!*"

Tank roared again. This time, I couldn't grasp the direction of the sound, but I didn't have to. A series of sharp *rat-a-tat-tats* cracked in the distance. Muzzle flashes popped like firecrackers. By their dim light I spotted bear form Tank, now towering over the corn, diving into the mass of black mist and tendrils.

I don't think she'd heard us, but Dawn's voice cut across the roar of rain regardless. *"Tank!"*

At least we all knew where Tank was. I pushed Larry and he took off again, the corn stalks flying out of his way by force of magic. With the adrenaline surging through me, I could've passed him, but there was something else coursing through my veins alongside the hormone. A cold, liquid fear, the fear of coming face to face with the same thing that had haunted my dreams and taunted me in a hospital chapel. Now it was here, on Earth, in Austin.

And it wanted vengeance.

Larry burst through the end of the corn into a patch of mowed grass. The dirt path curved in front of us. Beyond that stood the barn, which looked quite a bit more dilapidated then it had at a distance. The roof sagged, one of the front rolling doors was missing, and the entire building leaned to the left by more than a couple degrees.

Deep gouges scraped across the driveway, and I spotted a dull glimmer hidden in the mud. Tank's shotgun. Of the big guy, however, there was no sign.

"Tank!" shouted Larry. *"Tank!"*

I heard a rustling in the corn. My heart leapt into my throat as I reached for my pistol. I'd just undone the clasp over the grip when the stalks parted and out burst Dawn, her hair sopped and her tank top plastered against her skin.

"Where's Tank?" she asked.

"I don't know," said Larry. "I thought you had eyes on him. You were closest to him."

"I was—until he turned. You ever try to outrun a Kodiak?" She knelt next to the shotgun. "Damn. He was here. I saw the muzzle flashes, too. *Tank!* Where are you, Tank?"

A roar sounded in the distance. Tank's, as rage-filled and raw as ever, but I couldn't tell where it had come from. Behind the barn? Near the outbuildings?

Dawn nodded toward the far side of the barn. "Hear that? This way!"

"Wait!" said Larry. "That cry came from past the house."

Dawn wiped water from her face. "Are you batty? Put your magical smell aside and use your ears!"

"Guys!" I jumped between the two. "Stop fighting! And for the love of God, *DO NOT* split up. Haven't either or you ever seen a horror movie?"

Larry frowned. "Lexie, this isn't a horror movie."

"The hell it isn't! We're running through a corn field in the dark in the middle of a rainstorm in pursuit of a demonic dream monster and we already lost one of our party members. The black guy, no less. Shit! I don't think he even had a flashlight."

"Lexie, I don't mean to quibble," said Bill. "But if we were in a horror movie, the evil monster would be chasing *us,* not vice versa. As a zombie, I think I know horror."

"Shut up, Bill," said Dawn. "You're not helping."

Another roar cut through the air, perhaps more distant but it was hard to tell. A flash of lightning lit the sky. Shadows stretched from the trees at the roadside into the barn. One of the shadows inside loomed large, tall and vaguely man-shaped.

I stared at the open door as the thunder undulated over us. "Did you guys see that?"

Larry nodded. "Come on."

We jogged together to the open barn door. Larry called into the darkness. "Tank?"

He wriggled his fingers and a bright white light appeared between them. He flicked his hand and the orb he'd conjured hovered toward the barn's rafters, casting a cool glow upon the items within.

They creeped the hell out of me, now that I could see them. Past the green John Deere with bright yellow wheels and an attached rotary tiller were a host of older, more worn pieces of equipment that would've looked more at home in an eighteenth

century European barn than a modern Texan one. Next to a
giant pile of hay I spotted an old plow, all rusted iron and weathered wood with a heavy hitch for attaching the thing to a horse
or ox. Beside that were another couple contraptions, both of
them with hitches, one with a series of cruel, knife-like hooks
that curved toward the ground and another with sharper,
thinner tines, probably a horse-drawn hay rake. Dozens of tools
hung along the walls, both the normal stuff like rakes, hoes,
shovels, and pickaxes and a bunch of more obscure items that I
didn't know the names of: a tool with a flat, triangular tip,
another one with a heavy cone attached to the end, a short hoe
with a fork attached to the back, and something that looked like
a rake but had thick, wooden tines on both ends. Another wall-
mounted rack held a collection of knives and scythes. A dull red
color shone along the edge of most of the blades, either rust or
dried blood. I told myself it was just a function of Larry's
magical light.

Larry stepped cautiously around the edge of the tractor.
"Tank? If you're in here, now would be the time to growl."

"Wait. Is that...?" Dawn pushed past me, darting toward the
pile of hay. She rummaged around the base and pulled something out. A jacket.

Dawn spun, holding the thing out. "This is Charity's. She's
here. That thing brought her here!"

Water dripped from Larry's hat, leaving wet splatters in the
dirt. "Are you sure?"

"It's a jean jacket with roses embroidered along the edges.
It's hers. Wait... Is that *blood?*"

Larry gave me a nod. "Told you the spirit at Charity's house
and Benedict were connected. Wish they weren't, for Charity's
sake..."

Dawn bounded back and pushed the jacket at Larry. "This *is* blood. *God damnit!* This thing has Charity. We need to find her!"

"I agree, but at the moment, Tank's out there doing battle against Benedict on his own. Finding and helping him is our first priority."

"Tank's a werebear, Larry. He can take of himself."

"And Charity's a werehyena. What's your point? Charity is a client, and I'm worried about her wellbeing, but we take care of our own. Not to mention..." Larry trailed off.

Dawn stepped forward and grabbed his arm. "That what? She might be *dead?* You think that didn't occur to me when I found her *bloody jacket* next to a wall of *dull knives?*"

"Calm down," I said. "Remember the horror movie rules. First is don't get separated from the group, but a close second is not to think with whatever's between your legs."

Anger flashed across Dawn's face as she pointed at me, jacket in hand. "You don't get to tell me to calm down. Not about this. Not when you don't know the first *damn thing* about me and Charity."

I took a deep breath. "You're right. That was uncalled for. I don't know the extent of your relationship. It's not my place to say what you should or shouldn't be feeling, but you have to think rationally. You think Benedict isn't trying to play with our emotions? He already drew Tank off by taunting him about Kiara. We all heard it. You're on the same path, Dawn."

Lightning flashed again, sending shadows stretching from the farm equipment. Another laugh floated in on the thunderous wave that followed, one that included a bear-like growl.

Dawn perked. "You guys hear that?"

I nodded. "Sounded like Tank. Pretty distant this time. How far has that thing drawn him off?"

Dawn's brow furrowed. "What? No. That was Charity. I heard her cry out."

We both glanced at Larry. He shrugged apologetically. "I heard a bear. I'm sorry, Dawn."

Dawn threw the jacket on the ground. "Christ. Now you all think I'm going crazy."

"Not true," said Larry. "Look, we need to find Tank *and* Charity. Fair enough? Unless there's something hiding in the rafters, it's safe to say neither of them are here. If Charity's still on the property—" *And in one piece,* he left unsaid. "—she might be locked up in one of the outbuildings. Maybe in the house. We still don't know who this place belongs to. With luck, the entire property is abandoned."

I thought about the lights on the porch. "And without luck?"

"Hopefully that's a bridge we won't have to cross." Larry nodded toward the door. "We'll check the house out first. Follow me."

He headed back into the rain, and I hustled to keep up. "Hey. What about Tank?"

Larry spoke over his shoulder. "Dawn's right. He'll probably be okay. I least I hope he will. Either way, there's not a lot we can do to track him right now. Maybe I could enchant Bill to sniff him out, but that would take preparation. In the meantime, we need to get a handle on this situation. Setting up a base in that farmhouse, assuming the owners aren't opposed, is a better idea than running through the corn like chickens with our heads cut off."

Bill blinked in the rain, squinting as droplets slashed against his eyes. "And getting out of this rain would be a plus, too."

"You're the one who chose the mesh bag over the baby carrier."

"It's not like the baby carrier would've been better," said Bill. "Unless I'd put on a baseball cap and then I wouldn't have been able to see a damn thing."

Larry snorted. "Would you stop complaining? We're trying to deal with a hellish demon spirit here and you're concerned about getting wet.

The mud squelched under my feet as we walked, and I wished I'd worn my boots after all. Water oozed between my toes with each of my steps, and despite my raincoat, my pants had already soaked through from the thighs down.

Lightning crashed, making me jump. At least this time, when the thunder followed, it didn't carry any growls or roars or cries for help on its nebulous wings.

"You hear anything that time, Larry?"

He shook his head as he headed up the stairs to the farm-house porch. "No. What about you, Dawn?"

Rain pinged against the home's corrugated metal roof as I reached the steps, but Dawn didn't answer. A shiver ran up my spine. "Uh... Dawn?"

I turned. She was gone.

26

While I do suffer from personality quirks—I've been called hot-headed, my brutal honesty has cost me multiple friendships, and I tend to be demanding of others, in sports, classwork, and in relationships—I'm nonetheless not the sort to indiscriminately panic. I'd gone off the handles a few times when I first met Larry and the gang, but in my defense, learning the world around you contains mystical powers, supernatural beings, dark magics, and sundry things that go bump in the night merits a little freaking out. Since coming to grips with all of the above, I'd done a surprisingly good job keeping my wits about me even in stressful situations.

Until now.

I slipped and skittered up the porch steps backwards like a frightened spider. I stared at the empty path behind me as rain battered the ground. "Dawn's gone. *Where the hell did she go, Larry?*"

"How should I know? I thought she was following you." There was anger in his voice, but fear, too. At least I wasn't the only one.

I scrambled to my feet, taking deep breaths to slow my suddenly overactive heart. "She was right there. I swear she'd been right behind me. Jesus Christ, did Benedict grab her out of the bushes? She would've made a sound if he had, right?"

Larry stepped to the edge of the steps, scanning the corn and the road with narrowed eyes. "No question. Dawn's as tough as they come. If anything attacked her, she would've fought back. Which suggests she snuck off of her own accord."

"Why in the world would she do that?"

"Because she disagreed with us? Because she thought she knew where Charity might be? I don't know. It doesn't make sense."

"Unless she *didn't* wander off," said Bill. "Maybe something drew her off."

"How?" I asked.

"Your guess is as good as mine," said Bill. "But she heard Charity's voice on the wind whereas we heard Tank's. Who knows what magic Benedict can conjure in this realm."

I bumped against the front of the house. I hadn't realized I was still backing up. "I told you he was picking us off one by one, Larry. Christ, we just talked about sticking together!"

"Bill has to be right," said Larry. "It couldn't have been a conscious choice. Dawn might be concerned about Charity, but she has no reason to break off from us. And while it's not good that she's missing, it actually gives me some hope."

"Hope?" I blinked, confused. "The fact that we're being picked off like flies gives you *hope?*"

"It means Benedict fears facing us together," said Larry. "He's more confident dealing with us one at a time. That's a good thing."

"Not for Dawn, it isn't! If what you're saying is right, then

Benedict might be feasting on her entrails night now. We need to find her. We need to get ahold—" I paused, and my eyes widened. "God, I'm an idiot."

I pulled my cell phone from my pocket. We might've not had any way to contact Tank once he went full grizzly, and Larry couldn't touch electronics without starting the fourth of July in the palm of his hand, but at least Dawn was a member of the twenty-first century. I pulled up my contacts and punched her name.

My phone beeped angrily as I pulled it to my ear. "What the hell?" I glanced at the top corner only to see I didn't have any bars. "Oh, you've got to be kidding me. No service? We *are* in a horror movie."

"It's alright," said Larry. "Dawn's no were creature, but she's every bit as tough as Tank. You've seen her in action. I'm not sure Benedict could kill her if he tried. Trust me. She's going to be fine."

I stared at Larry, the rough feel of the siding behind me bringing me back to reality. "Are you really that confident, or are you putting this show on for me?"

"Would I tell you if I was?"

"Hey," barked Bill. "I don't care who's afraid of whom. You both need to snap out of it. The question is, now that Tank and Dawn are gone, what should we do?"

Larry adjusted his bag to get Bill more vertical. "I'm guessing your magical scent ability is still overwhelmed?"

"It's like I'm standing in a septic tank with the world's worst cold," said Bill. "I know the filth's all around me, but it's all muddled into an awful uniform background."

"Not the analogy I'd use, but close enough," said Larry. "In that case, I say we stick to the plan and check out the house. Charity might be inside, after all."

"Or a band of hillbilly cannibals, or a weird religious cult, or a bunch of creepy corn children with glowing eyes," I said.

Larry stared at me.

"Sorry. Hard to shake the whole horror movie feeling. But *do not* leave me behind, got it? We stick together, no matter what."

"No matter what." Larry stepped to the front door. Unlike the rest of the home which looked like it hadn't seen any upkeep in a quarter century, the front door had received a fresh coat of paint within the last year. He tested the tarnished brass doorknob.

It turned without a fight. Larry shot me a quick glance before applying force to the door. It swung open on squeaky hinges.

Together, we stared inside. Though the lights on the porch were lit, the inside was dark as night. I could vaguely make out the shapes of a stairwell and an entry table.

"Hello?" Larry called into the space. "Anyone there?"

The steady rain drumming off the roof was our only response.

Larry nodded. "Ladies first."

"So I can die first? How chivalrous."

"So you can turn the light on without an electrical shock blowing them to smithereens."

He had a point. I slid past him and fumbled on the interior wall for a switch. Eventually I found a group of three. One of them was already up, so I flicked the other two.

A flush mount over the entryway flared to life, as did another over the stairwell. Weathered wood creaked as I stepped inside. Faded floral wallpaper stared at me from every angle, and every piece of furniture had been covered with something hand sewn. Runners for the entry table. A throw for the couch. Even the drapes over the windows had a rustic flair.

The door creaked as Larry shut it behind us. "Doesn't look too bad."

"Don't get cocky," I said. "All houses in horror movies look like this. Not to mention we haven't seen the basement yet."

Something flickered across the opening at the end of the hall. A shadow, there one moment and gone the next. At the same time, something tickled the back of my neck.

I spun, but only Larry was there. "Tell me you felt that."

"Like a slight breeze? I don't think any of the windows are open."

"Definitely not a breeze." Almost as if in response, I heard a faint giggle, and I caught a rustle among the drapes. "Damn. How many ghosts are we going to get involved with?"

"Let's hope this one isn't as angry as the others." Larry crept into the room to our right. I turned the light on to find a study with a desk that looked like it had been pulled from a nineteenth century mail room. Letters covered it, but where the wood shone through, I didn't see much dust.

"I'm no detective, but this place doesn't look abandoned," I said.

"The only question is who's living here," said Larry.

A moan echoed through the house, a pained, joyful sound I hadn't forgotten. I reached for my demon tooth and found my pistol instead. I wasn't sure which I should pull. "I know that moan. That's the spirit who attacked us at Charity's."

A crackle of electricity appeared around Larry's fist. "Told you there are no coincidences, though I would've preferred it had stayed there."

Larry delved further into the house. The makeshift study merged into a dining room that looked more unused than the rest of the home. A layer of dust coated the table, and a milky film muddled the glass of a buffet against the far wall. We followed that into a small kitchen, the sort you found in old homes that was all closed in and barely had enough counter space to fit a single cutting board. I stretched my ears for sounds of the spirit, but all I heard was the continued assault of the rain.

I scanned my surroundings, gazing down the hall that fed past the staircase into the entryway. The lights were still lit, but the front door stood open, letting in some of the wind-swept droplets.

I froze. "Larry? Didn't you close the door?"

He followed my gaze. The electricity in his hand strengthened, casting a flickering glow. "Stay close."

He didn't have to remind me. I stuck to him like glue as we crept toward the door. I would've had to take lessons from a barnacle to get any closer.

Rain poured off the roof and whipped inside on a stiff breeze, bringing with it the scent of earth and rot and that same oily not-quite-a-scent of evil that coated the back of my throat and filled my sinuses. I slipped a hand into my pocket and removed my demon tooth as we approached the door, gripping it firmly but not tight enough to turn it into a bat.

Despite the omnipresent moisture, my throat felt dry, but Larry found his voice. "Dawn? Is that you?"

We stepped onto the covered porch. Rain battered the drive and the corn, but I couldn't see much beyond. The lights on either side of the door burned bright against the night that had now fully arrived.

A lightning bolt split the air, filling the darkness with unadulterated brilliance, and in that moment, I saw it. A dark mass standing inside the edge of the corn. In some ways, it reminded me of a man. It was the right height if a little tall, standing head and shoulders above the crops. There were features visible in its face, pools of fire that resembled eyes and a curved smile, like a knife's path traced through living flesh, but whatever stood there wasn't a man, or if it ever had been, it wasn't anymore. Dark mists swirled around the figure. Long tendrils of concentrated darkness undulated above and behind it, shifting tentacles so dense that even the bolt of lightning's flash couldn't penetrate them. What could penetrate the darkness was a glowing energy that erupted from the thing's chest, a bright circle of vibrant green energy that reminded me of Iron Man and Poison Ivy at the same time. Something about it niggled at the back of my mind, but it wasn't the feature that most caught my eye.

It was the fact that the creature was staring at us with a focused, feline hunger.

My grip on Larry's arm tightened. I hadn't even realized I'd grabbed hold of him. "L... L... *Larry?*"

He didn't say a thing, merely planted his leg against the floor and coiled his body. A static shock zapped me, causing me to let go of his arm. Within a second, the electricity from his hand crackled over his entire form, popping and hissing as droplets of rain hit him.

Larry spoke without turning, his voice hard. "Might want to shield your eyes, Lexie."

I got my arm up just in time. He stuck his arms out, and a

bolt of pure lightning, same as the kind splitting the sky, shot from his hands. Even prepared as I was, the intense light seared my retinas. A thunderous blast punched my eardrums, sending me stumbling into the siding. I shook my head, trying to clear the ringing from my ears and the spots from my vision.

I heard the laughter first.

I blinked a few times. Out in the rain, Larry's lightning had cleared a broad swath of the corn, vaporized it into ash and char —but Benedict remained. His laughter tunneled into me, cutting past the lightning-induced tinnitus as if it were a whole different sense, like the auditory equivalent of Larry's magical smell.

As he laughed, he started to walk toward us.

I wanted to whack Larry on the arm, to point and scream and tell him to do something, but my lungs wouldn't pull in enough air. My vocal cords wouldn't work, and my muscles were frozen in place. Fear gripped me.

For all the crap I gave him, Larry didn't let fear slow him. The air crackled as energy built around him. His arms whipped forward. A ball of fire erupted from his hands, the heat blasting me further back into the open doorway. A stream of hissing steam followed the fireball, then a beam of crystalline orange light, all of them directed right at the beast.

Benedict shrugged them off as if they were no more than a stiff breeze, his laughter growing as he methodically closed the gap. Between the blasts of heat and light, all I could hear was the laughter and the yelling.

"Do something, Larry! *Do something!*"

I'd thought my vocal cords had been too frozen to utter a sound. I was right, but it took me a moment to realize it was Bill who was screaming, not I.

"I am doing something, Bill!" Larry growled as he fired a cloud of some frothy, white liquid toward Benedict. What the hell was it? Glue? Spider silk?

"It's not working, Larry," I croaked. Apparently, my voice hadn't abandoned me.

"*I can see that.*" Another fireball. Another blast of heat, and a wave of renewed laughter. Benedict had closed to within thirty feet of us now.

I squeezed on my demon tooth, and it grew to full size. "Then try something different."

A blast of cold air hit me as frost erupted from Larry's hands. "Everything I've tried so far is different!"

Bill kept screaming. "Kill it, Larry! *Kill it!*"

Benedict's yellow eyes focused on Bill and hardened. "*You... are useless to me.*"

One of the black tendrils surrounding Benedict shot forward. I stumbled into the house, but it didn't come for me. It wrapped itself around the edge of Larry's mesh bag and jerked. With an audible rip, the strap tore, and Bill and the bag went flying. Bill's scream faded as he soared into the corn.

Larry steadied himself and took a step back. Benedict's eyes turned on us. "*Now... To finish the job you started months ago. Come to me.*"

Larry tells me there's a supernatural skill called compulsion that vampires use to coerce their prey into doing things they'd otherwise never consider. I don't know if the Benedict amalgam in front of me used it, but I sure as hell didn't listen.

I grabbed Larry by the back of the jacket and pulled him inside, slamming the door behind him. "Run!" I cried.

27

OUTSIDE, THE CREATURE BELLOWED IN ANGER. I TURNED and took my own advice, bounding up the stairs at breakneck speed. Larry followed me, nearly overtaking me. Behind us, I heard a splintering crash, and I suddenly realized that I hadn't thought my plan through. Running generally worked better when you headed *out* of a trap, not into one.

I paused, at the top of the stairs, frantically looking for a window or any way out of the mess I'd gotten us into.

Larry didn't give me a chance. He grabbed me by the arm and pulled me into the nearest room. "Here!"

I stumbled inside as Larry slammed the door behind us. The barest glimmer of pale darkness outlined a window on the far side, but otherwise the space around me was pitch black.

I spun in the darkness, gripping my demon tooth bat tight. I tried to keep the panic out of my voice. "Larry. We need a plan, quick."

A spark of light appeared between his fingers. "On it. Would've been better if you hadn't pulled us up the stairs, though."

I heard another crash of wood and Benedict's roar. "I figured that out after the fact."

Larry tossed the spark into the air as he pulled a small black rock from his pocket. "Get the lights. I didn't put a lot of energy into that."

The spark flickered, as if it was on its last legs, but it was enough for me to spot the switch by the door. A light flickered on as I batted it, revealing a bed, a desk, and little else. Another crash sounded downstairs, this one followed by a weighty slam. A roar followed, this one not as muffled as the last.

Footsteps pounded the stairs. *"Larry..."*

He scratched at the door with feverish speed, the rock in his hand leaving dark trails on the wood with each of his strokes. Only then did I realize he held a piece of charcoal.

Benedict's stomps rattled the house. The panes in the sconce in our room shook, and the desk along the far wall danced. I scrambled back from the wall, gripping my bat tighter as the footsteps and heavy breathing leaked through the drywall.

"Come out, come out, you two..."

Larry's arm whipped across the door, adding a final line to the dozen he'd already marked. As he did so, the hairs on the back of my neck sprung to attention, and his finished product, a rune, began to glow.

"Make us," said Larry.

Benedict howled and banged on the door, but the thing didn't budge. Instead, as he hammered on the it, I heard a hiss. The rune glowed brighter, and the howl outside turned to one of pain more than anger.

"Yeah, have fun with that," said Larry.

The howl intensified. I plugged my ears with my fingers and gritted my teeth.

"And shut up, while you're at it." Larry snapped his fingers. A ripple ran through the room, and the wailing faded to silence.

I shook my head and pulled my hands from my ears. "What did you do?"

"The rune established a barrier," said Larry. "From there it was easy to get it to exclude sound as well as physical force. Don't get cocky though. It won't hold forever. Probably would've been more effective if I'd drawn it over the front door. Then again, maybe not..."

Cockiness was the emotion I was furthest away from at the moment. "What do you mean?"

"Homes have a protective aura about them. Ever heard the term a man's house is his castle? That's not just common law doctrine. The roots of the phrase are magical in nature. Simply by establishing a place as your home, you create a protective shell around it. The longer you live there and the stronger the family connection, the stronger the shell. The rune I placed over the door was meant to tap into that shell, strengthen it against Benedict. It would've been more effective at the front door instead of on the door to this bedroom—or at least it would've been if this wasn't Benedict's home."

"What? That thing lives here?"

"Correction. This is that thing's *home.* Meaning it's lived here a while. I sensed it as I was writing the rune. But I don't think it's *Benedict's* home. He'd been attached to Romanov first and was obviously trapped inside the spirit realm until recently. Meaning we're inside the home of the vessel Benedict has now attached himself to. Thankfully, the room we're in must have belonged to a different family member or my rune wouldn't have done diddly squat."

I blinked, picturing Benedict in the corn, his glowing face and swirling mists outlining the shape of a man. "Yeah. Guess I already figured out he'd possessed someone."

"The news gets worse," said Larry. "My spells might not have been able to take out Benedict, but they should've done something to whoever he latched on to. The fact that they didn't suggests the person Benedict possessed isn't your average farmhand."

"Who then? Michael Myers?"

"Damnit, Lexie, we're not in a horror movie! I mean a magical being." Larry waved a hand and paced. "Doesn't matter. At least it doesn't right now. We need to get out of here and we don't have a lot of time."

The silence provided by the rune was lulling me into a false sense of security. "How much time?"

"I don't know. Ten, fifteen minutes?"

I swallowed hard. "Right." I pulled out my phone and pressed my thumb against the reader. *"Damn.* Still no bars."

"Really?" Larry eyed me with thinly-veiled contempt. "Your plan for defeating the monster that's trying to kill us is to call Dawn again?"

"I was planning on calling the police, the FBI, and the national guard, actually. You've got a better plan?"

Larry frowned. "No, sadly. But I have something better than a phone." He reached into his jacket and pulled his not-a-phone. He flipped it open and held it to his ear. The frown on his face deepened. "What the hell?"

"What is it?"

"There's nothing coming through. Just static." Larry held it out. I could hear the crackle from several feet away.

"Sounds like whatever has my phone on the fritz affects magic as well as technology," I said. "You want to revise that sentiment about being in a horror film?"

Larry snapped his not-a-phone shut and jammed it into his jacket. "What I'd *like* are thoughts on how we can stop Benedict before he bursts through that door and kills us."

"And you want *me* to tell you? I've got a whopping day and a half of training as a witch that *you* gave me, remember? I've been to the spirit realm precisely twice. Before today, I'd never even seen a ghost, much less tried to kill one. You're the one who should know what to do, not me. All I can do is beat it with my demon tooth bat or shoot it with the pistol Dawn gave me. Something tells me neither of those options are great." Although now that I thought about it, my demon tooth had turned several ghosts into ectoplasm at St. David's, and Benedict had hissed when I'd brandished it at him in the chapel.

Larry sat down on the bed. He sagged and put his head in his hands. "Christ. I'm not angry with you, Lexie. I'm just... I don't know what to do."

I glanced toward the rune-streaked door. The room didn't shake anymore and I couldn't hear any roars or shouts, but something told me Benedict was right on the other side of the drywall, probing at every point of Larry's shell. I took a deep breath and turned my attention to Larry. For all his foibles, confidence had never been something he'd lacked.

I released the grip on my bat and tucked the tooth back into my pocket as it shrunk. I knelt down before Larry. "You know, in softball, our coach always tells us the same thing when we're down big. Forget what's happened, and focus on how to win.

Doesn't matter if you're in the third inning or the ninth, there's always a chance. But your strategy changes depending on where you are in the game. So let's come up with a winning strategy. Start with the basics. How do you kill a ghost?"

Larry lifted his head. "With spirit magic. But I told you, we're not dealing with a ghost anymore. We're dealing with a possessed magic user. Big difference."

"So how do you kill one of them?"

"Same way you kill anyone else. With fire and brimstone. Hence the spells I cast."

"And when that doesn't work?"

"Having their true name would help," said Larry. "Would cut right through their defenses."

"The spirit's or the possessed host's?"

Larry shrugged. "Either."

I racked my brain. "Alright. That's a start. We're probably not going to figure out Benedict's name any time soon, but the host is another matter. We're in his house, right? We've got to be able to find something. A picture. A yearbook. Or the mail, on the desk downstairs! That can tell us his name."

"Possibly, if his common name is his true name. Wizards tend to be careful about leaving those lying around. Not to mention there's no way for us to get back down to the study, not without coming face to face with Benedict." Larry shook his head. "No. We can't kill him. Not yet. To use your analogy, we've got to play for overtime."

"How do you plan on doing that?"

"We run."

"Where? We shimmy out the window?"

Larry snorted. "That's a terrible idea. However, there's always the spirit realm..." He stood and lifted his charcoal.

I blinked. "You can't be serious."

"The rules there are different, Lexie. Spatial dimensions are different. It'll get us out of this protective shell and give us a shot. It's a risky strategy, but it's the one we've got." Larry started marking a circle on the ground. "Besides, I don't know how much longer my protective shell is going to—"

With a resounding crash, the door to the room exploded inward. Dark tendrils surged through the gap. One of them shot toward the flush mounted light in the center of the room, smashing it with a heavy thwack. Two more shot toward Larry, grabbing him around the ankle and wrist, and another pair stretched toward me.

Larry shot me a panicked glance and shouted my name. "Lexie!" He flicked his free hand at me. Before I could cry out in response, a ball of air punched me in the chest. My feet fled the floor and I sailed through the air backward. I heard a crystalline shatter and shards of glass tore at my raincoat as I sailed out the window. Rain battered me in the face as I landed on the slick metal roof with a thud. The impact knocked the air from my chest. Pain lanced through my back as I struggled to take a breath, but it wasn't like being hit with a pitch. I didn't have time to pull myself together and fight through the hurt. The shattered window sped away from me as I slid across the roof, and I heard Larry's cry. "Run, Lexie!"

I grunted as I rolled onto my belly. I made it just in time— sort of. The roof fell out from under me as I reached the edge. I scrabbled for the side as my feet fell into nothingness. A flicker of hope surged through me as my fingers grasped the cold, wet metal, but all the will in the world couldn't save me from the inescapable truth of momentum. My fingertips slid off the roof as if it were buttered, and gravity grabbed hold of me completely.

Luckily I was only on the second story of the house, but I wasn't in any position to prepare myself for a fall. My arms flailed as I fell, and I'd barely tilted my head toward the earth when I hit. My ankle twisted underneath me, followed immediately by a burst of pain that shot up my leg all the way to my hip. I crumpled and rolled, squelching to a stop in a puddle of mud.

Larry's cries cut across the patter of rain. Wood splintered and glass shattered. Hammer blows sounded, and an eruption of concentrated fire blasted what was left of the window into the night. Larry wasn't calling to me anymore. He was fighting for his life, but his words echoed in my mind, as strong as when he'd first shouted them.

Run.

It wasn't in my nature to flee. I was the type to stand my ground and tough things out, even when faced with overwhelming odds. Up until I suffered my shoulder injury playing softball, I'd always overflowed with an abundance of irrational self-confidence. My time with the Nyte Patrol had only helped reinforce that, despite the odds we faced at times. But Larry was right. The thing up there had picked us off one by one. I was the only one left. It was run or die.

I stumbled to my feet and nearly went down again as the pain coursed through my leg. I didn't think I'd broken anything, but I'd be lucky if my ankle only swelled to the size of an orange by morning. I hobbled around the edge of the house, ignoring the violent sounds above and focusing only on what was in front of me. The shrubs beside the farmhouse. The muddy driveway. My Suburban. I could see it now, less than thirty feet away.

I kept hobbling as I dug the keys out of my pocket. The pain in my leg hadn't dulled, but I'd become better at dealing with it as my brain pumped endorphins and adrenaline through my body to keep me moving. My shoe squelched in the mud as I ran. It stuck and I stumbled. Mud splattered across my face as I fell, but I scrambled back to my feet and kept going. I pulled open the truck door and flopped into the driver's seat. My hands shook as I crammed the keys into the ignition. I got them on the third try.

I turned them, and nothing happened.

Fear stabbed at my brain. I tried again, and still nothing. No electrical click. No strangled *chug-a-chug-chug* followed by a dying sputter. Nothing. Zilch. "You've got to be kidding me. *You've got to be kidding me.*"

I tried a third time with as little success as the first two. Rain pinged off my truck, creating an almost melodic tinkle. As the sound tickled my ears, I realized it was *all* I heard.

A shiver ran through me as I looked into my rearview mirror. The farmhouse door stood open, and on the porch stood the man turned nightmare. Tendrils of pure darkness swirled around him, but his yellow eyes and mouth shone through. They stared right at the truck.

I'd been raised Catholic, but I wasn't particularly religious. Exposure to demons and ghosts and alternate spirit realms had proved to me there were forces that existed above and beyond anything I'd ever understand. Perhaps the religion I'd been exposed to wasn't spot on with its predictions, but I believed there'd be an afterlife. I just wasn't ready to be a part of it yet.

My legs wobbled as I got out of the Suburban. Pain stabbed at my ankle as I propped myself on the side of the door frame. The truck wouldn't start. I couldn't run, and even if I could I sure as hell couldn't outrun the thing in front of me. I guess fighting was the only thing left. I wish my phone worked, though. Would've been nice to send a final goodbye to Heather and my family.

My arm shook as I pulled the Glock from my side. Fear wrapped my brain, but there was a new sensation growing there, too. An icy sense of finality, a sharpness of focus that crystalized and burst into a thousand pieces.

Benedict stepped off the porch and walked toward me at a leisurely pace, smiling as he did so. I lifted my pistol, gripping it tight in both hands and narrowed an eye along the sight. I waited until he was thirty feet out before I hammered on the trigger. *Bam bam bam bam bam bam bam bam bam bam.* Bullets whizzed through the air. Maybe some of them hit, maybe they didn't. I had no idea, but I kept squeezing the trigger until the magazine responded with a reluctant click.

The smile on the man monster's face spread. Fifteen feet out now. I tossed the Glock in the mud and pulled out my demon tooth. Benedict's eyes darted to it. He hissed as I squeezed on it, growing it to full size.

"Come at me," I snarled.

Unfortunately, he did. A tendril of darkness whipped through the air, catching me across the wrist. I cried out in pain as the bat twirled and flew into the woods, but my cry didn't last. Another tendril shot out and wrapped around my throat. My hands darted to it, but I couldn't quite grasp the mist. It pulled me off the ground and squeezed. I gurgled, feeling my body pulling me down, feeling the tendril constricting tighter.

My lungs burned. Rain splattered across my face as Benedict drew closer. Spots danced in front of my eyes, and the last thing I saw was the yellow smile spreading.

28

I'd always wondered what the afterlife might be like. Would I burst through clouds to find a set of pearly gates like in corny old movies and Bugs Bunny cartoons? Would I float through a dull, grey mist, seeing nothing, feeling nothing, a soul separated from a body without any sense of time? Or perhaps I'd be whisked straight to the spirit realm and find myself exactly where I'd left, standing outside my Suburban in the rain but without any way to return to the real world.

What I didn't expect was that the afterlife would be so cold and uncomfortable.

I blinked, or at least I think I did. Darkness surrounded me, but it wasn't perfectly monotone, not like the medium gray mist I'd envisioned. There were other sensations, too. An earthy smell. The faint taste of blood. A cool bite nipping at my nerve endings and the ache of sore muscles, not to mention the dull throb of my ankle. I shouldn't have felt any of that if I'd lost contact with my corporeal self.

I tried to move my body. Not only was it still attached to me, but it responded. My fingers slipped on cool, damp rock as I pushed myself into a sitting position. I blinked a few more times as my eyes adjusted to the darkness. Shadows engulfed most of my surroundings, but a square that was more charcoal than black distinguished itself. Thick black bars ran across it, dark as night.

Lightning crashed, and bright light flashed through the room. It outlined every crease in the dark stone walls, the rusted iron bars that held firm at the end of my cell, the wooden pail filled with water that had been shoved into a corner—and the man who stood in the hall outside the bars.

My breath caught in my throat and I scrambled back as the thunder pealed, muffled by the walls around me. The lightning flash had only illuminated the man for a moment. I'd caught a head of golden curls, broad shoulders, smooth cheeks, and a firm jawline before everything plunged back into darkness.

I swallowed and tried to keep my voice from shaking. "Who... who are you?"

The progress made by my eyes hadn't been totally ruined by the bolt of lightning. I could make out the stranger's form, if not his features, as he approached my cell. "The name's Dùghlas."

He spoke softly with an obvious accent, either Scottish or Irish, I'd never been able to tell one from the other. He didn't sound like a serial killer, nor did he sound like Benedict. Still, given that he'd locked me in a cage didn't give me much confidence about his intentions. "How did I get here?"

"My brother put ya here. Obviously."

Obviously? "Look, I don't know who you are or what's going on, but something attacked me. Out there, in the corn, assuming we're still on the farm. A creature of darkness, with powerful tentacles and the blackest of hearts that—"

Dùghlas leapt forward and banged on the iron bars. "Shut up, ya maggot. Don't ya dare speak about my brother dat way. Not you. Ya don't have dat right."

The gears in my brain groaned as they lurched into motion. I thought about what Larry had told me, that Benedict had possessed someone thereby turning into more than he'd been in the spirit realm. That whoever he'd possessed lived in the farmhouse along with a family. "That's your brother?"

"His name's Ciaran. Might wanna remember it, 'cause you'll be taking it with ya to yer grave."

Hearing such harsh words from such a soft voice took me aback. "Who are you? Why do you want to hurt me?"

Dùghlas let go of the bars and retreated to the other side of the corridor. I only now realized there were bars on that side, too. "Do I need to spell it out for ya? The name's Dùghlas. Dùghlas *O'Neill*."

"And my name's Lexie Rodriguez. So what?"

Dùghlas lurched and slammed his body against the bars, shaking them in their sockets. *"Damn ya, ya wagon!* Damn ya straight to hell. Ya kilt my brother, and ya don't even remember his name?!"

"Killed your...?" I blinked, confused, but the name O'Neill did sound familiar. Where had I heard it before? Suddenly I remembered. *"Angus."*

"That's right." A new voice oozed into my cell, cold and thick with malice. I recognized it as Benedict's, but it was different, too. More resonant. More human.

Dùghlas shrunk away from my cell door, slinking into the shadows. Into the spot he'd occupied came someone new. He was taller than Dùghlas, with broader shoulders and more of a russet tint to the curls on top of his head, but even in the darkness it was obvious they were brothers. A darkness swirled around him, though, and his eyes burned with an all-too familiar yellow fire.

"Angus was the best of us," he said. "And ya murdered him in cold blood."

"We didn't murder him." I remembered the incident. It was when I'd just joined the Nyte Patrol. We'd been in search of the *Librum de Virtute* for Ivan Romanov. After discovering it was housed in the University of Texas' Harry Ransom Center, we'd delved deep into its basement where we ultimately found it on top of a temple suspended over a pit of bubbling magma. As we'd prepared to grab it, several other treasure hunters had appeared out of nowhere to contest our claim to it. One of them had been Angus O'Neill, a druid who Larry claimed was immortal. Clearly, that had been a load of bull. "Angus fell into the lava as we fled the hell creatures that attacked us. That wasn't our fault."

"*LIES.*" The darkness around Ciaran intensified. His eyes glowed brighter, and he seemed to grow. As he did, a green energy pulsed from the center of his chest, the same as I'd seen coming from Benedict. I hadn't seen it clearly before, but now by its own light, I recognized it. It was Romanov's amulet of melding. Was it somehow behind his possession?

Ciaran gripped the bars of my cell, and the metal glowed faintly around his fingers. He spoke more softly, but the darkness didn't dissipate, nor did the yellow fire die from his eyes. "Don't deny yer involvement in Angus's death. It took us a few months, but we figured it out. You, yer wizard friend, Larry, and that reckless werebeast o' yers pushed him into the magma. We have first hand accounts o' the incident. *Ya killed him.* T'was no accident. Ya tore our family apart, all in pursuit of a useless arti-fact! Y'ave no idea what sort of pain you've put us through. But ya will. *Oh, ya will...*"

As Ciaran spoke, I pictured myself in Charity's house in the spirit realm. I pictured the poltergeist who'd attacked us, his body cracked and split by burns, his skin turned black and dry with magma leaking from his wounds. I could hear his moans, hear the pain in his voice as he's smashed and stomped around. "My God. Angus. I had no idea."

"O' the suffering ya put him through? And us? I imagine not. But trust me, ya will. Yer friend Larry has seen a glimmer o' it, even though he was able to save his niece. We'll rectify that afore we kill him. The bear finally knows what it's like to suffer the loss of a loved one, too. But you? Ya still haven't felt that pain. That fear. That agony. So it's time to change that. Lucky for us yer family lives so close."

The air bled from my lungs, and cold fear gripped me in an iron vice. "Wh....*what?*"

Ciaran's voice lowered to barely more than a whisper. As it softened, more of Benedict crept in. "Do ya know what revenge is, Lexie? Do ya understand *vengeance?* 'Cause I do. Having ya there to watch yer parents die'd be better, but I'll have to settle for showing ya the aftermath. Their broken bodies. Their pleas for mercy. I'll fill yer mind with the agony. Only then, once every fiber o' yer being cries out in sufferin' will I release ya to death. *And you'll beg for it.*"

The darkness intensified, swallowing Ciaran with Bene-dict's cloud of evil. His laughter filled my cell, growing louder as he released the iron bars and disappeared to the side, out of my field of view. I assume he left, but I couldn't hear his footsteps, couldn't hear his breathing, couldn't hear anything but the rush of blood in my ears and the echoes of his cruel laughter ringing through my mind.

Rough stone brushed my fingers. Only then did I realize I'd pitched forward, falling to my hands and knees under the weight of the truth. Benedict. Ciaran. Whoever was in charge, they both intended the same thing. They'd nearly killed Madison. They'd killed Kiara. Now they were going to come after my family, and there wasn't a damn thing I could do.

My breath caught in my chest. I tried to breathe, to gulp in big mouthfuls of air, but no matter how much I swallowed, I couldn't get enough. A tremble had taken hold through my spine that wouldn't let me be, and everything had gone fuzzy. I don't think I'd ever had a panic attack, but I was pretty sure I was having one now.

I felt wetness on my cheeks, and I realized I was crying. I heard a footstep, and I looked up. Dùghlas stood in front of my cell, his posture hunched, his face drooped. The anger I'd seen there was gone, replaced by a more complex emotion, some mixture of guilt, sadness, and suffering.

I crawled forward, reaching for him through the bars of my cell. My voice broke between my sobs. "Please. I'm sorry. Don't do this. Don't let him..."

Dùghlas pulled his leg back, and he stared at me with dead eyes. "Ciaran chose his path, same as ya did when ya murdered Angus. The darkness may have taken him, opened him up to things I ne'er thought were in him, but the agony ya receive is no less than that which ya deserve."

Lightning struck again, filling the room via a transom window at the far end of the row of cells. By its light, I saw

Dùghlas's face. There might be suffering there, but there was more determination than anything else.

He shrugged me off and headed to the far side of the room, where he mounted a set of rickety stairs. Thunder pealed, darkness returned, and I curled into a ball and cried.

29

I LAY ON THE COLD STONE FLOOR, TEARS CAUSING MY vision to swim. My chest rose and fell far too quickly, and I still hadn't beaten back the fuzzy, trembling feeling that coursed through me. Thoughts of violence filled my head, but it wasn't me I feared for. It was my mother, my father, my sister. Out in the rain with Benedict bearing down on me, my gun firing, the rain pouring over me, I'd accepted death. I'd acknowledged the moment and come to grips with it. The worst moment of my life, and I'd faced it head on.

I didn't think death could get worse, but I'd been wrong. My death bookended by the murder of those I cared about was a million times more painful.

As I sobbed, I started to blame myself. I knew I shouldn't. I wasn't an angry psychopath, bent on revenge after the death of a sibling. I wasn't an evil spirit whose sole purpose was to possess maniacs and force them to carry out their darkest nightmares. I wasn't going to kill my parents. And yet, I wasn't faultless. By refusing to talk to my folks about the Nyte Patrol, I'd put them in the path of danger. I'd lied to them. Told them I was interning in an engineering firm instead of tangoing with demons and spirits that thirsted for blood. Telling them might not have saved them. It hadn't kept Kiara or Madison out of the line of fire, but I should've told them. Heather had been right. I should've come clean. At least then they would've known. Would've been able to prepare for the worst, something I hadn't done either. I'd craved adventure and excitement, but I'd never considered the cost.

I squeezed my eyes shut and focused on my breathing, trying to do anything to stop the shaking and the nauseating tingle. In and out. Deep breaths. I wasn't sure if it was helping, so I cleared my mind. Out with the visions of violence and terror, in with happy thoughts. Good times. Memories. Bonding with Heather. Getting into trouble with my baby sis. My mom's smiling face. I focused on it, wanting to remember it forever. *Hey, Mom.*

"Lexie." She smiled back at me.

It was working. The pressure over my chest lessened, the tingle dulled. "Yeah, Mom. I'm here. I'm sorry. So sorry."

My mom's smile broadened, but when she spoke, the voice wasn't hers. "Lexie. *Lexie.* Can you hear me?"

I pushed myself off the floor, wiping away the tears with a cold hand as I blinked away the image of my mom. I looked past the bars to my cell. There, in the cell across from me, I saw a hunched figure. "Who's there?"

The figure approached the bars. It was a woman, but her face was covered in dirt and blood. She spoke in a low voice. "It's me. Charity. Dawn's friend?"

"Charity!" My exclamation came out louder than I'd intended. I tried again, quieter this time. "You're alive. My God.

Dawn found your jacket in a barn. It was all bloody. We feared the worst."

"Yeah, well, they roughed me up a bit. A lot, actually." Charity leaned against the bars and peered toward the stairs at the side. The lighting was awful, but some of what I'd thought was dirt on her face might've been bruising, too. "Where's Dawn?"

"I don't know," I said. "We lost her outside. She was supposed to be following us, but she disappeared in the rain. We figured Benedict grabbed her."

"Who?"

"Sorry. Benedict's the evil spirit who possessed Ciaran. Larry gave it that name. Don't ask."

"I won't." Charity quieted, tilting her head. She stayed that way for a second before relaxing. "Sorry. Have to be careful. Dùghlas comes and goes without warning. He's not as bad as Ciaran, but still."

"Speaking of, where are we?" I asked.

"Basement of the farmhouse," said Dawn. "You and Larry made one hell of a racket up there earlier. Is there even a house left to go back to?"

"I think so. I haven't been inside since Larry shot me out a window and blasted the room he was in with a giant fireball in an attempt to slow down Benedict." A lump formed in my throat. "God. I hope he's okay..."

"I don't know about okay," said Charity. "But he's alive. He's in the cell next to you."

My heart leapt out of my chest. "Are you serious? Larry! Larry, can you hear me?"

"Relax," said Charity. "If he was conscious, don't you think he would've said something? I can hear him breathing, but he's out cold. I thought Ciaran was rough with me, but he pulled a number on Larry."

The surge of hope I'd had flickered and dimmed. I slumped against the side of my cell. "Damnit. Here I thought he might be able to get us out of this mess."

"Not in the state he's in. What about Dawn? And your other friend, Tank?"

"They're still out there unless Ciaran captured and imprisoned them, too. But I have no way to contact them. My phone's on the fritz."

Charity sighed and slumped, too. "So much for that idea."

The spark of hope inside me refused to die. "But you're a werehyena, right?"

"Been there, done that, Lexie. I may be stronger in hyena form, but not strong enough to break through inch and a half thick iron bars. Trust me, I've tried."

A metaphysical hand reached inside me and snuffed the last spark of hopeful flame. I felt like crying again, but the embarrassment of acting like a baby in front of Charity kept the tears at bay. "Jesus Christ, Charity. I thought when Benedict came to kill me, things couldn't get any worse. I can't believe I was wrong. I'm so sorry you got dragged into this..."

"No need for apologies, Lexie. You're not the one who got possessed by a psycho demon spirit. This isn't your fault."

I sighed. "I don't know. It kind of is. When we battled Romanov on the South Congress bridge a few months ago—Dawn told you about that right?—we managed to kill him, but his spirit got away. I heard it laughing as it shot away from the crater he left behind when we killed him. I knew something had escaped. I told Larry about it, but we didn't do anything. We should've been more proactive. If we had, maybe we could have stopped any of this from happening."

Charity was quiet for a moment. I heard a creak upstairs, then nothing. "Well, if we're handing out unnecessary apologies, I should offer mine as well. I'm the one who told Ciaran what happened to Angus."

A knife twisted in my gut. "What?"

"While we fled the monster attack at that underground temple and Dawn and I got separated from you guys, I saw him fall into the lava from afar. That's why Ciaran and Dùghlas kidnapped me. Somehow they figured out I'd been looking for the *Librum de Virtute* at the same time you and Angus were. For the record, I didn't tell them you killed Angus. I told them exactly what I saw, that Angus fell to his death while he and Tank were battling the demons. I didn't offer up the information willingly, either. That's why the jacket you found was so damned bloody."

The pain of betrayal in my belly faded. "I can't fault you for that. I would've told them anything if they tortured me. Speaking of Angus, you know the ghost problem you called Larry about?"

"Yeah, I figured that out over the last couple days. Angus's spirit keeps popping up here, too, moaning and groaning and blowing air around when he's agitated. Horny bastard keeps trying to cop a feel, too." Charity shivered. "So you're saying he and this Benedict character are two different spirits?"

"I'm sure of it," I said. "Angus attacked us at your house. Benedict came after me in my dreams and in the spirit realm while we were at St. David's trying to save Larry's niece, Madison. I think he managed to follow us into the real world when we escaped. I'm guessing that's when he possessed Ciaran, because the same monster who attacked us outside is the one who came after Tank's ex-wife, Kiara."

Charity squinted at me. "When was this?"

"This afternoon. I don't know. Eight hours ago? I've lost track of time. Why?"

"It wasn't until this afternoon that those dark mists formed around him. There's been something wrong with him from the start—they tortured me day before yesterday—but it wasn't until today that he got the yellow eyes and that medallion around his neck started glowing."

"That's Ivan Romanov's amulet of melding. Larry procured it for him before I joined up with them. Ciaran must've used it to morph with Benedict somehow—or vice versa."

"He's had the medallion since he first kidnapped me, though."

"Wouldn't surprise me," I said. "If I had to guess, Benedict's been pulling strings from the spirit world for a while. He got someone to buy the crystals we delivered to Romanov and used them in an attack against Madison. Must've been either Ciaran or Dùghlas. He also placed a talisman over Madison in the spirit realm. Not sure how he did it, but he must've roped one of the O'Neills into that, too. It was a *druidic* artifact. I can't believe I forgot that Angus and his folks were druids. Now he's got the medallion, too, and is using it to increase his Earthly power. He must be trying to reclaim all the artifacts Romanov had so he can take over the world."

Charity looked at me across the bars. "Lexie, I already thought this situation was bad, but you're making it sound a million times worse."

"You think I don't know that?" My voice inched up in volume. "I'm stuck in a psychopath's basement with a bum leg, a phone that doesn't work, and the demonic spirit who put me here is going to kill my entire family. *Trust me, I know it's bad!*"

"Okay. My fault for saying something stupid," said Charity. "But don't think about your folks. No one ever saved anyone by panicking. Focus on solving the problem at hand, which is getting out of here so we can warn them to take cover."

I took a deep breath and pushed back the violent images that had surfaced again. "You're right. I told Larry the same thing earlier, but it's hard to take good advice when you're freaking out. Got any ideas?"

"Ciaran and his brother took everything I had when they abducted me. Did they do the same to you?"

I checked my pockets. "I lost my pistol and my demon tooth in my fight with Benedict. I've still got my phone, but..." I pulled it. "Yeah. Still no signal."

"Okay. What about Larry? Do you think he might have anything useful on him?"

"He might. He carries all kinds of magical crap in his duster." I pushed myself against the bars to my cell, trying to poke my head around to see. "Is he near the front of his cell?"

"No dice," said Charity. "He's a few feet back. You'll never reach him."

"*Damnit.* We really need his help."

"No kidding, Lexie, but he's out cold. You could scream bloody murder and he wouldn't notice, which is not something I'd suggest, by the way. If Dùghlas comes back down, we're more screwed than we are now."

A thought struck me. "Do you have a bucket of water like I do? If so, you could splash him with it. That might do the trick."

"And if it doesn't I won't have anything to drink. Still, it's worth a shot." Charity slinked into her cell and reappeared with a wooden bucket in hand. "Hope the noise doesn't alert Dùghlas."

She swung her arms and pitched the contents of the bucket across the corridor. Water ricocheted off the bars and splashed as it made contact with Larry and his cell.

I thought I heard a groan. "Anything?"

Charity sighed as she put her bucket down. "He twitched, and he's soaking wet now, but if you're asking did he wake up, the answer is a solid no. We need something more potent to wake him. Unless you've got smelling salts squirreled away in your shoe, I'm afraid we're out of luck."

"Something potent. *Smelling salts...* Charity, you're a genius." I scuttled back into my cell, looking around me. Besides the bucket, there wasn't much of anything there, not even moldy hay or a pile of dirt. Oh, well. The water would have to do. I dipped my hand in the bucket, getting it nice and wet.

"What the hell are you doing?" asked Charity.

"Making a magic circle." I traced my wet fingers along the stone underneath me, more in the shape of an oval than a circle. I made sure to add random corners and jags that shouldn't be there, too. "A really bad one, at that."

"You know how to use magic? Christ, Lexie, that's something you could've mentioned earlier."

"That's the thing. I don't know how to use it. Larry started training me yesterday. I can't even summon a fly, but I can sure as hell botch an incantation."

"That's a good thing?"

"Right now it is."

I finished drawing the wet circle on the stone and added a few lines that didn't even resemble a star. I stepped inside the wobbly circle. "Alright. What was it Larry told me to say the last time? *Vide praeter illam... velum...?* Screw it. The whole point is to butcher it. *Viva prattle Euler venti infernal apartheid!"*

The hairs on the back of my neck stood on end, and this time even *I* smelled it. A foul stench, part magical, part real, like rotten eggs and volcanic ash and week old fish all rolled into a putrid trash taco. I gagged, and I wasn't the only one.

From the cell next to me, I heard a groan, followed immediately by a hacking cough, a *hurrrrr*, then a wet splash. The stink of vomit joined the already foul mixture in the air.

I heard Larry. *"Oh God.* What... What is...?" He made another deep sound from his diaphragm, and more vomit splashed across stone.

"Sorry!" I grabbed my bucket and splashed water across the wet marks I'd left on the stone, hoping it would clear the super-natural stink. "Are you okay, Larry?"

Larry groaned again. *"Ugggghhhh.* God, my head. And that *smell.* What...? *Hurrrrr* ... Ugh, what *is* that? Where am I? Is this hell?"

"If only," said Charity. "We're trapped in the basement of a vengeful murderer who's been possessed by an even more evil, psychotic spirit who wants to murder Lexie's family."

I heard a rustle. "Charity? Is that you? And Lexie?"

I pressed against the bars of my cell. "It's me, Larry. Quick recap. You didn't beat Benedict, and I sure as hell didn't either. Turns out he's been influencing people from the spirit realm in an attempt to take over the world again with the items we delivered to Romanov a few months ago. He possessed Ciaran O'Neill, brother of Angus O'Neill, who happens to be the ghost we caught in Charity's house, and now the Ciaran Benedict combo is off to murder my family and Madison, too, before he comes back to finish us off!"

"Whoa, whoa, slow down," said Larry. "He's going after *your* folks now?"

"Yes," I said. "He knows where they live. He left probably fifteen minutes ago. If I don't get word to them quick, they're... *they're...*" My throat closed up at the thought.

"The point is, we don't have a lot of time," said Charity. "Can you get us out of here, Larry? We've been hanging our hopes on you."

Larry poked half his head through the bars, letting me get a glimpse of him. He looked like death warmed over. "I... I don't know, guys. I feel like I've been chewed up and spit out. Hell, maybe I was. I don't remember what happened after Benedict busted in on us. Maybe if you give me a few minutes to rustle up some energy."

"We don't have minutes," I said. "We're already way behind Ciaran. My phone still doesn't work, and my truck wouldn't start, last time I checked. We need magic, either to get us out of here or to contact my folks, *now!*"

Larry sighed. "Okay. Alright. Let's focus on communication. That's faster and easier than trying to outrace Ciaran, especially if your truck's busted. You sure your phone's not working?"

"I just checked, Larry. No service. None."

"I don't suppose either of your parents is a practitioner of the arcane arts, are they?"

"You can't be serious?"

"Hey, I'm just asking. You've got to understand, communication isn't a problem between magic users. It's magician to mundie where it gets tricky. How are they with smoke signals?"

"Larry! It's the middle of the night, and it's pouring rain! I know you feel half dead and I'm putting you under pressure here, but we need something that can actually work. Some way for me to communicate with my folks, person to person, or..." I glanced at Charity, and the thought struck me. "Or animal to person! Like how you sent birds and cats to Charity's place to get into contact with her."

"You did what now?" said Charity.

I heard a rustle. I think Larry sat up straighter in his cell. "Now *that's* not a bad idea. But I need an animal. Are there windows in this basement? If we lure a pigeon in here..."

"No need," I said. "My parents have a cat. Mr. Whiskers. We can talk to them through him!"

"Mr. Whiskers?" said Larry. "You're jerking my chain, right?"

"My little sister named him. She was seven when we got him. Cut her some slack."

"Sorry," said Larry. "Using your family cat isn't an option. I need the animal to be in front of me to be able to soulcast into them. At the very least, I need something from their body, a feather, a tuft of hair, hell, a whisker even. Maybe a charm they wore. No offense, but you don't seem the type to carry a tuft of your family cat's hair around in your purse."

"I don't even carry a purse," I said. "But I have pictures of Mr. Whiskers on my phone. Would that work?"

Larry snorted. "It needs to be something that connects directly to the animal. Your phone's not going to cut it, Lexie."

"How are you so sure? Every time you touch a smartphone, it blows up. I bet you've never tried."

"Of course I haven't tried, because it wouldn't work. I'm telling you—"

I ripped my phone from my pocket and held it between the

bars. "Try it. I don't care if it blows up, we've got to give it a shot. Unless you have a better idea?"

Larry didn't say anything.

"*Well?*"

"I'm thinking!" said Larry. "And no, I don't have any better ideas. But if this is going to have any chance of working, it has to be you performing the soulcast. Using a picture on a phone means the connection is going to be shaky at best. Maybe your love for the animal will be enough to get it to work. Maybe..."

"Well, I screwed up a spell just to get you to wake up, but sure. Tell me what I need to do. I'll give anything a shot at this point."

"No need for that," said Larry. "I'll cast the spell. Your soul will be the one that's cast, though. Are you looking at a photo of Mr. Whiskers already?"

I pulled one up. "Yeah. Now what?"

"Focus on the picture. Really focus on it. Look through it, as if it were one of those Magic Eye posters. I'll speak the incantation."

"Wait," I said. "How is this going to work? I'll be able to talk, right? How long will I have?"

"Well, if everything works out, you'll be you, just inside of Mr. Whisker's body. When I soulcast, I can talk, and I pull myself out when I'm done. How about I give you... ten minutes? Either that or I'll pull you if Charity says you start twitching uncontrollably. Now are we doing this or not?"

I shook my head, trying to banish any doubts. *Think positive, Lexie. This is going to work.* "Ready."

I stared at the photo on my phone, focusing on Mr. Whiskers but staring through him at the same time. I heard Larry's voice speaking in Latin. I had no idea what he was saying, so I ignored him. I poured every ounce of focus into the picture. The floor of my cell and the bars beyond faded into darkness. Only the photo existed in front of me. Only Mr. Whiskers. There was only him, except he was fading, too. The phone, my arms, now everything was fading to black.

Oh, no. What had I done?

30

I OPENED MY EYES, AND THE DARKNESS FLED, REPLACED instead by a field of white fluff. It looked soft. In fact, it *was* soft, and I was laying in it.

I blinked again, taking note of the gray white paws tucked in front of me, stretching from underneath me where my arms should've been. I twisted my neck, finding it far more flexible than I was used to, and gazed upon the rest of my body, a ball of fur curled among the fluffy bed. The edge of the cat bed beyond me rose to above face height, and beyond that, a massive great room loomed, with ceilings ten stories high and furniture fit for giants. Actually, on second thought, it was my parent's living room, but I'd never seen the thing from Mr. Whisker's point of view.

I'm not sure what I'd expected from Larry's soulcast. Perhaps I'd envisioned myself hovering over Mr. Whiskers, looking over him as if I were a ghost and pulling invisible strings to get him to act. For some silly reason, I hadn't anticipated I'd actually be inside him. See what he saw, felt what he felt, smelled what he smelled. Seeing everything from his position, the sheer enormity of it, made me want to curl up into a ball and go back to sleep.

So I did. I curled up, nestled my head among the fluffiest portions of the bed, and closed my eyes.

Hey. Wait a second. I didn't want to go to sleep. I had things to do. *Get up you stupid cat. Er… I mean, me.*

I lifted my head back up and yawned. My tongue rolled out and flapped in front of my face. *Holy crap that thing is long. That's so weird.* Then I arched my back and stretched. My back crackled and popped. *Ok, time for action, cat.* But instead of heading out of my bed, I flopped my back legs open and stuffed my face in between them.

Oh, God no. No no no. But I couldn't stop it. I started licking my privates. *Ugh. I can taste it, too. A little tangy. Gross! And is that fur on my tongue! Ack! Yuck! Stop it, Whiskers!*

I sat up and looked around, and I felt a strange sense of being watched. *Well, duh! It's because I'm here, Whiskers.* That's when I realized I wasn't totally in control. I was in Whisker's mind, but I also *was* Whiskers. And the things I wanted weren't the same as the ones he did.

I focused. *Alright, Whiskers. Me. Whoever. Listen up. We've got things to do and not a lot of time to do them. Let's find Mom, quick. Lives are on the line!*

I yawned again, flopped down, and sighed.

Fine. You want to do it the hard way, we'll do it the hard way. I forced my eyes at my paws. I stared at them, focused on the thought of moving them, same as I would with my arms and legs. I thought about putting one up and moving it forward.

Sure enough, it responded. *Great. Now the other.* I felt resistance in my brain, but whether it was an actual battle between me and Whiskers or the pervasive laziness of being a cat, I couldn't tell. Either way, I was moving. I hopped out of bed and padded off toward the couch. I wasn't sure what time it was, but it seemed like the time of night my mom would be watching TV.

Sure enough, I saw the flicker of the flatscreen as I rounded the edge of the sofa, and there, curled up in a corner, was my mom. A surge of relief flooded me as I saw her. *She was still okay!* But who knew for how long.

She saw me and smiled. *"Hola, viejo.* Want to come up?"

She held out her hands and leaned over to pick me up. *God, she's big. It's disorienting.* I shuffled back and sat down on my hind legs.

My mom looked at me. "No?"

This was my moment. I thought about how to break it to her gently, that I'd joined the Nyte Patrol, was training to be a witch, that I'd possessed her cat and come to tell her to flee the path of a nightmarish death spirit that planned to murder her and dad and my grandmother. *Whatever. There's no time to hesitate.*

I opened my mouth. "Meow."

My mom cocked her head. "What is it? I gave you dinner."

No no no. This wasn't right. Larry said I'd be able to talk. This couldn't be happening.

I tried again. "Meow."

My mom reached down to grab me. *"Venga.* Just come up."

I screeched, hissed, and jumped back, lashing out with my claws. My mom swore and kicked at me. *"Oye! Maldito gato!* Have it your way."

I ran, partly because I didn't want to get stomped on by a crazed human, partly because I needed to try something else.

Damnit! If I can't speak, how can I tell my parent to run? I needed to try something else.

I ran into my dad's study. As with my mom he was in his usual nighttime spot, parked in front of his computer. The screen flickered, illuminating his face with a pale glow as he read his online news.

I bounded up a sofa chair and onto his desk. "Meow."

My dad eyed me, smirking knowingly. "And what is it you want, Whiskers? *Un poquito de amor?*"

I sauntered toward the computer, feeling myself respond to my dad's cooing. *No. Damnit, Whiskers, not now!* I glanced at the keyboard as my dad reached out to scratch me behind the ears and had an idea.

Before his hand reached me, I sprung forth and batted the keys. I could spell it out for him. *Evil demon, coming for you, run! Now!* I hit the e key, then the v, but my paws were too big and too imprecise.

"Whiskers! What are you doing? I'm trying to read that."

I hissed and kept batting, desperately hoping my point was coming across. I glanced at the screen. In the web browser's search field, I read my message. *ewdrvfgbiujldewontsldptnf.*

My dad swatted at me. *"Vaya!* Get out of here. What's wrong with you?"

I jumped to the floor as my dad brushed me away. *Crap!* What could I do to get their attention, to get them to listen to me? I couldn't talk. Couldn't write. Time was ticking away, both time they had until Ciaran arrived and time I had left in Mr. Whisker's body.

I had to try again. Something. Anything. Or anyone.

I bounded off, racing around a corner into the downstairs guest room, though it had since become my *abuela's* room. I found her sitting on the edge of her bed, stooped over and dressed in a nightgown. She held her rosary beads and mumbled her Hail Mary's, same as she always did before bed.

I ran up to her. "Meow."

She smiled. "Ah, Whis-kers. *Que quieres?*"

She said his name in her Spanish accent. She leaned forward to pet me. As she did so, something slipped from around her neck out of her nightgown. The LifeAlert my parents had gotten for her, fearful she might slip and fall while they were out and about.

That was it! I leapt at her and swung at the dangling pendant, trying to bat the button with my paws.

My *abuela* jerked back and screamed. *"Ah! Dios mio! Ayuda, el gato esta tratando de matarme!"*

I heard a rustle from the living room and a curse muttered under my mother's breath. *How could I hear that? Are my ears that sensitive?* It didn't matter. I bolted from my grandmother's room as my mother's footsteps neared. Sounded like my dad was on his way, too. *Drat!* My cat instincts took over at the thought of being cornered. I shot upstairs like someone had threatened me with a bath and slunk into the nearest unoccupied room. It happened to be the one I'd shared with my little sister.

The lights were off, but I could see just fine. I didn't know what time it was, but I could hear the ticking second hand of a clock in my head, the relentless reminder of Ciaran's threat and the duration of Larry's soulcast.

I had to act quick. Luckily, my grandmother's LifeAlert had given me an idea.

I bounded onto my desk. At the corner was the old cordless phone I'd been forced to use through much of high school. I don't know why my parents hadn't ditched their landline—all they got on the thing was spam calls—but for the moment I was grateful.

I batted the phone off its receiver. I might not have been particularly dextrous with my paws, but I still had my face. I leaned down and pushed the on button with my nose, then carefully I punched in 9-1-1.

The call rang. I wouldn't be able to answer, but I was familiar enough with dispatch protocols to be reasonably sure it wouldn't matter.

A voice answered. "Nine one one. What's your emergency?"

I didn't make a sound.

"Hello? Is anyone there?"

Still nothing.

"Are you unable to speak or is it unsafe to speak? Hit any button on your phone. Once for yes, twice for no."

Perfect. I leaned down and pushed a single button with my nose.

"Alright. I'm sending law enforcement to your location now. If you can, please stay on the line. Are you—"

I ignored the dispatcher as there was work yet to been done. It wouldn't be good enough to have the police come to my parent's place. I needed a reason for them to stay, or for my folks to get out. Something to give them serious pause about their safety other than the wild actions of a demonically possessed cat.

Demonically possessed? Couldn't hurt. I jumped onto my bed and busted out my claws. I'd had plenty of experience with Larry drawing pentagrams, and I put it to use. I tore lines into the bed as quickly as I could, hoping beyond hope I wouldn't get yanked from my cat body before I finished shredding the blanket.

The circle looked awful as I finished it, but perhaps the visceral nature of it would help convince my parents I was truly possessed. *Sorry, Whiskers. I'll call them as soon as I can and explain everything. Promise you won't get sent to a shelter.*

The voice on the phone kept talking, assuring me they'd stay on the line until police arrived. That still wouldn't be good enough. I needed my parents to see what I'd done.

I ran to the door and perked my ears. My parents were both downstairs, talking to each other about what the hell had gotten into me.

What the hell, indeed.

I arched my back, puffed up my lungs, and started hissing and spitting. I heard my dad swear. The stairs creaked as he set foot to them, and I retreated into my bedroom.

Or at least, I tried to. I stumbled to the carpet as I back-tracked, suddenly feeling woozy. My world stretched, and a force picked me up from behind. I lashed out and grabbed hold, refusing to be sucked away, except I didn't. I didn't dig my claws into the carpet, not did I bite and latch onto the nearest chair. Rather the effect was in my head. It was as if my brain was being sucked by a vacuum cleaner from behind. I tried desperately to hold on, to force my way into my bedroom, but the force grew fiercer. It sucked, and sucked, and *POP!*

31

I FELL BACKWARDS, SMACKING MY HEAD AGAINST THE COLD stone of the basement. I cried out and crumpled, feeling the wetness underneath me. I blinked in the darkness, gritting my teeth as I willed away the pain.

"Lexie? You there?" said Larry.

I grunted. "Ugh. Yeah. I'm back. Christ, that hurts."

"Returning from the soulcast? It's disorienting, but I wouldn't call it painful."

"Hitting my head on the wall, genius."

"Well," said Charity. "Did it work?"

I rubbed the back of my head. Bet I'd have a nice lump there later. It would go great with my swollen ankle. "Yes and no. I couldn't speak, so that was a rude awakening."

Larry swore. "*Son of a...* Well, I told you a cell phone image wasn't an adequate focusing charm, didn't I?"

"On the bright side, I scratched demonic symbols into my room, called the police, and attacked everyone in my family, thereby ensuring they either lock Mr. Whiskers in a closet or kill him in fear. Your guess is as good as mine."

Charity leaned against the bars of her cell. "Lexie, I don't want to belabor the obvious, but the point of transporting you into the body of your family cat was to get your folks out of Ciaran's path. Even if the cops show up, what chance do they stand against him if you and I and Larry all failed to scratch the guy? They need to flee, not fight."

"You think I don't know that?" I said. "I mean, I do now. I had a hard time grasping the concept as a cat. The whole experience was a mess. It's like my mind was half cat, too. I couldn't control my baser instincts. Even now I feel like I'm waking up from a night of heavy drinking. I can't think straight. Crap... What are we going to do?"

"Warning your folks was the best option, but there's still plan B," said Larry. "Which in this case is fighting our way out of here and catching up to Ciaran. Maybe we'll get lucky. Maybe your truck will start now that he and Benedict are gone. Remember that time I supercharged your Suburban? We might be able to get to San Antonio in time, or at least to a place with a payphone. How long was I out?"

"No."

Larry and I turned our attention toward Charity. She stood at the front of her cell, her face set in stone.

"What do you mean, no?" said Larry.

"I mean, we're not going to succeed by chasing this thing all over central Texas," said Charity. "It has a head start on us, it knows where to go, and based on what I've gathered over the past couple hours, it can move in ways none of us are able to. We're not going to catch it, not before it does serious harm to a lot of people, either Lexie's family or your niece or anyone else. Taking the fight to it in the center of a dense urban setting is only going to make the carnage worse. Better to tackle Ciaran somewhere remote where the damage he'll do is minimal."

"You want to lure him back out here?" I said.

"Better here than in a city of millions," said Charity. "Besides, he set a trap for you here. This is his home. He's confident here. Maybe overly so. We might be able to use that against him."

Larry held up a hand. "Slow down. I'll acknowledge moving heaven and earth to race into downtown San Antonio after Benedict isn't a strategy that offers a high rate of success. And it's true. Benedict's been a step ahead of us for the last two days. We've chased him and yet he's the one who's always found us. Even after tracking him here, he sprung a trap on us and took us out one by one. I'm all in favor of turning the tables on him. However, unless you have a working cell phone and Ciaran's number on speed dial, we're shit out of luck as far as luring him back here is concerned."

"Maybe not," said Charity. "Even if we could contact him directly, there's no way he'd turn around. Benedict has too tight a hold on him, and he thirsts for blood. But if one of his own were in danger? If his lone surviving brother, Dùghlas, were to call for help?"

Hope flared in my chest. I'd gone so long without it, the spark felt like a fire. "Yeah. If we can capture Dùghlas, threaten him and let him call Ciaran, that might work. Of course, Ciaran would know it's a trap. He'd come back ready to fight."

"Only if Ciaran thinks we know he's coming back," said Charity. "If we let Dùghlas contact him on his own, Ciaran might return to free his brother, not to fight us. Then we strike."

"Kind of hard to slip Dùghlas a cell phone without him realizing what's up," I said. "Not to mentions there's no service."

Charity laughed, but there wasn't any mirth to it. "He won't use technology. He and Ciaran can communicate through their dead brother, Angus. Something to do with the family connection. I've been here long enough to see it in action. If we lock him up, he'll commune with Angus and that dude will zip across the netherworld and tell Ciaran what's up straight away. Don't ask me how."

"It's alternate universe physics. Spirits can traverse the spirit world quickly if they know what they're doing." Larry sighed and wiped his face with a hand. "Okay. This could work. But there's a gaping flaw in the plan. Namely that we have no idea how to defeat Ciaran and Benedict. You've got to remember, I hit that thing with every spell I had, and I ended up face down in a cell feeling weak as a babe. If we get Ciaran to charge back here in a fit of rage, chances are all we'll accomplish are swifter deaths."

Despite the muddiness left by the process of having my soul cast into a cat seventy miles away, the desperation swirling in my mind cracked the shell that hovered over the creative portion of my brain, and a shiny golden nugget appeared. "We don't know how to defeat Ciaran and Benedict, together, but Ciaran on his own is a man. Well, a druid, but still. Benedict is an evil spirit. Stronger than most, but you've tangoed with them before, Larry. If we can separate the two, we might have a shot."

Larry pressed his head against the bars. "And you have a plan to do that?"

"Ciaran is wearing Romanov's amulet," I said. "The amulet of melding! If we get it off him and destroy it, that should free him from Benedict's grasp, right?"

"Hopefully, otherwise we're all going to die." Larry groaned as he stood. "Alright. Imprison Dùghlas, lure Ciaran back, get the amulet off, destroy it and Benedict along with it. I'm not feeling a hundred percent by any means, but we're running out of time, so let's get this clown show on the road. Charity? What's the best way to lure Dùghlas? By being loud?"

"I could turn into were form," she said. "He hates that. If I start howling, he'll be here in no time flat."

"Perfect. Lexie? You're a mechanical engineer. Are these bars pure iron or steel?"

"Iron, I think, but it's dark, I'm a mechanical engineering *student,* not a trained metallurgist, and even if I knew what I was doing, I'd need equipment to know for sure. Why?"

"Just trying to figure out how much to supercool this lock before I karate kick my way through it as if it were made of ice. I don't want to overexert myself unless I have to. Charity? How's it going?"

She'd disappeared from the front of her cell. Now she reappeared, naked as the day she was born although with a lot more floral tattoos. Despite the fact that she was bloodied, muddied, bruised, and had been held captive in a cell for a few days, she still looked unbelievably, ridiculously good. What the hell was it about being a supernatural badass that made you look like a women's fitness cover model? Perhaps if I kept up with Dawn's training regimen, I'd look half as good some day.

"Ready when you are," she said.

Larry nodded. "Let's do it."

Charity growled, a cross between a howler monkey's whoop and a lion's roar coming from deep inside her. She dropped to her hands and knees as she barked out the strange sound. Fur sprouted from her skin, her nose stretched, her brow flattened, and her hands and feet warped into massive paws. The more hyena-like she became, the louder her growl grew. If anything, she transformed faster than Tank did. Within fifteen seconds, a hyena with vaguely rose-like spots on its hide paced the front of the cell, whooping and laughing in agitated glee.

At the same time, chill air wafted over from Larry's cell. His hand wrapped around the locking mechanism, and the metal glowed a cool blue. Mist leaked off it as if it were a block of dry ice.

Larry glanced at me. "Shouldn't be long now. I'll get you out as soon as I can."

I nodded. Barely had my head stopped moving before I heard the creak of a door. Dùghlas descended the steps at the end of the basement, a three and a half foot electric cattle prod in hand. Electricity crackled at the tip.

Dùghlas snarled. "If I told ya once, I told ya a hundred times, ya shtate, keep it down! Think Ciaran's gonna take it easy on ya if ya laugh up a storm? Wait till I tell 'im about dis."

Charity slammed her body against the cell bars before dancing back. Dùghlas cursed and stabbed between them with the cattle prod. A flash of blue danced off the prongs.

That's when Larry's door exploded off its hinges. The thing flew through the air and smashed Dùghlas square in the back. I'd thought he was only chilling the lock, but I guess I'd only seen his left hand. The right must've been busy working the hinges.

Dùghlas cried out and stumbled to his knees, dropping the cattle prod in pain. Larry darted out of his cell, swerving to avoid being hit by the falling iron door. He lifted a wooden bucket similar to the one Charity and I had in our cells and swung.

Dùghlas didn't stand a chance. The thing blasted him in the

cheek. Spittle and blood and perhaps a tooth flew as he grunted in pain and collapsed to the floor.

Charity's hyena laugh filled the basement as Larry flipped the guy over and rummaged through his pockets. He pulled a comically oversized key from Dùghlas's jacket and hopped to my cell.

"I figured you'd incapacitate him with magic," I said.

Larry shrugged as the key clicked in the lock. "I'm saving my strength for Benedict and Ciaran. Help me get him into your cell."

Sharp nips of pain bit my ankle as I hopped beyond the bars, but it wasn't as bad as I expected. Maybe I hadn't twisted as badly as I'd originally feared. Nonetheless, even with Larry's help, dragging a groaning and squirming Dùghlas across the floor wasn't pleasant. I cursed a few times before we pulled him far enough to close the door behind him.

The lock gave a satisfying click as Larry turned the key. He headed toward Charity's cell to free her. To my surprise, she'd already turned back and was donning her clothes.

Charity pulled her shirt over her head. "Nice kick, Larry. You take yoga?"

Larry shrugged. "I'm naturally flexible."

As Charity's door squealed open, Dùghlas's spoke, his voice wracked with pain. "Ya gobshites. You'll pay for this. Just wait."

"Well, you didn't knock him out." I nodded at Charity and lowered my voice. "How will we know if he... You know."

"No need to wonder. He already is."

Charity pointed. Within the cell, Dùghlas had started to mumble. His eyes had rolled into his head, and his fingers twitched. Suddenly, a breeze stirred, despite the fact that the window was still closed. Something flitted past me. Goose-bumps prickled my arms, and I heard a pained laugh.

"Angus," I said.

The laughing intensified, and then the breeze whisked past —but not before touching me on the ass.

"That was him alright," said Charity. "He's on his way. Time to get ready."

32

THE RAIN HAD SLOWED, BUT IT CONTINUED TO BEAT A steady rhythm against my jacket. I'm not entirely sure why I still wore it given how wet and muddy I was. The hood kept the water out of my eyes, at least. Perhaps that was it.

Larry walked beside me, a stick in hand. The end of it glowed with cool white light, illuminating the forest floor underneath us. For some reason, he preferred turning twigs into magic flashlights in lieu of balling light together. Maybe it was easier to control.

Larry waved the wand back and forth across the water-logged brush. "This is useless. We're never going to find it."

"We have to find it. It's our only shot at defeating Benedict."

"I wouldn't say *only* shot," said Larry. "I'm a wizard for Christ's sake, and you're a witch in training. There are other options."

"Such as?"

Larry grunted. "Nothing's coming to mind at the moment."

"Then quit wasting time and help me look."

"What do you think I'm doing with this wand? Conducting an orchestra of will-o'-wisps?"

"Larry..."

"Sorry." He followed me as I pushed into a grove of beech saplings. I pushed them to the side, my feet squelching in the mud.

Larry looked over his shoulder. "You sure it flew this way?"

"Seeing as I thought I was about to die, the moment is pretty much burned into my memory," I said. "Ciaran whacked my demon tooth bat out of my hand. It spun and flew into the woods, somewhere in this general area. Probably would be easier to find if it hadn't shrunk back down to tooth size, but it's here somewhere."

Larry was smart enough not to question me. "What time is it?"

I pulled my phone from my pocket. Water beaded across the screen. "Quarter till eleven."

"Which is, what? Twenty minutes since Angus took off?"

I stuffed my phone back into my pocket. "What's your point? That we need to hurry? That Ciaran could be back any minute? *You think?* Maybe you should stop complaining and start helping. Something beyond waving your magic stick in the air."

"You know it doesn't work that way," he said. "I'm not adept at tracking magic, as I've proven on more than one occasion."

A canine laugh sliced through the trees, drowning out Larry's complaints. My heart leapt. "I hope that's a good laugh."

I took off toward the sound and instantly regretted it. My ankle shook its fist at me. I only made it about four steps before I slowed back down to a hobble.

Luckily, I didn't have to go far. Out of the darkness, Charity splashed through a stream, something held between her pale yellow teeth. She stopped in front of me and spit it into the wet leaves at my feet.

"Oh, thank God." I leaned over and picked up the demon tooth. Other than being coated in slobber, it didn't look any worse for wear. "You're a lifesaver, Charity. Perhaps literally."

Charity barked. She stretched into the downward dog position, but as she came up, her body leaned and smoothed out. Her paws and snout shrunk. Within a few seconds she stood in front of me, once again naked, though the rain had washed most of the dirt off her.

She shook her head. "You're welcome. I found it in a stream past that hundred year old red oak over there."

"Thanks." I didn't want to stare, but I couldn't help myself. I'd kill for abs that flat. Did she do like two hundred crunches a day, or did all the running in hyena form carry over? "You, ah... didn't have to transform to tell me that."

I don't think I fooled anyone. Charity lifted an eyebrow. "Does my nakedness make you uncomfortable? Dawn told me you were an athlete."

"I am," I said. "That doesn't mean I chat with my girlfriends naked in the locker room all the time. Plus, given you and Dawn are... *you know*. It's kind of weird."

"I figured given how much time you spend around Tank, you'd be used to it by now."

"Hey." Larry beckoned from the edge of the beech grove. "You remember how I was saying we don't have a lot of time? Maybe discussions on social norms for paranormal folk can wait until we're not fearing for our lives anymore."

I wiped the demon tooth on my pants and stuffed it into my pocket. "Fair enough. Everyone clear on the plan?"

Charity nodded. "I'll go hide in the corn, though I'd rather be out looking for Dawn."

"Dawn won't be safe until we stop Benedict and Ciaran, regardless of whether or not you find her," said Larry. "And for the record, Lexie, let me state unequivocally that I *hate* this plan. I don't have a better one, so don't ask. I'm just voicing my displeasure."

"Hate it all you want," I said. "This is the best plan we've got, and it's a good one. Remember how my tooth tore through the spirits who attacked us at St. David's? Benedict recoiled when I pulled it out in the chapel. He hissed and batted it away when I made my stand at my Suburban, and that was with it in bat form. He's afraid of it, and I'm the one in the best position to use it against him. You have to trust me."

Larry's face grew grave. "I *do* trust you. I've trusted you for a long time. I trust you'll act when the time comes, that you won't back down, and that you won't crack under pressure. But that doesn't mean you're going to win, Lexie. This plan is risky. If anything goes differently than you're expecting, you may not have a chance to act, and if Ciaran or Benedict pull a rabbit out of a hat? I won't be able to protect you. You saw how ineffectual my magic was against him. If he gets those spirit tentacles on you..."

"Believe me, I'd rather not put my life on the line," I said. "I'd rather be home, safe and warm and surrounded by friends and family who aren't going to get murdered within the next few hours, but I'm stuck here instead. It may not be a perfect plan, but it's the best we've got. Someone has to carry it out."

"Exactly." Larry took a step forward. "So let me do it."

"*What?*"

"I'm serious," said Larry. "Let me be the one to do it. I know you're brave and you're strong and I believe you'll be a kick-ass witch one day, but you're not one yet. I can protect myself with magic, at least to a degree. Let me do it."

It was a tempting offer. I didn't have a death wish, but I'd also meant what I'd said. I wanted to protect my friends from further harm, Larry among them. "No. Ciaran thinks I'm helpless. You should've seen his grin as he bore down on me. He won't expect it from me. I have to be the one."

Charity tilted her head to the sky. "Did any of you hear that?"

"Hear what?" The rain pattered down relentlessly. It might've strengthened since the last time I paid it any mind.

Charity shivered. "I don't know. Maybe it was nothing. Still... I'm going to head to the corn. You should return to the house."

I nodded. "Let's go, Larry."

Charity transformed again and took off at a run. I wasn't able to do the same thanks to my bum ankle. Larry and I picked our way through the beech grove, back through the underbrush as the edge of the forest, and to the path. I don't know if it was an effect of leaving the protective cover of the forest canopy, but the rain hit us with a wallop as we reached the field.

A crack of lightning split the sky, booming with thunderous intent. "That can't be good. I thought we'd gotten over the worst of the storm."

Larry frowned from under the brim of his hat. "I know it feels like Benedict is controlling the weather, but I'm pretty sure it's coincidental."

As I set foot to the farmhouse porch steps, another bolt of lightning turned my world white. The blast exploded in my ears with concussive force. I stumbled as a jolt of fear lanced up my back.

I turned, blinking away the spots from the searing white light. There, standing at the foot of the corn in almost the exact spot we'd faced off with him the first time, stood Ciaran.

33

SEEING CIARAN IN THE DRIVING RAIN, THE TENDRILS OF darkness swirling around him, the glowing yellow eyes, the way the air rippled around his body, making him seem larger and more dangerous than before—it made me question my choice. Perhaps it would've been better to run. I could've convinced my parents to move to Siberia, I bet.

"Then again," said Larry. "Maybe he does have something to do with the storm."

Ciaran's voice slithered across the space separating us, an amalgam of his own and Benedict's. It was oily and alive and more powerful than it had any right to be. "Ya *dare* threaten my brother. After all you've taken from me. After everything you've done."

Larry stepped into the rain. "What did you think we would do, Ciaran? Lay down and wait to die while you ran off to murder our families and friends? That thing inside your head must've ripped away every shred of humanity you ever had if you think we wouldn't fight tooth and nail to protect the people we love."

"*NO.*" The roar nearly knocked me to my knees. "Ya don't get to use that against me. I'm the one who lost a brother. You're the murderers. *I'm the one fighting back, not you!*"

"Maybe *you* are, Ciaran," called Larry. "But that thing inside you begs to differ. It's evil personified. It doesn't care about Angus. It doesn't care what happens to you or Dùghlas or anyone else. It only cares about death and destruction, and it chose you to carry it out."

"*LIAR!!!*"

"Prove me wrong," said Larry. "Cast him off. Banish him. Remove the amulet. Talk to me, man to man. I know what happened to Angus. It was an accident, and I can prove it."

The air around Ciaran thickened. The tendrils around him coalesced, turning from mist into opaque black streaks. I don't think an earthquake hit at that moment, but Ciaran shook, as did the space around him. A violent growl seeped out of him, and even in the rain, I could see his cheeks darken with rage.

After a few moments, the shaking died. Ciaran's eyes brightened, the yellow crowding out any hints of normal color that had been there. He opened his mouth. Bright yellow light poured out, and the voice that spoke was devoid of any humanity. It was Benedict's slithering tongue, through and through.

"*I would've relished your agony upon seeing everyone around you broken and dead, but I suppose there are more important things than such joys. Still, I guarantee I won't spare them simply because I've already taken the pleasure of killing you.*"

Larry dug his heels into the mud. Electricity crackled from his fingertips. "Let's see you try."

Ciaran jumped. Dark tendrils burst from around him, stretching forward as he soared through the sky, but Larry shot off the ground with a superhuman leap, too. They met in the air with a violent clash, like something off a cover of a Spider-Man comic. They cried out, Ciaran in rage and Larry in exertion. A shield of white light spread before Larry, flashing like a lighthouse beacon as Ciaran's tendrils pounded away at it. Fire danced, lightning split the air, and some weird violet energy I'd never seen before whipped about the pair like a swarm of purple martins.

I don't know who held onto who, but the pair fell to the earth with a weighty thud, neither giving an inch. Benedict screamed. The air wobbled, driving Larry halfway to his knees. Larry responded by summoning a burst of wind to dissipate the fouled air, then countered with a spray of supercooled mist that turned the falling raindrops to hail. Every hair on my body stood on end, lifted by the energy that radiated off them.

I simply stood and watched. Part of me wanted to dive into the fray, to squeeze on my demon tooth bat and start swinging, even if I might strike Larry as easily as Ciaran. I wanted to help, to give my friend a fighting chance, but I couldn't, and not because I was petrified by fear. I had my part to play, and it involved staying rooted in place, eyes wide and with a tremble in my leg. I had to sell it.

At least Larry wasn't on his own. I heard a familiar laugh as a blur shot from the corn. Charity darted out, teeth bared as she dove into the fray. Given what she was up against, I didn't expect her to do much, but she proved me wrong. I lost track of her as she entered the sphere of darkness behind Ciaran, but a fraction of a second later, Benedict cried out as he was knocked twenty feet to the side. Larry dove on him, his fist glowing in preparation of a magical super punch.

I don't know if Benedict was fueled by adversity or if he simply needed a kick in the pants to reach his potential. Either way, Larry's blow never landed. A *whump* pulsed from Ciaran, knocking me to the ground even at a distance. Larry and Charity fared worse. Both of them flew through the air. Larry slammed into the side of the farmhouse, the siding cracking behind him, while Charity howled as she sailed even further, past the edge of the house before crashing through the side of the barn.

Ciaran stood in a fresh crater. His chest rose and fell, his eyes flared, Benedict's spirit rippling over him like a midnight black current.

He turned and stared at me.

This time, I didn't have to fake the icy fear that gripped me. I felt it for real. I scrambled to my feet, turned tail, and ran.

Or at least I tried. My ankle didn't let me. I winced as my foot slipped in the mud, and I went down in a pile.

It probably wouldn't have mattered even if I was Usain Bolt. A second later, my skin crawled as one of Benedict's tendrils slithered over me. With a quick flick, it wrapped around my neck. I barely got in a quick gasp before it squeezed and yanked me to my feet.

My neck and spine ached as the tendril whisked me through the air. Rain splattered against my head as I flew backwards, and a force pulled on my shoulder. I spun and jerked to a stop, my body swinging beneath me as I came face to face with Benedict.

The spirit had consumed Ciaran's face, turning it black, smoothing the features, eating the eyes and mouth from within. Benedict smiled, light pouring from his mouth as he held me high. *"Well, well, Lexie. Once again we find ourselves in this position. Did you think you could beat me with brute force? Didn't you learn anything from our first fight?"*

I gurgled, and Benedict shook me. The smile on his face grew. *"That's the difference between hunters and their prey, Lexie. The victors learn from their mistakes. You can be sure this time, when I squeeze, I won't stop until every drop of life in you is extinguished."*

The tendril dug into my flesh. The entire weight of my body pulled at me, straining the muscles in my neck and shoulders, but I didn't bring my hands up to ease the burden. I couldn't breathe, and my vision blurred at the edges. Fear crept into me, gnawing at me. *Larry had been right. This was a terrible plan.*

"Do you want to know one more thing, Lexie?" Benedict's tentacle tightened as he pulled me close. *"I thought I'd miss bathing in the agony of you reliving your family's deaths, but this moment? It's just as sweet."*

As my lungs burned for air and my vision failed me, I could feel the evil radiating off him, feel the stink of his breath on my face. It was the moment I'd been waiting for, the reason I was sure my plan would work despite the fear that nibbled at me. Unlike Larry and despite his assurances to the contrary, I *knew* I was in a horror movie. Maybe not literally. I hadn't spotted any hidden cameras, but metaphorically? You bet. And the monster in every movie always trapped the heroine, always brought her close and sneered at her with his stinky breath as he guaranteed her demise. Benedict had already wrapped his tendrils around my throat once. This time, when he meant to kill me, I knew he'd do it again.

It was why I hadn't bothered trying to rip the tendril free. I was too busy grabbing the demon tooth from my pocket.

With Benedict inches from my face, I lashed out, slicing at an angle with the tooth. It tugged in my hand as it tore through the thong holding the amulet of melding in place, then it caught along Ciaran's neck and bit deep into his jaw. Benedict and Ciaran both cried out, the latter in pain and the former in surprise.

The amulet slipped and fell to the mud, as did I. The tendrils of darkness vanished into an inky mist. The light faded from Ciaran's eyes and mouth as he, too, crumpled to the dirt. Ciaran groaned and put a hand to his neck to staunch the flow of blood, but his gurgles were drowned by Benedict's cry. It reverberated through the sky. The earth started to shake again, same as it did when Benedict took over and swallowed Ciaran's will entirely. I thought he might come back, might manifest himself as a creature of nightmares on his own, but the cry swallowed itself, rushing into a point somewhere close to Ciaran's head. Wind buffeted me as it went, and in a fraction of a second it was gone. Vanished, as if it had never been there in the first place.

Ciaran sputtered and rolled onto his side, but I didn't stick around to check on him. I jammed the tooth into my pocket and hobbled to the farmhouse. "Larry? *Larry!*"

I heard a weak cough and a pained grunt. "Ugh... Over here."

I found Larry amid a pile of broken planks and shredded insulation, his legs sticking from the battered siding and his butt stuck inside the house. His hat had been lost to the storm, and blood ran down the side of his face from a cut on the top of his head.

"My God," I said. "Are you okay?"

"I can still feel my legs, so I'm pretty sure I didn't break my back." He gave me a nod. "Help me out?"

"Yeah." I took his hands and stuck my good foot in the dirt.

With a grunt and a pull, I yanked him out. Scraps of wood and vinyl fell off him into the mulch at his feet.

Larry cast a dubious glance toward Ciaran. "Is that it? Did you beat him?"

I nodded. "The sly bastard couldn't help but bring me close to lord his victory over me. Told you it would work."

"And Ciaran?"

"I don't know. I got him pretty good along the neck. He's still alive, but—"

Air rushed around me, and I heard a moan and a giggle. I swiveled about, trying to locate the source.

Larry must've heard it, too. "I don't think we're out of the woods yet, kid."

I shook my head. "Maybe not, but I don't think that's Benedict. Matter of fact, I'm pretty sure that's—" I jumped as something groped me between the legs. "Yah! Angus. *Son of a bitch!*"

The laugh echoed off the side of the farmhouse, and a gust of wind flitted off toward the corn. I was half tempted to take off after it, but another sound caught my attention. The roar of an engine, getting closer.

I turned toward the forest in time to see an old Ford F150 tearing around the corner onto the drive. Mud kicked up from the tires as it barreled down the path toward us. I pushed Larry toward the house reflexively, but the thing wasn't aiming to run us over. Its tires slid as it skidded to a halt some ten feet from Ciaran's side.

The door flew open, and out jumped a woman in a forest green Carhartt jacket. She was tall and broad shouldered, with curly golden-brown hair that hung to her ribs. She raced to Ciaran's side, oblivious to the rain as she called out. *"Ciaran!"*

A breeze whistled past me, and again I heard Angus's laughter. Seeing the way the woman dove into the dirt at Ciaran's side and cradled his head in her lap gave me a bad feeling. Combined with her resemblance to him and Dùghlas, it wasn't hard to figure out who she was.

"Ciaran has a *sister?*" I said under my breath.

Angus flitted past again. As he touched my backside, a whisper carried on the wind. *"Beitris..."*

"Dùghlas," said Larry. "He called to Angus for help. Not just to Ciaran. He must've called to *all* his siblings."

Beitris's sobs carried over the relentless patter of rain. She glanced at her brother's weakened, mud-streaked body. She surveyed the gouges and blast marks on the road before stopping upon the fallen amulet in the dirt at her brother's feet.

"No." The word escaped my mouth as a whisper.

Beitris couldn't have heard me, but she looked at me as she grabbed hold of it. A potent, green energy pulsed from the amulet as soon as her flesh made contact, and I heard an all too familiar cackle.

"Yes. YES. LEXIE!!!"

The air near Beitris thickened and darkened. Tendrils of black mist formed out of nothing as cruel yellow light spilled from her mouth and eyes.

"No," I said. *"No no no..."*

Beitris rose from the ground, growing larger than her six foot frame. The amulet's glowing green energy danced through the air as it fled the pendant into Beitris. Hatred radiated off her like heat from a sun, and she flew into motion—but not toward us. She dashed to her truck and threw open the door. She leaned inside and ripped something from the back seats. A gleaming four and a half foot claymore that I'd seen before.

"Oh, God," said Larry. "That's *Gwyriad*. Romanov's magic sword."

The crystals, the amulet, and now the sword. I'd been right. Benedict was gathering them all. I simply hadn't realized he was using an entire family to do so.

I didn't have time to think about the ramifications of it. Beitris hefted the sword, belted out a bloodcurdling scream, and rushed us.

34

Beitris closed the gap between us at a sprint, *Gwyriad* held high overhead as she roared in rage. I fumbled at my pocket for my demon tooth, but I wasn't as quick as Larry. He gave a weary grunt as he dove back into the fray to meet Beitris head-on. He threw up another shield of pure energy, same as when he'd clashed with Ciaran in mid-air. This time when Beitris brought *Gwyriad* down upon it, the thing flickered and groaned. The sword bit a few inches into the pulsing energy of the shield instead of being rebuffed, and Larry staggered under the effort of keeping it intact.

I finally ripped the tooth free from my jeans and squeezed. The thing swelled to bat size, but having the familiar weapon in my hands didn't unroot my feet. Questions swirled through my mind as Larry battled Beitris, fire and ice and lightning flying. Where should I attack? Was I putting Larry in danger by trying to help? Would I be better off attacking with the tooth rather than the bat? That's what had harmed Benedict, after all. But the biggest question that screamed at me with unyielding urgency was *how?* How in the world could we beat the demonic beast in front of us? I'd already gone through hell and back to put myself in a position where a well-timed strike would defeat Benedict, all for naught! Now he knew the only ace I'd help up my sleeve. Larry couldn't beat him. Even now I could see the concentration in his face and the creases in his brow. Sparks flew off his shield as he grunted in effort, his spells crackling and popping. What could we possibly do? I had to think. I had to come up with *something*.

Yet I had nothing. Not a single idea came to mind. No daring plan that might work if the cards fell our way. Nothing filled me except a cold dread and a wave of fear that swept over me like a tidal wave. *This is it. There's no way out. We really* are *going to lose.*

A breeze swirled about me, and I heard Angus's titter. There was more joy in it now and less pain. I could almost hear the vindication in his voice. He flitted back and forth as Larry fought, pressing against me, touching me on the butt, on the breasts, anywhere he could, laughing all the while. A sense of pure malice surrounded me, the aura of arrogance and charm Angus had exuded in life twisted by the agony of his death.

Even paralyzed as I was by fear, I wasn't about to let a sex-crazed ghost have his way with me in my last moments. I swung my bat through the air, the rage and pain and fear all forcing their way through clenched teeth. *"Get the hell off me!"*

Angus hissed in my ear. *"As you wish..."*

The breeze whisked off, straight toward Beitris and Larry, who was barely holding his own. He'd given up fifteen feet of ground, pushed back by the relentless sword strikes and whipping tendrils. Rain soaked his hair, his muscles trembled with exertion, and his teeth were set in a grimace that was equal parts pain and exhaustion.

I took two hobbled steps toward the battle, a sudden panic gripping me. "No!"

I don't know what he did to Larry. All I know is one moment Larry stood there, arms whistling though the air, lips moving as he spoke incantations in Latin, and the next his eyes widened. He doubled over and wheezed, his hands dropping to his groin as if he'd been kicked in the family jewels. His spells flickered, and he wobbled.

Beitris didn't hesitate. She lunged and drove the claymore forward, stabbing with it at the heart of Larry's shield. In that moment, the concentrated magic might as well have been made of folded paper. The sword sliced through it without resistance —and continued right into Larry's ribs.

I stared in horror as the gleaming blade burst out his back, blood streaking the steel. Larry uttered a pained grunt, his body tensing at the pain and shock. Beitris stood in front of him, both hands on the hilt of the sword. Benedict's spirit coursed over her, turning the air thick with dark mists, turning her eyes into pools of molten gold.

Larry turned his head toward me. His jaw dropped in shock and fright. His lips moved, but I couldn't hear what he said. I only saw a spatter of blood come out.

Beitris's head turned my way, but it was pure Benedict who glared at me. The sword twisted in her hands. Larry jerked and cried out. His body went limp, the life fled his eyes, and I screamed.

"NOOOOOOO!!"

I lunged forward, stumbling as pain lanced up my leg with each of my steps. "You murderer! *MURDERER!*"

Beitris ripped the blade free from Larry's torso, tossing him to the ground like a side of beef. She arched her back and laughed, but it was all Benedict's voice that emerged. His dark energy surrounded her, consumed her, rippling over ever square inch of her body. *"You act surprised, Lexie. I told you I would do it."*

My knuckles cracked as I squeezed my bat tight. My teeth could've ground rocks into dust. "I'm going to kill you, you rotten, disgusting, worthless piece of garbage!"

Beitris twirled the claymore in one hand, Benedict's energy granting her supernatural strength. *"Oh really? How do you plan to do that?"*

"I'm going to—"

A dark tendril whipped out and grabbed my bat. It yanked on it violently before I had a chance to pull back, ripping it from my hands and twisting my wrists in the process. I cried out in pain as I lost my hold on it. Benedict sucked the thing in and wrapped more tentacles about it, two on each end. With a violent jerk, they torqued on the bat. First it bent, but as the strain built, the thing snapped with an audible *crack*. A burst of energy leaked from the broken ends and faded, like dust on the wind.

"You were saying?"

I stood my ground, breathing hard. What did he want me to say? That I'd lost? That I didn't stand a chance? Was he hoping to revel in my death, same as he had before I'd slashed him? I'd felt fear then. I'd felt it as Beitris pulled up in her truck, as she'd grabbed the discarded amulet, as Benedict flowed into her, as Larry darted forth to try and save us, but no more. I didn't feel any fear. Just rage. I'd come to grips with my death. I'd done it not once, but twice. What was the prospect of dying to Benedict a third time? Nothing. Even if I couldn't fight back, I'd never give him the pleasure of having me run and cower before him and plead for mercy. Maybe if there was a purpose to it, something to be gained by running, I would, but I could barely move with my ankle the way it was, and besides, where would I go? There was no place I could escape him, no place to gather my strength and fight in any meaningful way. Better to stand and face death with bravery and sneer in his face as he choked the life out of me.

But if there *were* a chance to escape... If there *were* a chance to fight back...

Thoughts swirled in my mind as Benedict howled with laughter. *"What's the matter, Lexie? Lost your nerve?"*

I gritted my teeth against the pain I knew I would suffer, but better to suffer with a sliver of hope than suffer with none at all. I turned and bolted for the house, putting my full weight on each of my feet as I ran. Pain lanced up my leg, and I thought my ankle might buckle, but I didn't care. I pushed through, regardless of the consequences.

Benedict's cackle grew behind me. *"Yes, Lexie. Run. Run."*

The heat of Beitris's presence intensified on the back of my neck as I flew up the porch steps and blasted through the front door, but I didn't bother looking behind me. I knew Benedict was hot on my heels, knew he could overtake me whenever he so chose. I only hoped he'd relish in the chase long enough to give me the precious moments I needed.

I stumbled into the entry hall, past the stairs, around the corner, and threw my shoulder into the door to the basement. A darkness crowded me from behind. Benedict's evil mist licked my ankles. *"You can't escape, Lexie."*

Beitris's blade whistled, and I ducked. A crash of honed steel on wood filled my ears, and I tumbled down the basement stairs. Hardwood steps battered my shoulder, my shin, my collarbone. Pain blossomed with each strike as I bounced to the cold stone below, but I ignored it. With one last surge, I pushed off of my good leg and dove into the nearest cell, grabbing the iron bars and slamming the door shut behind me.

No lights were on in the basement, but the space none-theless grew darker as Benedict descended the steps. Beitris's eyes and mouth blazed with unholy fire. It was only by their light that I could see anything. *"Trapped by your own hand, Lexie. How ironic. How delightful..."*

I ignored the taunt as I ripped my keys from my pocket. I raked them violently against the palm of my left hand, stifling a cry as they cut through flesh. Without hesitation, I dug two fingers into the wound and raked them across the gash. I dropped to my knees and started drawing.

Benedict's eyes flared. *"What are you doing?"*

I wiped more blood from my hand and kept drawing, the circle almost complete, but I couldn't slow. I didn't have the time.

The sick joy fled Benedict's booming voice, replaced instead with rage. *"No. Stop it!"*

Beitris lashed out, striking the iron bars with her sword. Sparks flew and a metallic clang reverberated off the stone floor, but I kept drawing. I only had two lines to go.

Beitris blasted the door with her claymore. I heard a sharp crack, then another. *"You cannot escape, Lexie. You cannot!"*

He might be right about that, and then again he might not. I was sure Benedict had escaped the spirit realm when Larry and I jumped into the real world at the St. David's chapel. I didn't think he could exist in two places at once, but maybe I'd be wrong. Only time would tell.

There were a few things I knew for a fact, though, things

Larry had told me that I'd never forget. That a magic circle made of something close to the user was more powerful than one that wasn't, and there wasn't anything closer to me than my own flesh and blood. That a circle constructed with a whiff of death in the air was as powerful as they came, and the stink of Larry's blood still hung in my nostrils. And more than anything else, that a person's *will* determined their strength in the spirit world, and I'd never wanted anything so much as I wanted to destroy Benedict, once and for all.

I finished the last of the lines in the pentagram and stood, ignoring the sword that smashed against the cracking iron bars in front of me. I stared Benedict in the eyes, and then uttered in flawless Latin, *"Vide praeter illam velum. Inferis, aperta."*

35

THE WORLD TURNED UPSIDE DOWN AS I PLUNGED INTO A cold pool, then flipped right side up equally as fast. Blacks and whites flipped before settling back, the brights brighter, the darks darker, the colors more muted—which in the confines of the basement mostly meant everything lay along a color spectrum between charcoal and midnight.

Including Benedict.

He stood in front of me, *Gwyriad* in hand, his vaguely mannish shape outlined by the reflected light creeping through the door at the top of the stairs. Mists didn't swirl around him here, nor did tendrils of darkness sprout from his back like octopus tentacles. He lacked any facial features, either of Ciaran or Beitris, but he did have those same fiery yellow eyes and jack-o-lantern mouth that each glowed with yellow fire.

He smiled. *"Surprised? Did you really think I wouldn't be here waiting for you, Lexie?"*

I smiled, too. "Honestly? I was hoping I'd find you here."

His face didn't have the capacity to show surprise, and I

probably couldn't have made out the change in facial features in the near total darkness even if he had. Still, his eyes stretched a little. *"You want to face me? Really, Lexie, it would be more fun if you cry and squirm until I crush the last speck of life from your tortured soul."*

"I'm sure it would be," I said. "But I'm done playing the victim. I'm done being afraid of you. You want me? Come get me."

The yellow smile widened. *"Gladly."*

He dropped his sword and reached out, wrapping thick fingers of darkness around the iron bars. His shoulders bulged. The iron bars groaned and popped. *"You see, Lexie, for all your newfound bravado, there is still no escape. Nowhere for you to run. Nothing you can do to stop me."*

"Wrong on all counts."

The bars snapped, and I jumped. I'd never been great at basketball, but I didn't need muscles to launch me. Not in the spirit world, not when my will and desire propelled me. I reached out as I leapt. My fingers brushed the rough beams of the ceiling, and in that moment, I remembered the sensation of dropping through the bottom of the elevator shaft at St. David's. I willed the same sensation through my entire body. The beams and flooring above them gave way, turning to a mirage of reflected light under my touch. Still I flew upward, onto the first floor of the farmhouse into the middle of the entryway. Benedict roared from the basement as the floor coalesced underneath me. I flicked a hand at the basement door, pictured myself as a Jedi, and *pushed*. The door swung as if grasped by a gust of wind and slammed shut, but I kept pushing. Metal groaned as the refrigerator flew out of the kitchen and slammed against the backside of the door, followed by the oven and a cabinet that still had a chunk of drywall attached to its back.

I turned and bolted out the front door, slamming it behind me. I willed it to stay shut, but I didn't expect it to last. I might have the desire, but I still didn't know what I was doing. Instead I darted into the rain, straight toward the carnage I knew I'd have to confront.

Larry knelt in the dirt at the base of the corn, his face drawn as he gazed at his own body, bloodied, covered in mud, and split in half by the sword strike to his sternum. Close to him stood Angus, his body a mass of cracked, blackened skin, as hideously disfigured as before. He wasn't attacking Larry, though. Wasn't trying to choke him or splatter him with flecks of burning hot magma. Instead, he was doubled over, clutching his stomach and pointing at Larry as he brayed in laughter.

Rage burst through me at seeing the pain in my friend's face and the joy in Angus's. The world blurred around me as I ran faster, anger fueling me. I reached back, pumping energy into my arm. Angus barely looked up by the time I reached him.

I slammed a fist square into the middle of his face. Bone cracked as the full force of my assault drove through my hand into his nose. What was left of it caved inward. Angus flew backward, slamming hard into the dirt as he slid into the field of cornstalks. I shook my hand, figuring flecks of burning hot magma would've stuck to it, but it was fine. It didn't even hurt.

Larry looked at me. He blinked in shock. "Lexie? What's going on? Am... Am I...?" He looked down at himself, and I think he realized for the first time that he was covered in blood. A deep wound cut his chest across the sternum, same as the body on the ground.

Benedict roared, and I heard a crash within the farmhouse.

I pulled Larry to his feet. "No time to explain. Hopefully there will be soon enough." I scanned the road as rain battered me, looking for what I hoped would still be there. It was half hidden under mud and hard to see because it had stopped glowing, but I found it.

I stooped and grabbed the amulet of melding. I took Larry's hand and pressed it over mine atop the amulet. "Soulcast into me, Larry."

He blinked. "What are you talking about?"

"Like you did with Mr. Whiskers and the animals you sent to talk to Charity. Do it to me. Use the amulet."

His brows furrowed. "But... I don't know if it works that way. And why? What's—"

I heard another crash, much louder this time, and Benedict's scream of anger. *"LEXIEEE!"*

Larry's head turned toward the house, but I grabbed his chin and forced his eyes onto mine. "Soulcast. Do it, Larry. *NOW.*"

Larry's eyes hardened. He twirled a finger around a lock of my hair and chanted in Latin. A green light leaked from the amulet, growing in strength the more Larry spoke. The world about me wobbled, and for a moment I saw the farm from two distinct perspectives, mine and Larry's. A bright flash of green light swallowed us, and Larry was gone. Only I remained.

Except Larry wasn't gone. I could feel him inside me, not in a gross sexual way. More that I could feel his thoughts, feel his presence in the same way I'd both been myself and Mr. Whiskers simultaneously. More than his presence, I could feel his *energy*.

I'm sure Larry would tell me that it was battered and drained from his fights with Benedict, but to me it felt as if someone had uncapped a geyser. A flood of magical sensations rushed through me, heat and light and sharper hearing and a tingling that ripped through my fingertips all the way into my toes. So *this* is what it felt like to be a wizard.

Witch, Lexie. You're a witch.

Not now, Larry. It was weird having him there in my mind, but I didn't have time to worry about it. The door on the farmhouse burst open with an ear-splitting crash, and Benedict bounded through. He took several leaping steps toward me before slowing.

The rain disappeared into the shroud of darkness that surrounded him. His pale yellow eyes flickered. *"Lexie?"*

I glanced at my hands and willed weapons into them, but I had more than will working for me now. I had magic, too. A shield of bright light grew from nothing and strapped itself to my left forearm, and in my right grew a brilliant falchion.

I smiled and gave the spirit a nod. "Shouldn't have left your sword in the basement, Benedict."

"Benedict?"

I cried out as I burst into a run, the sword held tight in my fist. If Benedict's eyes had stretched in the basement, they truly widened now. He stepped back and threw up a shield of darkness, perhaps for the first time in his existence thrown off by an assault against him. I lowered my shield and rammed through it, Captain America-style. It shattered like glass, revealing a stunned Benedict behind it. Benedict's arms rose, and I slashed at them with my sword. The edge bit deep into the condensed darkness. Something fizzled and spat, and white sparks poured from the wound.

Benedict hissed in pain and darted back at lightning quick speed. Light continued to flicker from the gash in his arm. His mouth narrowed into a sneer, and he growled in a feline manner. *"No more games. I will* END *you, Lexie."*

I twirled my sword. "Go ahead and try."

Benedict roared. Bolts of dark energy shot from him like fireworks, rocketing through the air toward me. I launched myself into them, batting them away with shield and sword alike. My feet pounded the earth as I ran. More projectiles screamed from Benedict, gouts of goo, bolts of black lightning, wispy streamers that smelled of rot and crackled like logs in a fire. Some I deflected with sword and shield, others I pushed away with gouts of concentrated air, same as I'd done with the fridge, and still others I dodged. I spun and twirled, my falchion flashing in the night. I could feel Larry's energy growing inside me, adding to my iron will, but there was more in me, too. A fleetness of foot and ease of movement that I'd gained from training with Dawn, a strength of spirit and raw brutality that I'd picked up from Tank, even a bit of Bill's reckless drive.

The spells flew at me, hot and thick. The air pulsed with energy, and still I advanced, plowing through them as easily as did the raindrops cascading upon me. I jumped, and my run turned to flight. Benedict's mouth yawned open. He roared in defiance. His arms rose to block me, but I moved too fast. I plunged down with my sword, stabbing deep into his core.

Benedict's cry turned from one of rage to a howl of pained disbelief. A burst of light erupted from his chest, bright and white and smelling of freshly spun wool. *"No!* NOOOOO!*"*

I stared deep into his cruel yellow eyes. "How does it feel, you sick son of a bitch? This is for Larry!"

I leaned my weight onto the blade and pushed. The light

intensified, as if I'd torn a hole in the sun but without the heat. Pure, white light filled my field of vision, swallowing everything else, but I could still hear and feel what was going on around me. Benedict's scream rose in pitch, undulating wildly. My arms vibrated as I held onto the sword, and I had no idea if it was Benedict or the entire world that had started to shake. As the scream reached a fever pitch and I thought my arms and legs might be turned to jelly by the vibration, I heard a resounding *POP*. Benedict's scream died, swallowed from existence, and I pitched forward. My arms hit the wet dirt, but nothing moved. As I blinked, I regained sight. I saw the outline of my hands, then the texture of the mulch underneath them, then the creases in my skin as everything returned to normal, at least for the spirit world.

My sword and shield dissolved as I pushed myself to my feet. I stared at the spot where I'd stabbed Benedict, but he was gone. No crater. No black scorch where he'd stood. He'd simply vanished without a trace. His burning eyes, evil cackle. All gone.

Something else seemed to be fading, too. I turned my head toward the night sky, feeling the droplets hit me with slowing frequency. I closed my eyes and let the drops wash over me. For the first time all night, I relished in their touch.

Lexie?

"It's alright," I said. "You can come out now Larry. We got him."

Something tugged at my brain, and a burst of green light flared behind me. When I turned, Larry stood there, albeit with a bloodied shirt and the gaping wound that birthed it peeking from underneath.

Larry smiled. "You did it, girl. You killed him. And you used my magic like a pro. I knew you had it in you."

"Do you think he's really gone?" I asked. "For good? Forever?"

Larry shrugged. "There's no way to know. Evil like that has a way of lingering, of attaching itself to folks who are the most miserable, the most vulnerable. Folks like Ciaran and Beitris. Still... I don't know how everything works in the spirit world, but that felt pretty final to me."

He sighed and stared toward his body, sprawled in the mud by the corn. "Speaking of... I guess I'm really dead, then, aren't I?"

Raindrops rolled down my face, but some of the ones on my cheeks felt hot. It was only by the temperature difference that I realized I was crying. It seemed like an eternity since I'd felt any emotion other than fear and rage, but now that Benedict was finally gone and I stared at Larry's broken body, the full impact of it hit me.

"Larry, I... I couldn't stop him. Christ, I wanted to, but my legs were frozen to the ground. I didn't know what to do, and... I was so afraid. Oh, God. I'm so sorry." I couldn't stop the sobs from coming out. I didn't want to stop them either.

"Hey. Hey, now." Larry reached out and grabbed my shoulder. "It's okay. You did win. You beat Benedict. Not only that, you saved your family. And mine."

"Yeah, but I didn't save you!" I shrugged out of his grasp and stumbled into him, wrapping him in a hug. The tears poured freely now, and I buried my face into his bloodied duster.

Larry squeezed me, the strength of his arms as real as if he'd still been alive. He patted me gently with one hand. "It's going to be alright, Lexie. Being a wizard has its advantages, but one of them isn't longevity. I'd never figured I'd die in bed, old and gray and with loving children at my side. Not in this line of work. I knew it would happen, sooner or later. I'm okay with it. Besides, wizards like me don't just disappear. I'll putter around for a while, see what the spirit realm has to offer, and then? The next phase of the journey will start, and I'll finally get to see what's past the veil."

I shook my head, refusing to let go. I sucked back the snot forming in my nostrils. "But what if we're not ready to let you go, Larry? What if *I'm* not?"

Larry's hands moved to my shoulders, and he pushed me back gently. He smiled as he looked me in the eyes. "You're strong, Lexie. Stronger than you know. You've showed it to me more times than I can count. You'll get through this. I know you will. Trust me when I say that I would've loved to spend more time with you, with Dawn and Tank and Bill. I'm going to miss the hell out of you guys, but you can't change this. You have to accept it. Part of accepting is knowing there's still work to do. Tank is out there. So are Dawn and Charity. You need to check on your family. You need to go back to the real world—and I think the universe agrees with me."

I wiped the tears from my face. "What are you talking about?"

Larry put a palm to the sky. "Feel that? Storm's over. It's time to go, Lexie." He nodded toward a puddle at my feet. A single droplet plunged into it from above, sending ripples through it. Then it stilled, showing me a faint reflection under a sliver of moonglow.

I shook my head. "Not yet."

Larry squeezed my shoulder. "You can't stay forever. It'll only make it harder."

I took a deep breath. My chest shook as I let it out. "I'm going to miss you, Larry."

Larry's smile spread. "Likewise, girl. I'll see you on the other side, I guess."

Fresh tears sprung to my eyes, but I knew Larry was right. Waiting would only make it harder, so I trained my eyes on my reflection and stepped into the puddle.

36

MORE THAN THE COLORS, IT WAS THE STEADY CROAK OF frogs looking for mates that reminded me I was back in the real world. I stepped across the sodden driveway, my feet leaden. Rain no longer poured down, and like in the spirit would, a sliver of moonlight forced its way through the clouds.

Neither could do anything to lift my spirits. As I stopped in front of Larry's corpse, fresh tears welled in my eyes.

I still couldn't wrap my head around his loss. It was crazy how the mind worked that way. Even having seen the murder take place, having talked to him, having him reassure me he was going to be okay, none of it mattered. The chemicals that my limbic system pumped into the rest of my brain made me deny his loss nonetheless. I couldn't believe he was gone, no matter what the logical portion of my brain said. Soon enough, I'd be bristling with rage, cursing Benedict, cursing myself for not stopping him after Romanov's defeat, cursing every twist of life that had put Larry and me in this position at the moment of his demise. Then I'd start bargaining, trying to come up with any way to bring him back, no matter how impossible it might be. It was the way human physiology worked.

And it sucked.

As I stood there crying, I heard an electronic ding. I pulled out my phone and saw that my cell service had returned. Beyond that, a message was waiting for me.

I pressed play and pulled the phone to my ear. It was my mom. *"Hola, mi amor.* I, ah... just wanted to talk to you. It's been a very strange night. I already talked to your sister, but... well, there's no easy way to say it. I think Mr. Whiskers might've gone crazy. I refuse to believe it's anything more than that, no matter what your father or your *abuela* think. Anyway, we'll talk more later. Give me a call when you get a chance. *Adios."*

The message ended, and I slipped the phone into my pocket. I'd give them a call and explain everything—tonight, no less, but not right now. They wouldn't be able to understand me over my crying, and I couldn't do justice to everything I'd gone through over the phone, anyway.

I stood there, taking deep breaths, trying to slow the waterworks by thinking logically. What could I do now? I couldn't leave Larry there, but I didn't think I could move him, either. Would my car start? What about Ciaran? He lay there by Beitris's car, not moving. I hoped he wasn't dead, despite what he'd tried to do to us. Speaking of which, what had happened to Beitris? Had she died when I'd killed Benedict in the spirit world? Of everyone involved, she seemed the most like an innocent bystander.

Somewhere in the distance, I heard a cry. I wasn't sure what it said at first, but as it repeated itself, it became clearer. "Lexie? Larry? You there?"

I twisted around. It was coming from the direction of the barn. "Tank? Tank!"

He must've heard me. "Lexie! Hold on, I'm coming!"

It took a few seconds, but Tank rounded the corner of the farmhouse, jogging my way. He wasn't in bear form, which made sense given his calls, but he wasn't naked either. He'd found some blue jean coveralls that hung off him loosely, as if they'd been made for a guy with a fifty-inch waist. In his arms he held a limp form with jet black hair drawn into a tight braid.

"Jesus," I cried. "Dawn!"

I took off toward them and pulled up after about three steps. For all my powers in the spirit world, my ankle hadn't been magically healed back on Earth. My leg cursed me as pain sprouted anew.

Dawn tilted her head toward me and waved a hand weakly. "It's okay. I'm alright. Took a... gash to the leg. Benedict... almost got me. Took off instead of trying to... finish me off. Lost some blood. I feel a little weak, but... I'll be fine."

I glanced at her leg. Sure enough, a bandage made of strips of cloth had been wrapped tightly around it. It might've been the remains of Tank's shirt. Either way, they were a dark red in color.

Dawn flicked her wrist at me, her eyes fluttering. "Did you... find Charity?"

"Yeah. She's fine. At least, I think she is." I wiped tears from my face. "She got knocked away during our fight with Benedict. Over toward the barn."

Tank looked at me, concern in his eyes. "Are you okay, Lexie?"

I shook my head. "No. I'm not."

Tank looked past me, and for the first time his eyes landed

on the body behind me. Air left his lungs in a quiet gasp. "Larry...?"

He rushed past me, Dawn jostling in his arms. "No. No, Larry. It can't be."

I hobbled after him. "It's no use, Tank. Benedict killed him. He died to save me."

Tank lay Dawn gently on the road beside Larry as he knelt. He picked Larry up, cradling his head in his lap. "No. Come on, pal, wake up. *Wake up, Larry!*"

Dawn stirred, moving her head slowly. "Wait, what? Larry?"

I caught up to the pair, my ankle hurting something fierce. "I'm telling you, he's dead, Tank! Okay? I saw it happen."

Tank's face darkened and his muscles tightened. "Well, you saw wrong, Lexie. *You saw wrong!*"

"Yelling at me isn't going to change it! He's dead. Nothing can bring him back, okay?"

Tank burst into tears, hanging his head as he rocked back and forth. "No, no, it can't be. It can't. Larry, old pal... No."

Dawn scooted forward, the confusion on her face evident. "Wait. Is he really...?"

I didn't have anything else to say. I'd felt the exact same way, stood there crying just as he had. He had to get it out. We all reacted the same way. We all started with denial.

And we all transitioned into anger. Tank lay Larry's body down gently and rose from the driveway, looking like a super villain rising from the ashes. The muscles in his jaw bulged, and even in the darkness I could see the veins popping in his neck. "First Kiara, now Larry. Where is it? Where is that thing?"

"I killed him, Tank," I said. "Benedict is dead. Gone. He won't be coming back."

"Revenge was supposed to be mine, Lexie. I wanted to kill him. *Me!*"

Blood rushed into my cheeks in response to his raised voice. "You think I wanted this? You think I wanted to take him on alone and see Larry die in the process? I didn't want any of this Tank. If I could change it, I'd do so in a heartbeat!"

Tank's hands balled into fists, and he shook with rage. "No. It's not fair. It's not—" He looked about him desperately, maybe for something to smash or to punch. Instead he spotted the discarded amulet of melding on the ground. He ripped it from the dirt and grunted as he squeezed on it with both fists. "You piece of junk! This is because of you! You and that damn sword and those crystals!" Tank squeezed harder. He twisted and torqued on the thing, but it wouldn't break. With a roar of sheer anger he wound up and threw it into the corn, yelling as it flew. *"GRAAAH!"*

The amulet's whistle through the air faded, leaving nothing more than the sound of Tank's heavy breathing behind. And something else. Another faint cry, this one coming from the corn. "Hey? Hello?"

"Who the hell is that?" said Tank.

"Oh my God. It's Bill. I'd totally forgotten about him." Then my eyes snapped open. *"It's Bill."*

I took off into the corn, skipping as best as I could on my bum ankle. "Bill? Bill, where are you?"

"Over here!" he cried.

The vague instruction didn't help me much seeing as I was surrounded by foliage, but I followed the sound of his voice. "Bill? Bill!" I slapped aside a stalk to find him, still in his mesh sack and half hidden in the mud. The earth slurped as I pulled him free.

"Oh, God," he said. "That was the worst! I thought I was going to be stuck there forever."

I turned and headed back toward the house, running as quickly as I could.

"Hey," said Bill. "You going to acknowledge me here? What's going on? I heard a crazy *whump* a while ago, and was that Tank roaring? Did you kill Benedict?"

"Not now, Bill."

I burst onto the driveway and hopped to a stop in front of Larry.

Bill flicked his eyebrows at everyone. "There you are, Tank. And Dawn. And... *oh, God.* Larry? Tell me he's okay."

I ripped open Bill's bag, grabbed him by the hair, and tossed him on top of Larry's chest. "Bite him, Bill."

Bill's eyes flew open. "What? What are you talking about? Is... is he dead?"

I knelt in the mud. I picked up Larry's arm and moved it to Bill's mouth. "He's dead, Bill. Stone dead, but his spirit is nearby. I talked to him. He told me he wished he could spend more time with us, that he wished he didn't have to leave. So bite him. You're a zombie, for Christ's sake. Bite him and bring him back!"

Bill's eyes rolled as he tried to look at his friend. "Jesus, Lexie, he's really... *dead?* God. I mean... Look, you don't know what you're asking. I don't even know if it works that way."

Tank stood nearby. He'd had his back to us as we approached, but now he moved closer. "Lexie, what are you doing?"

"I'm training to be a witch, but I'm not a necromancer. I'm not a god, either. I can't bring him back, but damnit Bill, if you don't bite him and give this a god-damned try, I swear I'm going to bury you to your eyes on a beach full of crabs!"

Bill looked at me, then at Larry. I stuffed the hand closer to his face. Bill's brow furrowed. His nostrils flared. He opened his mouth and chomped down hard on the meat of Larry's palm. He growled as he dug his teeth in. His tongue flicked over Larry's digits, and somehow Bill managed to shake like a dog despite not having legs.

Finally, he let go. Blood oozed very slowly from the wound. Bill's eyes rolled, trying to get a look at Larry's face. "Well? What's happening?"

I picked him up and stood, holding him so he could see. "Nothing's happening. What's supposed to? How long does it normally take?"

"I don't know," said Bill. "The only times I've ever bitten someone, I never stuck around long enough to find out. That was way back when I had a body, too."

I stood there, watching intently. I couldn't bear to look away, couldn't bear to blink. "Come on, Larry. Come on. Come back. I know you can. You wanted to."

In the distance, a bullfrog gave a hearty croak. A gust of wind whistled through the corn, rustling the leaves. Tank's breathing shifted from heavy to barely audible.

Dawn's tired voice cut the tension. "It's no use, Lexie. You were right. We can't bring him back. We have to accept that."

And then Larry's eyes snapped open.

37

Red and blue light flickered over me from all directions. Emergency vehicles packed the side of the dirt road, stretching from the edge of the forest to past the farmhouse. I'd had to move my Suburban before they arrived, and someone had since parked Bietris's Ford F150 by the barn. A few cars had already left from the peak, notably the ambulance carrying Ciaran. The medics had refused to tell me if he'd pull through, but the fact that they were actively treating him as they pulled away gave me hope.

A second ambulance sat behind the spot vacated by the first. The back doors were open, and the lights inside shone brightly. Dawn lay on the gurney inside, sitting up as she spoke to the paramedics inside. She'd regained a little of her color, though she was still moving slowly. Charity sat beside her on the bench, her bruises more evident in the artificial light, but she didn't look any worse than she had before being ejected from Benedict's presence and tossed a couple hundred feet into the barn. Dawn's arm dangled off the edge of the gurney, and Charity grasped it lightly from her perch. Lines of exhaustion creased both of their faces, but every now and then, they'd sneak a glance at each other. In those moments, their eyes would twinkle and the edges of their mouths would turn up in smile. Their joy was a beacon of light in an otherwise mirthless night.

I heard the slam of a car door and turned to see Frank Connors standing next to one of the police cruisers. He slapped the top of the car a couple times, the engine roared, and the car took off. The darkness made it hard to tell, but I caught a glimpse of golden-brown curls from the back seat.

As the cruiser rumbled along the gravel, Frank turned and caught me staring. He nodded and approached.

I nodded back. "So that's the last of them?"

The grizzled cop brushed a couple fingers through his thick mustache. "Bietris, Ciaran, and Dùghlas, all in custody. According to state records, them and their brother Angus were the only four siblings. My officers are still finishing their search of the house, but it doesn't appear as if any of their extended family were involved in this."

The cruiser curved around the bend, disappearing into the trees. "What happens to them now?"

"They'll get charged, prosecuted, and probably go to prison for a long time, pending your testimony. Kidnapping and attempted murder are serious crimes."

"But how does the fact that they were possessed play into it?"

Connors snorted. "You haven't sat in on a lot of trials, have you? Lawyers have presented crazy arguments to keep their clients out of jail for centuries. Some of them have argued demonic possession in court before, but I don't think any of them have done so successfully. The O'Neills are going to prison, plain and simple."

"I know," I said. "It's the moral implications of it that bother me. Is it fair to incarcerate them when it was Benedict pulling the strings?"

Frank sighed. "Lexie, I know you've had a rough night, but you need to put emotion aside and look at the facts. You said this Benedict guy entered our world earlier today, right? The O'Neills kidnapped Charity two and a half days ago. They tortured her, and they attacked Madison Flemming and nearly killed her, too. Heck, they've been seeking revenge for their brother's death for months. Ciaran admitted as much, right? Maybe a spirit somewhere picked up on their anger and rage and used that as a conduit to get to Earth, but Ciaran and Bietris and Dùghlas made their own bed. Now they're going to lay in it."

I was silent for a while, mulling over the detective's words. Eventually I nodded. "You're right. I don't know why I'm so conflicted. Survivor's guilt, I guess." I stuck out a reluctant hand. "Thanks for coming to help, Frank. I didn't know who else to call."

We shook. "Not a problem. Well, technically it was. Caldwell County is out of my jurisdiction, but once I called the sheriff, explained to him what was going on, and told him how this tied into an active murder investigation, he was happy to let me take it. I wish you'd all stayed out of it like I told you to, but I can't argue with your results. Mostly I'm just glad you're safe and that this mess is finally over."

I grimaced and hummed with uncertainty.

"What? You think it's *not* over?"

"I don't know," I said. "I'm confident Benedict is gone, but I don't know about Angus. I punched him pretty hard in the spirit realm, but things are weird there. Who knows if he'll be back."

Frank snorted again. "Well, at least you all pulled through."

I stared at Tank, who sat by himself at the edge of the road past the trail of police cars. He hadn't moved in about an hour or said anything to anyone. "More or less. We're going to need time to process and heal, though."

"Speaking of which..." Frank glanced at my Suburban. "You ever going to tell me what's going on with Larry?"

It wasn't easy to see in the darkness of night, even with the flashing police lights, but Larry sat in the back of my Suburban. He'd taken Bill in with him. Like Tank, he'd barely moved since finding his seat. He's said even less.

"He pushed himself the hardest against Benedict. Gave everything he had so the rest of us could defeat him. He's going to need the most time to recover."

"But he's going to be fine, right?"

I felt a pang in my heart, still unsure if I'd made the right decision. "Only time will tell."

ABOUT THE AUTHOR

Hi. I'm Alex P. Berg, author of *Nyte Terrors*. Lexie may have put herself in a bit of a pickle at the end of this one, but her adventures certainly aren't over. Be sure to pick up the third installment in the series, *Nyte Prowler,* in which Larry adjusts to a new normal and Lexie tests the limits of her powers.

Need more adventures, mysteries, and laughter? Try my Daggers & Steele series, featuring homicide detective Jake Daggers and his clever new partner, Shay Steele. The complete ten book series is now available on Kindle Unlimited. Read it now!

Word of mouth is **critical** to my success. If you enjoyed this novel, please consider leaving a positive review on Amazon. Even if it's only a line or two, it would be a *huge* help. Thanks!

Want to connect? Visit me at www.alexpberg.com or contact me on social media.

For a complete list of my books, please visit: www.alexpberg.com/books/.